# Gypsy
## WEDDING

Kate Lace met her husband while they were both serving in the army. She left after eight years and had three children. She has written 13 books under several different names, but this is her eighth as Kate Lace.

# *Gypsy*
## WEDDING
## kate lace

arrow books

Published by Arrow Books 2011

2 4 6 8 10 9 7 5 3 1

First published in Great Britain in 2010 by
Arrow Books
Random House, 20 Vauxhall Bridge Road,
London SW1V 2SA

www.randomhouse.co.uk

Addresses for companies within The Random House Group Limited
can be found at: www.randomhouse.co.uk/offices.htm

The Random House Group Limited Reg. No. 954009

A CIP catalogue record for this book
is available from the British Library

ISBN 9780099564539

The Random House Group Limited supports the Forest Stewardship
Council® (FSC®), the leading international forest certification organisation.
All our titles that are printed on Greenpeace approved FSC® certified paper
carry the FSC® logo. Our paper procurement policy can be found at:
www.randomhouse.co.uk/environment

MIX
Paper from
responsible sources
FSC® C016897

Typeset by SX Composing DTP, Rayleigh, Essex SS6 7XF
Printed and bound in Great Britain by
CPI Bookmarque Ltd, Croydon, CR0 4TD

# Acknowledgements

I owe thanks to Jenny Haddon and Cat Cobain for suggesting that I ought to write this book and to Gillian Holmes, my editor, for keeping me on the straight and narrow. I also owe a big debt of gratitude to Katie Fforde and Judy Astley for inviting me to join them on a writing retreat in Scotland so I hit my deadline, and finally to Elizabeth Garrett who provided the cottage we retreated to and showered us with the most wonderful hospitality.

To Ian, Penny, Victoria and Tim, with love.

# PROLOGUE

Vicky O'Rourke looked across the short grass at the front of her family's trailer to where Liam was standing. *Bless him*, she thought as she watched him being almost swamped by her father's huge hug. Mind you, her father, Johnnie, would swamp anyone. He was a massive bear of a man who still kept himself in shape even though his days as a prizefighter were long past, while Liam was just – well, ordinary. Lovely, fit, gorgeous but when it came to size, he was definitely ordinary. She felt a warm glow of love sweep through her as she looked at the two men in her life: her father who treated her like a princess, and her fiancé who, as he had slipped the big diamond on her finger, had told her that he loved her and would never let her want for anything.

For the millionth time she glanced down at the ring, admiring the sparkling diamond in its white-gold setting. 'Betrothed,' she whispered to herself. 'Really, *really* betrothed.' And to Liam. She could still hardly believe it. She was so lucky that, out of all the boys on the trailer park, Liam had asked her, *her*, to marry him. Her parents, and his, had always assumed they would

1

end up together, but just because they'd known each other from birth didn't mean that it was a done deal. Being friends was a long way from being man and wife. Besides Liam was so good-looking he could have had his pick from any of the girls. And it wasn't as if the other girls of marriageable age hadn't made it obvious that they wouldn't have said no to getting grabbed by him.

She looked back across at him where, now released from his future father-in-law's embrace, he was drinking from a can of lager. She felt her insides go all fluttery again. What wasn't there to love about him? Not only was he hot, with a smile to die for and a naturally buff body, he was also kind, funny and a brilliant carpenter. Liam and his dad Jimmy had a shed on the trailer park where they turned out all sorts of wonderful stuff. Most of their bread-and-butter work was for the building trade – hanging doors, fitting skirting boards and the like – but when business was slow, especially in the winter months, they would turn their hands to more skilled joinery, making pieces of furniture for their fellow travellers or repairing traditional bow-topped wagons.

Vicky just knew that their babies would be beautiful – both Liam and her had the colouring of the Black Irish: dark hair and skin that tanned with the first rays of sun. She could see his biceps bulging under his white shirt and there wasn't an ounce of fat on him; she knew that from watching him when he was out and about with his shirt off, as he often was in the summer months, loading up his father's van with timber, sawing wood on the workbench outside their shed or just playing football with the lads.

Vicky shoved her dark curls back behind her ears and flashed a smile at her fiancé, pushing her shoulders back as she did so to give him the full benefit of her curvy figure. His blue eyes sparked back at her and he gave her a slow sexy smile in return. Vicky licked her lips and then ran her tongue over her gleaming teeth as she looked coyly at him from under her thick black lashes, a look she'd practised a number of times in the mirror in her bedroom, often while slathering on the mascara. Not that Liam needed mascara to have lashes to rival hers. She giggled to herself at the thought of Liam using mascara.

'What are you laughing at?' said her sister, suddenly appearing by her elbow.

Vicky turned to look at thirteen-year-old Shania, already a beauty with her copper-coloured hair and milky skin, a younger version of their mother, Mary-Rose. Shania had classic Irish colouring, so different from Vicky herself, who favoured her father's side of the family with her dramatic mane of luxurious curls and olive skin. In fact, if you didn't know the family it was hard to believe the pair were sisters, they were so different: Vicky looked not unlike Cheryl Cole while Shania had been compared to Doctor Who's new assistant, Amy Pond.

'I'm just happy,' said Vicky.

'As you should be, getting engaged to the gorgeous Liam. God, you're so lucky. Still,' said Shania, flicking her auburn ponytail over her shoulder, 'it'll be me next.'

'And why not? Have you got anyone in mind?'

'Maybe,' said Shania, a blush reddening her cheeks.

3

And although her younger sister didn't give a name Vicky noticed the way her sister shot a glance to Liam's cousin Michael. Not that he noticed, he was busy admiring the new Beemer that Liam's dad had recently bought.

Which was a shame, thought Vicky, as her little sister was looking especially hot in a minuscule outfit of pillar-box red, which made her pale skin almost translucent. Most of the girls at the party, also dressed in brilliant colours which showed off their young bodies to their best advantage, were dancing in the huge tent Johnnie had put up for the occasion. The DJ, hired especially, was playing a Shakira track and her friends were all gyrating madly, swinging their hips and throwing sexy glances at the group of boys standing on the sidelines. The boys were transfixed, tongues virtually hanging to their knees. Vicky reckoned that if the music stopped suddenly, all you would hear would be a desperate panting and slavering coming from the edges of the dance floor. *They're like a pack of horny dogs*, she thought with a grin. And not one of them would get more than a kiss, and only that if they were lucky. The boys were nudging each other and obviously discussing among themselves who they fancied – when they weren't being distracted by new cars.

Vicky herself was dressed in a long gown of brilliant turquoise silk, which showed off her colouring to perfection. It had a big net underskirt that puffed the dress out and made her waist look tiny. Vicky had slaved over it for days to get it finished in time although her mother had insisted that she didn't have to make her own dress.

4

'Your daddy'll buy you one,' Mary-Rose had said repeatedly in her heavy Irish brogue, as Vicky sat hunched over her whirring sewing machine.

'But I want it to be special. If I make it myself I can be sure that no one else will ever have one quite like mine.'

'If that's what you want we can get it made for you.'

'I want to do it myself. Truly, Mammy, I'm happy to do it. I want it to be perfect and if I make it myself it will be.'

Her mother had stood and watched her in silence for a while as she pushed the fabric under the darting needle. After a few seconds she said thoughtfully, 'But you'll have your wedding dress made by a proper dressmaker, won't you?'

Vicky took her foot off the treadle of her old machine and looked at her mother, seeing the worry in her eyes. She knew that making her own dress for *that* occasion would be a step too far. 'Yes, Mammy, but I'm going to make the bridesmaids' dresses. Is that a deal? I know exactly what I want and I know I can do it. Please, Mammy.'

'If it'll make you happy,' Mary-Rose conceded, but there was still an uncertain note to her voice.

'I *know* I can do it. And I'll have time. It isn't as if we're setting the date for tomorrow.'

'If you're sure then that's okay with me. I'll tell your dad. I'll get him at a good moment. You know what he can be like.'

Vicky nodded. Her dad was a lovely man but he had a temper on him and once he'd made up his mind about something nothing would shift him. They all knew he'd never hit them but they were terrified of his rages all the same. 'Now leave me be, Mammy. This dress won't make itself.'

Now Vicky looked down at the finished product with pride. The work and effort and pricked fingers had been worth it: it was beautiful. Everyone had admired it and she knew that Liam had been blown away by it.

'I can't believe how clever you are,' he'd said when she'd emerged from the trailer earlier that evening, looking stunning.

'Then that's both of us with a real skill, Liam. You with your woodworking and me with my needle.'

'We'll be the envy of everyone on the park when we're married.'

*And I'm the envy of everyone right now*, thought Vicky as her gaze once more fell on Liam.

'I'm off for a dance,' said Shania, interrupting her sister's reverie. 'Coming?'

Vicky shook her head. 'I'm going to sit this one out.' Besides, she had no need to try and attract a boy any more. She'd caught the biggest and best prize of all: her Liam.

Around them the warm evening air was filled with noise, laughter and music and the space around their trailer was crowded with a colourful swirl of people who were making the most of celebrating Liam and Vicky's engagement. Not that they needed much of an excuse. They'd party at the drop of a hat but a betrothal, a christening or any major milestone in a gypsy's life had to be marked with a full-on shindig, and given the status of Vicky's family as Johnnie was one of the elders, travellers from far and wide had come to join them. And the party exactly reflected their friends who were attending: raucous, brash and fun. Everyone was having a wonderful time.

The marquee was right in the middle of the site, just by the trailer that the O'Rourkes lived in, and the party was being enjoyed by babies and grandparents and every age in between. The menfolk dressed in clean shirts and slacks or jeans but the girls – the girls were something to behold. Traveller girls liked to look their best at a gathering like this and they all wore their favourite or newest dresses, which were all in the brightest fabrics. There were reds and oranges, yellows and lime greens, purples and pinks; every shade of the rainbow was on display and every dress was either made from satin or Lurex or sparkled with sequins or crystals. The disco lights bounced off the dresses in the same way it reflected off the revolving glitter ball above their heads. And, just like Shania, most of the girls were exposing as much of their bodies as they could in order to attract the attention of the lads. Even the youngest of the girls knew how to pout and pucker and use her body to maximum effect. Poor lads, thought Vicky as she watched. They were never going to stand a chance if a girl set her heart on one of them.

She wandered over to her mum, who was sitting on a garden chair by the door to their trailer, a glass of champagne in her hand, chatting to Liam's mother Bridget and some of their other neighbours.

Vicky bent down and gave her mother a kiss.

'Thanks for the party, Mammy.'

'Get away with you,' said Mary-Rose. 'And why wouldn't a mother give her daughter a party to celebrate her engagement? You and Liam will make us proud, isn't that so, Bridget?' She turned to Liam's mother, who was nodding in agreement. 'And just think, in a year or two we'll be celebrating your wedding day.' Mary-Rose's face was lit up with the excitement of the thought. 'I've been waiting for this day ever since you were born. My own daughter getting wed!' She hauled herself out of her chair. 'Give us a hug, darlin'.'

She put her arms around Vicky and pulled her to her big squashy bosom. As she enveloped Vicky, her daughter breathed in her mother's scent: freshly washed clothes, the soap she used and Devon violets, her mother's favourite perfume. This smell had been a part of Vicky's life for all of her fifteen years. It was the smell that meant love and warmth and kindness. It was the smell that filled their trailer.

Suddenly Vicky realised that when she married Liam she would have to leave her family trailer for ever and live apart from her mammy. She buried her face against her mother's neck. She wanted to get married, she truly did, but she couldn't help feeling scared at what it meant to her life, and how much everything would change.

There was no going back now. She'd taken the first step towards getting married and the wedding now had to be the focus of her life. It was certainly going to be the focus of her mother's.

Two years later . . .

Baby Kylie, the most recent addition to the family and a little sister for Vicky and Shania, had woken from her nap and was grizzling. Now eighteen months old she was more than capable of letting her family know if she was happy or miserable, or grumpy like she was at this moment.

'I'll get her,' said Shania, jumping up from the rug she'd spread on the grass beside the trailer so she could sunbathe. 'I expect she'll need changing,' she said as she adjusted the straps of her tiny bikini top.

'Thanks,' said Vicky, rolling over and reaching for her bottle of sunscreen. As the oldest sister it was really her job to look after Kylie but since Shania loved doing it so much it seemed a shame to deny her the pleasure. *She'll make a wonderful mother*, thought Vicky. She caught sight of her sister's shoulders as she disappeared into the shade of the trailer. 'And when you come out again I need to put some lotion on your back. You look as if you're beginning to burn. You don't want to go to that wedding at the weekend looking like a lobster.'

'I certainly don't,' Shania called out of the open door.

There came sounds of rustling and then the baby stopped crying. All she needed was a bit of a cuddle and she was as happy as Larry. Such a placid child.

Vicky finished topping up the protection on her shoulders and lay back on the rug and let the peace of a perfect August afternoon wash over her. She could hear an insect buzzing nearby. It was probably on the big tubs of flowering plants her mother had placed either side of the entrance to their trailer. In the distance was the muted roar of the dual carriageway. There was a field between their trailer park and the road but the sound easily carried across the grass. The rumble of the traffic was so much a part of the soundtrack of the park that it was rare that she noticed it. Above her, out of sight in the flawless expanse of clear periwinkle blue sky, a lark was singing his heart out. She squinted her eyes to try to spot it but gave up after a few seconds as the sun was just too bright. Somewhere the lads were having a kick-about and she could hear the yells of triumph and disappointment as the game ebbed and flowed. She imagined that her two much younger brothers, Billy and Jon-Boy, would be right in the thick of it. They'd been going stir-crazy all week with the weather being rubbish so they'd been off out with their mates as soon as they'd grabbed their breakfast that morning. With them out of the way she and Shania had got their caravan cleaned in double-quick time, which was why the two girls now had time to laze about, soaking up the rays.

However, being idle was niggling at Vicky's conscience. She should really be getting on the with dresses she was making for her mother and her sister for a friend's wedding they were going to at the weekend but this weather was too good to waste. It was the first decent day in an age. Still, the weather forecast was set fair for the weekend, which would be nice for the prospective bride. *It should be the law*, thought Vicky, *that the bride should always have the sun shine on her on her big day*.

Vicky sat up. No, this wasn't getting those dresses finished. She jumped up off the rug and followed Shania into the relative cool of the trailer. Baby Kylie was on the bench seat by the door, kicking her chubby legs in the air while Shania changed her nappy.

'Who's a good girl, then?' cooed Shania. Kylie gave her a smile in response as Shania pressed down the sticky tabs, and then straightened the pretty pink smocked dress, all flounces and frills – another one of Vicky's creations. With ease she swung the baby up off the changing mat and onto her hip.

'I can't wait to get married and have babies of my own,' she said. 'I think I'd like more than five.'

Vicky wasn't surprised. If there was anyone on this planet who was born to be a mother, it was Shania. 'I think Mammy would have liked more too but she always said that she didn't fall pregnant easily.' Vicky opened a cupboard and got out her sewing box and one of the two dresses she was working on.

'I hope that doesn't happen to me. I want ten.'

'Oh my God, ten! You'll be needing a big trailer with all them.'

'What about you and Liam? How many kids are you going to have?'

11

Vicky took her sewing box from the kitchen counter. 'Shan! I'm not even married yet. That's putting the cart before the horse.'

Shania grabbed a feeder cup off the table with one hand and handed it to Kylie, who began sucking on the spout contentedly. She stowed the changing mat away, disposed of the dirty nappy, made sure she'd tidied up properly, then moved to the door. Vicky followed her.

'When are you going to set a date?' Shania said over her shoulder. 'You're almost seventeen.'

'That's hardly ancient.'

'I want to be married when I'm sixteen.'

Shania put the baby on the rug where she sat placidly still drinking her juice and then plumped down beside her sister. Vicky sat on the aluminium step by the door, her open sewing box at her feet, the lime-green dress she was making for Shania draped over her knees.

Shania stretched luxuriously on the rug and then said in an artificially casual way, 'I reckon Michael's going to grab me at the wedding.'

'You reckon?'

'Sure of it. He keeps looking at me.'

'You could do worse.' Vicky concentrated on threading a needle

'I know. He's lovely.' Shania sighed, wistfully.

'You mustn't look too keen, though. You've got to put up a fight if he does grab you.'

'Oh, I will. It wouldn't be proper to give in to a kiss right away. I'd look a right slapper if I did that. And think what Dad would say.'

Vicky, who'd started hemming the sleeve, put down

her sewing as she contemplated just how angry he would be. No, her dad's temper wasn't a happy thought on a day like today. She smiled at her sister, pleased that she'd got her eye on a good man and even more pleased that her sister knew how to behave. She caught sight of her sister's reddening shoulders. 'Hey,' she said. 'You've forgotten about the sunscreen. You'll be burnt to a crisp if we don't get that on your back and then no one, not even the sainted Michael, will want you.'

She dumped her sewing onto her sewing box and moved over to the rug where she could help Shania slather on the factor twenty.

'It's so unfair,' said Shania. 'Why don't I tan like you?'

'Because you've got beautiful Irish skin like Mammy's.'

'But I always look as if I've just crawled out from under a rock,' wailed Shania.

'You so don't,' said Vicky. 'You're a beauty, you're pale and interesting whereas me? I'm so dark after the summer I look like I could be related to that guy Jordan.'

'Jordan?'

'Yeah, you know him. In my year, hangs around with that bitch Chloe.'

'Oh, him. He's well fit.'

'Yeah, but his dad is from somewhere in Africa.'

'Can you imagine if we married a black man?' said Shania.

The girls giggled at the enormity of the idea.

'Can you imagine if one of us married a gorgio?' said Vicky, going one step further. The idea of marrying a non-traveller was so unthinkable that they both shrieked. 'Oh my God,' yelped Vicky. 'Dad would go ballistic.'

'Mental,' agreed Shania.

The family car drew up in front of the trailer; their parents were back from a shopping trip to the local superstore. Mary-Rose waved at her daughters and then heaved her bulk out of the white saloon. Their father got out of the driver's seat.

'Give your mammy a hand with the shopping,' he said, although the girls didn't need telling. They were already on their way over to help bring the groceries into their home.

Mary-Rose settled down in a plastic garden chair outside and pulled Kylie onto her lap while the girls ferried all the carrier bags inside and got busy stowing away the food in the fridge and the larder cupboards. They switched the kettle on as they worked and took their mother a cup of tea. Their father had decided to slake his thirst with a can of beer he'd liberated from one of the carriers as the girls had passed him by.

'Oh, that's grand,' she said, accepting the steaming mug with a grateful smile. 'I'm that parched.'

When the girls had finished Vicky went back to her dress, neatly sewing the hem on the sleeve and then nipping off the thread with her teeth.

'Go and try this on, will you, Shania?' she said as she handed the frock over.

Shania retreated to the tiny space that was the room she shared with her big sister. A few minutes later she emerged clad in the skimpy creation.

'Oh, what a picture,' said Mary-Rose, clapping her

14

hands. 'I love it. Give us a twirl.' Shania pirouetted. 'That colour's lovely with your hair. Do you think it needs more sequins?'

Vicky put her head on one side as she considered her mother's suggestion. 'I've got plenty left. We could put some around here.' She pointed to the bottom of the short bodice top that left most of Shania's midriff bare.

'Yeah, I'd like that,' said Shania. 'If it's not too much trouble.'

'Of course it's not. Nothing is too much trouble for my sister. And not if it means she catches a certain someone's eye.' She gave Shania a nudge. 'Now go and take it off – I don't want to accidentally sew a sequin onto you!'

Her sister disappeared to change once again.

'Daddy,' said Vicky.

'Yes, my angel.' The sunshine and the chilled lager had made her dad mellow and content with his lot.

'Are you still all right to give me a lift into school tomorrow?'

Johnnie gave his daughter a quizzical look and then he remembered. 'Oh yes. It's your results day, isn't it? What time have you got to be there?'

'Any time after nine. It *is* okay, isn't it?'

'No bother.'

'Just think,' said Mary-Rose, shaking her head. 'One of our kids with GCSEs.'

The tone of her voice made Vicky smile; pride and bewilderment in equal measure. 'I haven't got them yet. For all we know I might have failed everything.'

'You won't,' said her mother with a smile. 'But I still

can't work out why for the life of me you bothered with them. None of your cousins has got a qualification to their name. In fact, I don't think most of them can even read. And what does it matter – all this book learning? Will it make you a better wife or mother? To be sure it won't.'

Shania emerged back in her bikini and gave her nearly finished dress back to her sister.

'I can't see why on earth you think staying on at school is going to do you any good. I'm glad I left last year,' she announced. 'What's the use of book learning when I'm keeping a house? In fact, if you hurried up and tied the knot with Liam, I could think about marrying too.'

'Well, you can't,' said her mother firmly. 'Not just yet. I want Vicky settled before we think about you.'

'You can't stop me getting engaged,' said Shania, defiantly. 'If the right boy asks me I shall say yes as soon as blinking. And if Vicky doesn't get a move on I don't care if it wouldn't look right; I'll get married before her.'

'That's enough,' barked her father, who didn't like to hear his family bickering. 'Vicky will marry next year and you can be wed the year after and that's an end to it.'

'Next *year*,' said Vicky, appalled. 'But . . . but . . .'

'But nothing.'

'But I've got plans,' she muttered.

'Plans? What plans?'

'Plans like what Mrs Truman suggested,' she admitted slowly.

'You mean that nonsense about going to college,' said her father.

'It's not nonsense.'

'Yes it is. College is no place for our kind. It's just a waste of time.'

'But it wouldn't be,' pleaded Vicky. 'I'd learn a real skill, a useful skill.'

Johnnie narrowed his eyes. 'I'm not going to discuss this, Vicky. You won't need no dressmaking qualification when you're married to Liam. Jesus, can't you already make lovely dresses? What could college teach you that you don't already know? It would just be a waste of time. Time that would be better spent planning your big day and, once that is out of the way, starting a family.'

Vicky felt her eyes filling with tears. Dad didn't understand. She could make dresses just fine but she always had to buy paper patterns for the designs and finding anything that was suitable was almost impossible. If she went to college she'd learn to pattern cut and how to design her own garments. Ever since she'd been tiny she'd been dressing her Barbie dolls in her own creations and more than anything she wanted to learn how to do it properly. Professionally.

She knew full well that she wouldn't be allowed to do it as a *job* once she was married. It would bring disgrace to Liam if she earned money. Earning money would be his role, just as her role would be that of wife and mother, but she could make outfits for her friends and family. She'd help people choose the fabric and then she'd make it up. There couldn't be anything wrong in that, providing she didn't ask for more than the money

17

to cover the costs. Just like Shania could think of nothing but keeping house and having babies, Vicky's head was filled with ideas for lovely dresses and outfits. It was her passion. But her dad refused to listen to any of her ideas. As far as he was concerned she was out of order.

Rather than cry in front of her mother and upset her too, Vicky put down her sewing and took off. She wandered aimlessly down the main road that led through the centre of the park. It was so *unfair*. And her dad didn't get it. It wasn't as if she wanted to do anything *wrong*. It was only dressmaking, when all was said and done.

Walking and the warm sunshine calmed her slowly and she let her feet carry her to Liam's shed. Well, it was his dad's shed really, but it would be Liam's one day. As she approached it the pine-scented tang of wood shavings drifted on the slight breeze accompanied by the rhythmic rasp of the sound of sawing. She leaned against the doorjamb and watched her fiancé working. He'd stopped sawing and was holding up the piece of wood he was working on, caressing the grain with his long, tanned fingers, almost as if he were playing an instrument. Her annoyance and frustration with her family was swept aside by a big surge of love for her fiancé. Her Liam really was one of the best. *I am so lucky*, she told herself, *to have him*.

'So what's that going to be?' she said softly.

Liam jumped and put the wood down, almost guiltily. 'And what are you doing creeping up on me like that?' But his words held no anger and his smile was one of pure pleasure at seeing her.

Vicky ignored the question and moved across the floor of the shed to his workbench. 'What are you making?'

'Never you mind.'

'It's nice wood. Pretty colour.'

'It's cherry.'

'That sounds lovely.'

'It is. It's a grand wood. One of the best.' Liam picked up the plank and took it over to the side of the shed where he put it with some similar timbers. Vicky, used to seeing the component pieces of a garment laid out before she put them together, could see that Liam was working in the same methodical way. He obviously had a commission to make something more complex than a simple cupboard.

'You nervous?' he said, returning to her side.

'Nervous?' Vicky shook her head. What was Liam on about? 'Why should I be nervous?'

'Big day tomorrow – your results.'

Vicky's feelings of frustration barrelled back. 'Oh, them,' she snorted. 'Yeah, well, it's not going to matter now whether I pass or fail . . .' She shrugged.

'Of course it matters. And it matters to me. I want to be able to boast I've got the cleverest wife in all the world.'

'Liam, a few GCSEs doesn't make me a brainbox.'

'It does to me. Anyway, why don't your results matter all of a sudden? That wasn't what you thought when you were working for them.'

'Daddy says I can't go to college. He says I've got to get married.'

19

Liam frowned. 'But . . .' Now he was confused. 'But you still *do* want to get married, don't you?'

'Oh Liam, of course I do. It's just . . . it's just . . .'

'You want everything,' he finished for her.

She nodded. 'Is that so wrong?'

'Darlin' girl, as far as I am concerned you can have whatever you want. If I can make it or buy it for you, it's yours.'

*But,* thought Vicky sadly, *going to college doesn't fall into either of those categories.*

Liam went over to the corner of the shed where there was a fridge and a sink and where the kettle lived. He picked it up and waved it at her. 'Tea?'

She nodded. 'Let me,' she said, moving over to join him. She took the mugs off the shelf and a pint of milk from the little fridge and busied herself, filling the kettle from the tap.

'What if . . .' said Liam. He paused, clearly thinking through what he was about to suggest.

'Yes?'

'What if,' he said slowly, 'you told your father that you need to go to college to make sure the bridesmaids' dresses are perfect? I mean, I'm right that he's only said he's unhappy with you going to college. He hasn't said you can't make those dresses, has he? He's still okay about that, isn't he?'

'Yes, but—'

'Couldn't you tell him you need the sort of machines they'll have at college to work with. I mean,' Liam gestured around him, 'Dad and I need all sorts of special tools to do what we do. People think chippies just need a hammer and a saw but to do a proper job you need all sorts. You've only got a sewing machine.' He laughed and added, 'Not that I know anything about dressmaking, but isn't your machine a bit basic for the sort of dresses you girls like at your weddings? I need all sorts for the different jobs I do. Isn't that the same for you?'

Vicky nodded. At school in the textiles department she had a whole range of machines from overlockers to ones that did computer-aided embroidery. The one she had in the trailer was really old-fashioned and just stitched in a straight line. It didn't even zigzag. Anything fiddly she had to finish by hand, which took time.

And,' he added, 'if I told your dad that I don't mind you going if it means making you happy, means you can make those dresses you've set your heart on . . . well, it can't do any harm, can it?'

'You'd talk to my dad? Really?'

'I'll talk to him, but that's no guarantee he'll change his mind.'

'No, but . . .' But it was a ray of hope.

Johnnie O'Rourke sat by the barbecue checking on the meat he was cooking. The girls were in the trailer getting the rest of the food ready. On the next plot their neighbour, Jimmy Connelly, Liam's father, was doing the same and the men chatted across the space as they sipped their beers and turned the meat. Liam, fresh from the shower block, came across to join them, pulling on a clean shirt as he walked towards them.

21

'Hello, Uncle Johnnie,' he called.

The O'Rourkes and the Connellys weren't related by blood, but it almost felt as if they were, having been neighbours since before Liam had been born.

'Evening, Liam. Would you like a beer?'

'You're all right, I'm good, thanks. But I'd like a word.'

'A word, eh? Would it be about the wedding? When are you going to get my daughter to set a date? Neither of you is getting any younger and Mary-Rose is desperate for grandchildren.'

'My ma's the same, to be sure. In fact it's funny you should mention it as me and Vicky were talking about the subject only this afternoon. Which is why we need to talk.'

'Praise be,' said Johnnie with feeling. 'So she's scrapped that stupid notion of going to college, then.'

'Well, not exactly.'

Johnnie stopped attending to the steaks on the barbecue and turned to look at his future son-in-law. 'Not *exactly*? How does that work?'

'You know she's set her heart on making her bridesmaids' dresses.'

'Yes.' Johnnie said slowly, narrowing his eyes.

'And you agreed that she could do it.'

'Yes.' Johnnie was sounding increasingly wary.

'Well, Vicky's worried about it.'

'Then I'll pay for her to have them made.'

'I know you would, and so does she, but she wants to do it herself. You know what women are like when they get a notion in their heads.'

Johnnie did, only too well. Mary-Rose was always getting ideas for things to do to the trailer – 'improvements' – as if it wasn't perfect already. And she was never happy until he'd forked out for her latest whim. However, in Johnnie's world, he found that most problems could be solved by throwing a bit of money at them. 'So, either she can make these fecking dresses or she can't. If she can't, I'll pay, if she can, what's the problem?'

'The problem is she *can* make them, but she'll need specialist machines.'

'Then I'll buy the fecking machines.' Johnnie was beginning to get irritated.

'I don't think it's as simple as that. She'll need to be taught how to use them.'

Johnnie gave Liam a long stare. 'So what you're trying to tell me is that she's convinced you that she ought to go to college just so as she can make some dresses that by rights I should be paying a proper dressmaker to make.'

'Well . . . yes, that's the size of it. But it'd make her so happy to do it herself. And you did say she could.' Liam leaned forwards and looked earnestly at Johnnie. 'And isn't her happiness what we both want for her? It'd only be until June, then we'd get married, promise. She'd be happy, the wedding won't be delayed more than a few months . . .' Liam shrugged. 'So, Uncle Johnnie, what do you say?'

'To be sure I want her happiness too but I worry about this college business. School is one thing but college?' Johnnie sighed. 'At school there were kids from here with her. Safety in numbers and all that, but she'll be alone at college. I don't like that idea at all.'

'But Vicky always said that no one really realised that she's a traveller, especially when she stayed on to take her GCSEs. She said she was very careful to keep a low profile.'

'I don't know.' A big frown creased Johnnie's forehead.

'In fact, I reckon she'd be safer. Let's face it,' said Liam. 'No kid from here has ever gone to college. It's the last place they'd expect a traveller to show up.' He could see Johnnie was wavering and decided to try to press home his advantage. 'And you could take her in the car each morning and pick her up in the afternoon.'

'I don't know. I'm not happy with the idea, not at all. If she doesn't go, she'll get over it.'

'Okay, Uncle Johnnie. I just promised myself that I'd ask you. I just hate to see her miserable and it'd break my heart if I didn't think I'd done everything in my power to make things perfect for her.'

He got up and left, leaving Johnnie with his barbecue.

Night was falling by the time the O'Rourkes had finished gorging themselves on the mounds of food they'd prepared. Kylie had long since been bathed and put to bed. The boys were playing with a swingball set, Johnnie and Mary-Rose were sitting by the still-glowing coals sipping cold beers and the two older girls were doing the washing up and tidying up the trailer at the end of the day.

Across the park were the sounds of kids playing, people laughing, music coming from someone's trailer –

the sounds of happy people enjoying a balmy summer evening.

'Young Liam had a talk with me earlier,' said Johnnie.

'And?'

'He says that our Vicky will be unhappy if we don't let her go to college.'

Mary-Rose tutted. 'She'll get over it. There's lots of worse things that can happen in life than not going to college.'

'He says she mightn't be able to make those dresses like she'd planned.'

'What's Liam doing worrying about the dresses?' Mary-Rose was outraged. 'That's women's business. How would he like it if I started on about carpentry?'

'He wasn't talking about the actual dresses themselves, just the making of them. He says Vicky'll need special equipment.'

'Then she'll have to manage without.'

'I know. But Liam's right: she's set her heart on doing it.'

'Then she can *un*set it.'

'That's what I thought, Mammy, but now I don't know. Liam said that they could get married this time next year so she could go to college, get the dresses made, she'd be happy, he'd be happy . . .'

'But college?'

'Our Vicky's a good girl.'

Mary-Rose nodded in agreement.

'She's never given us a jot of trouble,' continued Johnnie.

25

'That she hasn't.'

'If it doesn't work, she could leave.'

Mary-Rose nodded again. 'So you're thinking of changing your mind?' Which was a rare occasion. And if Johnnie was thinking along different lines then Mary-Rose knew it was okay for her to do similar.

'I'm not sure. What do you think?'

'Well, it's only till next year. It's too late for her and Liam to be thinking of marrying this summer and I've never liked the idea of a winter wedding.'

'So shall we tell her?'

'She needs to know before she gets her results,' said Mary-Rose, still a bit thunderstruck by her husband's change of mind.

'Call her out here, then.'

Mary-Rose heaved herself out of her chair and asked her eldest to come outside. 'Your daddy wants a word.'

Shania and Vicky exchanged a glance. What was this about? Why did her dad want a talk? Dutifully Vicky went outside while Shania hung around the entrance to the trailer, agog with curiosity.

'I've been thinking about college,' said her dad.

Vicky nodded, and desperately tried to keep her hopes from soaring like a lark.

'I don't know nothing about the place, and I don't understand why you want to go but I can see it's important to you.'

Despite Vicky's best efforts her expectations that this was a 'good' talk began to rise.

'But I need you to promise me that if . . .' her dad paused. '*If*,' he repeated for effect, 'I let you go, you promise me you'll do nothing to disgrace me or your family or bring shame on our community.'

'Daddy,' said Vicky, almost crying with happiness. 'I promise on my life. If I do anything, *anything* that anyone here would worry about I'd kill myself, so I would.'

'But you won't,' said her mother. 'You're a good girl and you know how to behave.'

Vicky nodded so hard she felt her teeth clatter together. 'Mammy, I'll be such a credit to the family.'

Shania could bear it no longer. 'College?' she cried, jumping out of their trailer and ignoring the step. She leapt forward so that she was right in Vicky's face. '*College*? But you should be getting married. What about me?'

'Hush, you'll wake Kylie,' reprimanded her mother.

'Blow Kylie. What about me?' she repeated, her voice shrill with indignation. 'I just know Mikey is going to ask me to marry him soon and I don't want to hang around once he has.' She turned to her mother for support. 'Just because Vicky can't get her act together I don't see why I should suffer.'

'You haven't been asked yet and you're only just fifteen,' replied her mother, reasonably.

'But I can be married at sixteen. And if Vicky doesn't get going I'll be seventeen before I'm wed.'

'That's not old,' said Vicky.

'Do you know something?' Shania squared her shoulders at her older sister. 'I don't think you want to get married at all. If you did you'd just be getting on with it. You're just playing at getting married.'

'How dare you say that? Of course I want to wed Liam. Who wouldn't?'

'You, apparently. You seem to be looking for problems.'

'I so am not.'

'You so are – I mean, *college*? What the heck is that all about?'

'It's about . . .' Vicky just couldn't voice her dream. It was her innermost ambition, her innermost hope. The idea of being a professional dressmaker one day was just too big a deal to talk about. And it certainly wasn't something to go into with her father present.

'It's about just getting my wedding perfect,' she lied. She wasn't going to let on about her true motivation. 'I know the dressmaker will do her best but only I know *really* what I want for my bridesmaids and if it takes a bit longer to create . . .'

Shania shook her head. 'It sounds like an excuse to me. You're just finding reasons to not set a date.'

'Vicky,' roared Johnnie, 'will get married in under three hundred and sixty-five days from now, and that's an end to it.'

Silence fell. Vicky was contemplating the fact that she'd never take the A level she'd set her heart on and Shania was thinking that she had a whole year to wait at the very least, which, as far as she was concerned, was just totally unfair.

# 2

The next morning Vicky was awake at dawn, her stomach churning with nerves at the realisation that this was results day. She crept out of the bed she shared with her sister, praying that Shania wasn't going to wake up. She had enough to worry about today without a re-run of the row they'd had the night before. They had both got ready for bed still spitting tacks, hissing harsh words at each other in low voices so as not to antagonise their father further – Shania making it plain that she thought her sister's attitude was unbelievably selfish and Vicky shooting back that Shania was being completely unreasonable. She'd never gone to sleep without making up with her sister before and this morning she felt bad about it. She'd sort it out later. Vicky hardly ever fell out with her sister and she didn't like the atmosphere between them, but she wasn't going to back down on the subject of college. Liam supported her and now that her father had changed his mind she didn't care that it didn't suit Shania. Tough – she'd have to get over it. That was assuming that she got the grades, because if she didn't . . .

29

No, she wasn't going to think like that. Mrs Truman was sure she would pass her textiles GCSE with flying colours. A couple of the other subjects were a bit iffy but she didn't care two hoots about science or history. Just as long as she got her English, maths and textiles then she could go on to college. Anything else would be a bonus.

She glanced down to check her sister was still sleeping, grabbed her dressing gown, towel and sponge bag and then slipped out of the tiny room they shared in the family trailer, shutting the door behind her silently. Equally quietly she let herself out and breathed in the fresh, chill morning air. It was going to be another glorious day. Above her the sky was milky blue and cloudless, there wasn't a breath of wind and the grass under her bare feet glistened with dew. The birds in the trees around the park were singing almost loud enough to drown out the traffic noise and at the edge of the park, where the grass grew long and lush, rabbits were foraging. Fingers of mist were rising off the field and the low sun cast long shadows. It all looked so perfect, Vicky almost thought she was on a film set.

She stood for a moment enjoying the sheer peace and loveliness of the morning before she skipped across the grass to the shower block, leaving a trail of dark footprints in the silver dew. As she had got up so early, she had the block to herself and she luxuriated in the shower, taking her time, knowing that she wasn't keeping anyone waiting. She washed her thick dark hair and then combed conditioner through it. If she was going to be meeting all her classmates she wanted to look as neat and tidy as possible. Her best friend Kelly knew where she lived, and so did some of her teachers, but the fact that she was from Irish traveller stock was a secret she kept from everyone else.

Of course, the kids at school weren't stupid and they'd picked up on one or two of the kids from the trailer park, Shania being one of them, and had given them a hard time – name calling and bullying to the extent that those children had left the school completely, their parents telling the authorities that they were moving on. Since outsiders were less than welcome on the site no one ever checked up; as far as the local education authority was concerned, if the traveller children couldn't read or write adequately it was their parents' lookout.

So Vicky had known all her life that if she wanted to pass unnoticed she needed to tone down her Irish accent when she was away from the site and do nothing to draw attention to herself. The fact that she was naturally bright and a quick learner had also helped her to blend in, as did the uniform. Looking the same as the other kids, wearing the same clothes and doing absolutely nothing to stand out Vicky became almost invisible.

Quite how her schoolfriend Kelly had guessed about Vicky's background she didn't know, but when Kelly had stopped her on her way to lunch in the canteen one day and asked her outright if she was a gypsy, she and Vicky were close enough for Kelly to agree to keep the truth to herself.

'I can't believe it!' Kelly had said in a shocked

31

whisper. 'You, a gyppo! I mean I know I asked if you were but I really didn't expect the answer to be yes.'

'Well, there you go and please don't call me a gyppo, it's really rude.'

'I am sorry, I didn't realise. Blimey, that explains a bit.'

'Maybe it does but you mustn't tell a soul. Please,' Vicky pleaded, taking Kelly's hand and looking into her eyes. 'You know what some people are like and just because they have accepted me here don't mean their attitude won't change once they know where I live.'

'Surely not?'

'Well, I don't want to find out that I'm right.'

'No, I can see that. There's one or two who just love to make other people's lives miserable.'

'Chloe for one.'

'Exactly.'

Kelly had been true to her word and a couple of years on no one else had guessed. There had been a couple of dodgy moments when other kids noticed that although Vicky was one of the oldest in the class, as she had a September birthday, she seemed to have to obey much stricter rules than some of the youngest. One or two of the boys had also wondered why she was so uptight about going out with anyone but Kelly had always jumped to her friend's defence and said that her father was really strict. Which was true, but the way Kelly told it made him sound just old-fashioned rather than the fact that Vicky's whole lifestyle was so different to theirs, that her schoolmates would never understand.

Vicky rinsed the conditioner out of her hair, switched

off the shower and dried herself carefully before winding her towel round her wet curls. When she left the shower block she could see signs of life springing up on the park. A couple of the trailer doors were open and hooked back, a dog had been let out and was rushing up and down the hedge trying to find the rabbits that had been there a few minutes before, and there were footprints other than Vicky's in the grass.

When she got back to her trailer the family was awake. Kylie was in her high chair with a beaker of warm milk and Shania was cooking bacon for her father and brothers. The smell was delicious but Vicky was feeling so wound up with nerves that instead of making her feel hungry she just felt sick.

'Cut the bread,' said Shania.

No 'good morning', Vicky noticed, so clearly Shania was still in a mood with her. Not wishing to upset her sister further, Vicky put off drying her hair and expertly cut half a dozen slices off a new loaf. She slathered them in butter and passed them to her sister, who flipped the bacon from the pan onto the slices and made up three big sandwiches.

'Breakfast,' she called.

With the men being fed Vicky was free to sort herself out. She had hours before she was due in school but she had to think about what to wear; no more school uniform for her, which meant that the anonymity of black trousers and a white shirt wasn't available.

In the end she chose a pair of jeans and a bright green T-shirt and tied back her hair in a neat ponytail. She checked her appearance in the long mirror on the wall. Good, nothing about her that would make her look any different from the one hundred or so other girls also getting their results. Neat, tidy, plain and unremarkable. Job done.

'What time do you want to leave?' asked her father, watching breakfast TV as he finished the last of his bacon butty.

Vicky glanced at her watch. 'About quarter to nine. Ages yet.'

And in the meantime she had to find something to do to keep herself busy or she was going to end up a basket case with worry and nerves. She'd be all right for a few minutes and then the memory that this was results day would come crashing back into her mind and her stomach started to churn once again. In fact, she thought that her stomach was whirling so much someone could use it as a cement mixer.

She filled the sink with hot water and began on the washing up, then she made the beds while Shania got on with cleaning all the windows. Although the two girls largely ignored each other the atmosphere thawed. And when the clock had finally crawled round to the time for Vicky to leave, Shania even wished her a grudging 'good luck'.

'I'll wait for you here,' said Vicky's dad as she got out of the car around the corner from the main entrance and well away from the school car park where most of the kids got delivered. While Vicky didn't look different from anyone else at the school, her dad, with his skin colouring, gold earrings and tattoos, certainly did.

34

When, on her first day at the comp, she'd suggested that driving up to the school gates wasn't a good idea, he'd wanted to know if she was ashamed of who she was.

'Of course not, Dad, but you know what kids can be like. Remember how it was at primary. I don't want it to be like that here. There's no point in me going to school right across town if it all kicks off again, is there? And if I get bullied then so will Shania and then it'll be the boys. They're always in fights with other school kids as it is.'

Since Johnnie adored his children and wanted to protect them from harm as much as possible he'd accepted Vicky's argument. There was no point in deliberately looking for trouble and if parking several hundred yards away was going to help, then so be it.

'I'll be a bit,' she said. 'Maybe thirty minutes.' Her dad sighed. Vicky got the message. 'Okay, I'll be as quick as I can,' she promised.

As she walked the few hundred yards to the entrance she slipped her engagement ring off her finger and onto the chain around her neck with her crucifix. Along with her accent and her normal style of dressing, her engagement ring, which she'd had since she was fifteen, would have raised tricky questions. Outside the traveller community girls that young didn't get engaged. Kelly knew the situation but not a soul else in the school had the smallest clue – and as far as Vicky was concerned it was going to stay that way. And it was going to have to stay that way if she made it to college.

Oh God – thinking about going to college set off her nerves again. With trembling fingers she texted Kelly.

'U here yet,' she sent.

'Yes w8ing 4 u b4 I open mine hurry.'

The girls had sworn that they'd open their envelopes together. Vicky couldn't bear the thought of keeping her friend waiting a minute longer than necessary so she broke into a trot. A couple of minutes later she raced through the door and skidded to a halt in front of the desk where the Head was handing out the results.

'Vicky O'Rourke,' he said as he glanced at her and began rifling through the alphabetical pile. By the time he'd found hers Kelly was beside her. Together the two girls, who were so similar in colouring and curves they could be sisters, went off to a quiet corner to find out the truth. Around them were shrieks and laughter as those who had received good grades celebrated, phoned home and shared the news. But these were also a couple of pupils staring at their slips ashen-faced, as they realised that whatever hopes or ambitions they had had, had just slipped away.

'Oh my God, this is it,' said Kelly.

Vicky looked at her envelope clutched in her shaking hand. 'One, two, three.'

The girls ripped open the flaps at the same time. And took out the slips. Both stared at their results for a couple of seconds, taking in the grades, and then they looked at each other.

'And?' breathed Vicky.

'I got three Bs and five Cs. You?'

'A star for textiles, A for art, three Bs and a couple of Ds.'

'Did you pass English and maths?'

Vicky nodded.

'So we're both going to college,' they shrieked in unison, their voices adding to the cacophony. They hugged each other, jumping up and down.

'Ohmigod, ohmigod, ohmigod,' chanted Kelly, the words running into each other in her excitement.

'We've done it!' Vicky laughed.

'Someone's pleased,' said a male voice.

The girls broke apart to see who was talking to them. 'Jordan,' said Kelly. She clocked his smile. 'You look happy. I suppose that means you did okay.'

'Yup, got the grades.'

'So you'll be going to college too,' said Vicky.

'First one in my family to stay in education beyond sixteen.' He gave her a huge happy smile.

'Me too,' said Vicky.

A tall blonde with a sour expression joined their group and put her arm around Jordan. Her body language was unmistakable. He's mine – keep off.

Vicky and Kelly exchanged a look. Neither of them liked Chloe very much. Whenever she turned up she always seemed to put a downer on things. Kelly and Vicky couldn't work out why but there was an atmosphere whenever she was about. It was like she came with her own personal rain cloud. Today was no exception.

'So, did you two pass?' Her tone of voice clearly indicated she was expecting a negative answer.

'Yes, great, isn't it,' said Vicky, refusing to be intimidated.

'Oh.' Chloe failed to hide the surprise in her voice. 'Well done,' she added grudgingly.

'It's fantastic, isn't it?' said Jordan. Was he ignoring

his girlfriend's rudeness or had he just not picked up on it? 'We're all going to be at college together, won't it be great?'

'Lovely,' said Chloe flatly, looking down her nose at the other two girls. She snuggled up even closer to Jordan.

Over the top of her head, Jordan winked at Vicky, who had to pretend to cough to cover up the laugh that burst out of her. Chloe looked at her with narrowed eyes, making her appear even more bad-tempered. Vicky wondered, not for the first time, what on earth a fitty like Jordan saw in her. When the pair had first started dating Kelly had suggested that maybe Chloe's knickers came down more easily than most, which was why he'd asked her out.

Which was possibly quite true although, at the time, Vicky had refrained from mentioning pots and kettles because she knew for a fact – because Kelly herself had told her – that Kelly had gone with Bradley Brown when they were only in year nine. Vicky had been horrified. If a gypsy girl wasn't a virgin on her wedding night then the disgrace and the shame were intolerable. But non-travellers had a very different set of values. Which made it odd, Vicky had thought, that they treated Romanies and travellers like they were the scum of the earth when their kids were behaving like harlots and gigolos. But she loved Kelly far too much to let her know what she really thought about her friend's behaviour. However, passing judgement on a cow like Chloe was a whole other matter. Chloe deserved it.

'Come on, Jordy,' Chloe said, 'I want to tell Jenna

how I did. Bet it was better than her,' she added smugly.

After Chloe had dragged Jordan away from them, Kelly turned to Vicky.

'I saw that wink that Jordan gave you. I keep telling you he fancies you. Do you believe me now?'

'Don't be silly.'

Kelly raised her eyebrows and sighed. 'You could have him like that,' she snapped her fingers, 'if you wanted.'

'Don't be daft. And anyway, I don't want.' Which she definitely didn't. Not with the lovely Liam firmly in the picture. However, there was a little bit of her that, treacherously, couldn't help feeling flattered. And, although outwardly she rubbished Kelly's words, she knew deep down that her friend had a point. Jordan was often finding an excuse to chat to her, if he managed to get away from Chloe. They'd done geography together, which Chloe hadn't taken, and Jordan had sat next to her for that. He was just being nice, she'd told herself, they were just mates. You could like someone without fancying them, couldn't you? And anyway she didn't fancy him – even if he was drop-dead gorgeous. One thing was certain, though, he was the fittest boy in year eleven and, quite probably, the whole school.

Not that he was completely perfect. On the downside, he'd already dated quite a few girls from their year – Chloe was hardly his first love, although she was the one who seemed to have got her claws into him deeper than anyone else. Jordan might be gorgeous but Vicky didn't think he'd win a Mr Faithful contest and, judging by the way he kept giving her the eye, maybe he was already trying to dump Chloe and move on. But he'd picked on the wrong girl if he thought Vicky was going to be next in line. No way.

'What's wrong with you? I'd go with him,' said Kelly, looking wistfully in the direction of where Jordan and Chloe had gone.

'You'll have to get Chloe out of the picture first.'

'And you,' Kelly pointed out.

'Do me a favour. I keep telling you I'm not interested.'

'That's not the point.'

Vicky frowned. 'I know I'm not thick – hey, I've got GCSEs to prove it now – but which bit of *I'm Not Interested* don't you get?'

Kelly shrugged. 'But it isn't *just* about you. If Jordan escapes from Chloe's clutches, he's not going to come looking for me, he's going to head for you. I could have a neon sign strapped to me flashing "Come and get it here, Jordan" with a big arrow pointing straight at my fanny and he wouldn't pay any attention. Not while he's got the hots for you.'

Kelly's outrageous comment made Vicky giggle. That was one of the things she loved about her friend – she was so upfront. Kelly would say what she meant, no mucking about with weasel words, and she expected her mates to be equally straight with her. If she asked if she looked rough she wanted an honest answer, not some fudge about looking a bit peaky or any other sort of crap.

Vicky shook her head. 'Then he's going to be disappointed because he's not in the frame.'

Kelly looked exasperated but could tell that her

friend wasn't going to budge. She changed the subject. 'I know it's unlikely but any chance of you being
allowed out tonight? A bunch of us are going out on the
lash.'

Vicky sighed. 'Come on, Kel, what do you think?'

'That'll be a no then.'

Vicky nodded. 'I don't know how you get away with
it. I mean, I know your mum and dad aren't as strict as
mine but don't bars and clubs want ID? Your mum and
dad mightn't mind you having a drink but the coppers
do.'

'Some bars do, some don't. Me and the other girls
have sussed out the ones that don't care. Besides
some of us have got fake IDs.' She gave Vicky a knowing
wink.

'You are so naughty, Kelly Munro! And you know I'd
love to come out but . . . well, it isn't going to happen, is
it.'

'Not even tonight?'

Vicky shook her head sadly. 'Not even tonight.' Her
phone bleeped. 'Shit,' she said guiltily, hauling it out
from her pocket. 'That'll be Dad wanting to know where
I am.' She looked at the caller ID. 'Aw, no it's not.' She
checked the text. 'Bless him.'

'The lovely Liam?'

Vicky nodded. 'He's desperate to know how I've done
but says that whatever the results he's more proud of me
than I could possibly guess.'

'Aw, sweet.'

'Isn't he just?'

'You know, he needn't know.'

41

Vicky looked bewildered. 'Needn't know? But I want to tell him my results. I'm dead proud.'

'Not that. What I mean is he needn't know if you had a fling with Jordan. It isn't as if your two worlds overlap. Liam and Jordan will never run into each other. So have some fun and just don't tell Liam.'

Vicky's jaw dropped at the enormity of what Kelly was saying. 'You don't get it, do you?' She began to tick points off on her fingers. 'One, I have to be a virgin on my wedding day; two, I don't fancy Jordan; and three, I love Liam. So can we drop this crazy idea you have about me and him?'

'And just how is Liam going to tell if you're a virgin? I bet he wouldn't have a clue. If you tell him you're whiter than white, he'll believe you.'

'Hush your mouth, Kelly Munro. That's the most disgraceful suggestion I have *ever* heard! I couldn't lie to Liam. For a start I just couldn't live with myself and also I'll burn in hell for all eternity.'

Kelly shrugged. 'It was just a thought.'

'Well, keep thoughts like that to yourself. Now I have to go. My dad will be wondering where I am. Have a good one tonight.' She gave Kelly a quick hug to show that she forgave her for her shocking suggestion. 'I'll text. Maybe, if I can get Shania to come too, we can meet in town and go shopping together.'

Vicky rushed out of school and raced back to find her dad before he got too antsy about being kept waiting.

'Well?' he asked as she climbed into the car.

'Pretty good,' she said. 'I passed five and got an A for

art and an A star for textiles. And with English and maths I've got enough to go to college.'

Johnnie's face broke into a huge smile. 'Well, I never, my daughter, a college girl. Who'd have thought it?'

'You pleased, Dad?'

'Since it's what you've set your heart on, yes. Yes I am, princess.'

On the journey home Vicky texted Liam with her results and he was there to greet her when the car drew up. As she got out he picked her up and spun her round and round, pride in his fiancée's achievement beaming from his face.

'I can't believe my girl is so clever,' he said. 'And an A star! Isn't that like top marks?'

'It's a good grade, yes,' said Vicky with a laugh. Liam's joy was infectious.

'Vicky! Vicky!' Her mother was shrieking at her from the door of the trailer. 'Vicky, your daddy's just told me. Come here, me darlin', and give me a hug.'

Vicky ran across to her mother, who enveloped her. She kissed her daughter's hair repeatedly. 'Clever, clever, clever girl,' she said between the kisses. 'To think, a daughter of mine with real, proper qualifications! Where do you get it from?'

'I thought you said your great-granny was a seamstress. I think wanting to sew is in my blood.'

'That may be the case but the other exams? Great-granny couldn't read or write and no one else in your family has ever got past the basics.'

'Reading and writing isn't that tricky, you know, Mammy.'

43

'Maybe not but you won't be seeing me learning to do it properly. Not now. But I'm glad you have, although what you'll do with all these exams is a mystery to me.'

'I'm going to college, Mammy.' Vicky could still barely believe it and saying the words again gave her a thrill.

Her mum smiled at her. 'To be sure you are, although I still don't see the need. Great-granny Bernadette made clothes for all sorts before she married – gentry and everything – and she didn't need no college education.'

'I know, Mammy, but times have changed.'

Her mother heaved a sigh. 'You're right there, sure enough.'

Her father appeared from behind their trailer lugging a crate of beer. 'Come on, Liam,' he said. 'I think our Vicky deserves a toast. Mary-Rose, get some apple juice for the girls and grab a glass of something for yourself.'

The noise and happiness that exuded from around the O'Rourke trailer brought others out of theirs in curiosity. The news of Vicky's results soon whizzed around the site and other families came to congratulate her on her new qualifications and slap her father on the back for producing such a clever daughter, although there was a certain amount of private head-shaking when they heard she wanted to go on to do more learning.

'So when's the wedding?' asked Fergal McMahon, one of their neighbours. 'I was expecting it any day now. You and Liam have been engaged for quite a while.'

Vicky slapped on a smile. Why couldn't people mind their own business? She'd had enough of this sort of talk last night and really didn't appreciate Fergal dragging it all up again. 'Not so long, really, and I've promised to tie the knot next year. And my dad says it's okay to wait till then and Liam does too.' *Put that in your pipe, you interfering old duffer.*

'As long as your daddy is okay with your plans that's all that matters,' Fergal went on, interferingly.

'As if I'd be planning on going to college if he didn't want me to.'

'Of course not. You're a good girl, Vicky, we all know that.'

Vicky's phone bleeped to alert her to a text. She excused herself and checked it out. It was an unknown number. Curiously she opened the text.

'Come out 2nite. Wld love 2 c u. Jordanx'

Vicky stared at the screen transfixed. What the heck was he playing at? As if he didn't have a girlfriend already. Chloe would kill her if she found out that her man was texting another woman. *And frankly*, thought Vicky, *I wouldn't blame her*. Suppose the shoe was on the other foot and she found out that Liam was playing fast and loose behind her own back? She'd be livid.

'Something wrong?' said Shania, coming over to her with the jug of juice to refill her sister's glass and clocking the expression on her face. 'Was that the school saying they've made a mistake and you're not the smarty-pants you think you are after all?'

'Miaow,' said Vicky. She tried to keep her annoyance in check. It was a great day for her and she wasn't going to have Shania spoiling it. 'Can I get you a saucer of milk?'

Shania had the decency to look shamefaced; she'd gone too far with that catty comment. 'Sorry, I mean I know you've done well and all that but I just don't see why on earth you want to go off to college. I'm glad you've got your grades. To be sure you've worked hard enough for them but . . . well, I think you're mad.'

'So you've said. It's not like I'm in any doubt about how you feel.'

Shania looked down and shuffled her feet. 'No, well, like I say, I'm glad you've got the grades.'

'Here, give us a hug. And no, as you were asking, it wasn't the school.'

'Oh, that's okay then. And I was only joking.'

'I know. If you must know, it was a text from another girl telling me how she'd done,' she lied. No way could she let anyone on the park know that she was getting messages from a boy from school. Deftly she pressed a couple of buttons and the text disappeared.

Shania shrugged. GCSE results, with the exception of her sister's, were of no interest. She'd given up school ages back and had only ever cared about becoming a housewife and mother.

The impromptu party swirled around Vicky. Someone brought out a CD player and plugged it into their trailer. A couple of others brought more beers and the women got together and began to organise some food. Suddenly the celebration had gone from a couple of beers with friends to a full-on knees-up.

Vicky realised she was completely underdressed. The

clothes that had seemed so suitable for popping into school now seemed drab and boring. Telling everyone she was going to change she nipped into her room in the trailer and shut the door. Besides, she didn't just want privacy to get changed, she wanted to check out something on her phone.

She sat down on her bed, opened her phone and clicked on the buttons to bring up the call history. There was Jordan's number. Vicky stared at it. Should she answer his text or ignore it? She made up her mind. It would do no harm to tell him 'no'. It wasn't as if she was doing anything wrong. It was only a text. Except she knew in her heart that her dad and Liam wouldn't see it like that. Having a secretive text conversation with another boy would be stepping right out of line. As far as they were concerned it would be almost as if she were having sex with the lad.

She began to text back. 'Cant come . . .' She stopped. What could she say? My dad won't let me? I'm engaged? No, either of those would spark too many questions. But if she just told him she was busy he might text again and now he had her number he might keep pestering her and she couldn't risk that. What if Liam found a message from him, which was a real possibility, as he often borrowed her phone when he'd run out of credit on his own. On the other hand she didn't want to be rude. She deleted what she'd written and instead put, 'No don't want to hurt Chloe.' That should make him think twice. Satisfied with her answer she hit send. It was only when she'd done so she wondered who on earth had passed on her mobile number to him. There were very few people at school who knew it and one of them was Kelly.

She was going to have to have a really strong word with Kelly about trying to set her up with Jordan. She might think it was clever, or possibly funny, or maybe she really thought she was doing them both a favour, but as far as Vicky was concerned she was wrong on every count. It had to stop.

Vicky changed into the shortest shorts she could find and a skimpy top of neon pink. Tucking her mobile into a pocket she sashayed out of the trailer and into the sunshine and back into the gathered crowd of friends and well-wishers.

The cooking was getting going, despite the fact that it was still only mid-morning, and the smell of barbecuing sausages was fabulous. She realised that she hadn't eaten since the night before as her nerves had got between her and any thoughts of breakfast. It wasn't quite lunchtime but Vicky was starving.

A table had been brought over and plates and cutlery were piled on it. Someone had produced a load of soft rolls and Vicky pinched one, buttered it and added a dollop of tomato sauce for good measure before wolfing it down. She was just licking her fingers when Liam came up to her.

'Where've you been, gorgeous?'

*In my trailer texting another boy.* 'Changing into something nicer. Didn't want to party in those dull old trousers.'

'It doesn't matter to me what you wear. You'll always be the prettiest girl around.'

Vicky gave his hand a squeeze. 'You do say the nicest things.'

'But I was thinking, Vicky.'

Oh yes? Why did Vicky think that this didn't sound good? 'Really, babe?'

'We could get married soon. I'm earning enough from carpentry to support us and I've got money saved for our very own trailer. So what do you say, hon? Now you've got your exams you don't really want to do any more studying, do you? I mean, why?'

What could she say? That she felt like he'd kicked her? This was a complete turnaround from what he had suggested the night before. She took a couple of deep breaths while she thought about her answer.

'But Liam—'

'I know yesterday I said I'd help persuade your dad, and I am proud of your results, really I am . . .' he paused.

'But?'

'But . . . well . . .'

Vicky thought she knew what he was going to say. She thought she'd better help him get his doubts out in the open. 'But you didn't think Dad would agree to letting me go to college or you didn't think I'd get the grades. That's the truth of it, isn't it?'

'No. Not really.' But he wasn't looking her in the eye.

'That's *exactly* it, Liam. I can't believe you're doing this to me.'

'But we could get married so much earlier if you didn't go to college.'

'But what about the dresses?'

'Are you telling me you want to make some dresses more than you want to be married to me, is that it?'

Was it? Vicky didn't know what to say.

'Because,' continued Liam, his voice getting louder, 'that's what it looks like from here. Your dad would happily pay to have them made by a *proper* dressmaker who wouldn't take a whole year to do them.'

His phrase about a proper dressmaker cut her to the quick but she couldn't let him see it. She knew that by wanting to learn a skill, a craft – other than that of being a good wife and mother – she was going against every traveller tradition. She thought quickly, trying to find an argument that would make sense and give her some breathing space.

'But it would still take time – months. You can't run up a whole load of wedding outfits overnight. Even a *proper* dressmaker,' she tried to keep the bitterness out of her voice as she repeated his phrase, 'would take several months by the time we'd done the designs and the fittings and all. We're going to be looking at November at the earliest now and I don't want to be married in the winter. I want to be a June bride, is that unreasonable? Is it unreasonable to have a half-decent chance of sunshine on my big day? You may think it's fine to trail around in the wet on your wedding day but I'm not going to do it on mine.' Vicky stared at him defiantly.

Liam sighed and shrugged. 'I hadn't thought about it like that.'

'No, well, I have.' The atmosphere between them eased slightly. 'Liam, I have thought about little else than my wedding day ever since you asked me to marry you. It's going to be the biggest day of my life and I want it perfect. This isn't just about the dresses, it's about everything, and that includes the weather. I know there's a chance the sun mightn't be out, but we can give ourselves better odds if we don't have it in the middle of winter.' The last thing she was going to mention was that waiting for summer would give her at least the first year at college, and once she was there, she might just be able to persuade her family to let her hang on for the second. It was unlikely but it was worth a shot. But did Liam believe her argument? She held her breath and stared at him, pleadingly.

He nodded. 'You've got a point.'

Vicky breathed a sigh of relief. 'So in the meantime I might as well make some use of my time.'

'I suppose.' Liam sounded grudging but at least she'd made him see sense.

Vicky leaned in and gave him a quick peck on the cheek. 'You're a darling and I love you.'

Liam smiled. 'Love you too, babe.'

He walked back to the party and grabbed another beer. Sometimes, thought Vicky as she watched him go, life might just be easier if she was engaged to someone like Jordan who would understand about having a bit of ambition. She loved Liam, of course she did, and of course she wanted to get married, but . . . no. She loved Liam and she was going to marry him and that was that.

# 3

The Saturday of their friend Theresa's wedding dawned warm and clear. The weather that they'd all enjoyed a couple of days earlier when Vicky had got her results had held, as promised, till the weekend. Vicky had worked long hours on the Friday to finish the outfits for her mother and sister and now the family were almost ready to set off, dressed in their new clothes, to the local Catholic church for the wedding mass and then the party after.

Shania was jigging with excitement at the thought that Mikey would almost certainly be at the wedding too. She smoothed the brilliant green fabric of her dress over her hips and turned left and right to see her reflection in the long mirror. She had to admit that Vicky had done a fantastic job. The extra sequins emphasised her slim waist and the green made her auburn hair look even more vivid. She knew she looked hot and as she admired herself she practised looking seductive and mysterious as well.

Vicky, brushing her hair in front of the other mirror that hung over the shelf that served as their dressing table, watched her sister in the reflection. It was so obvious what was going through her mind – she was rehearsing how she'd try to get noticed by Mikey and maybe get grabbed by him.

'You just remember not to give in too easily,' warned Vicky.

Shania blushed, giving her alabaster skin rare colour. 'And just what sort of girl do you think I am? Of course I'll fight . . . for a bit.' Shania let out a naughty giggle. 'Don't want to overdo it and have him think I don't fancy him, now do I?'

'I don't think, given the way you were making sheep's eyes at Mikey on Thursday, he can be in much doubt.'

'But he *is* buff, isn't he. You have to admit that.'

'Yes, he's buff,' she agreed. Although to Vicky's taste he wasn't as fit as Liam – or Jordan for that matter. *Now what*, she thought angrily, *has put that thought into my head?* Jordan had no business there. Her irritation with herself transferred to her sister.

'Quit jabbering about Mikey and do my eyeliner for me.'

Shania took the pencil from her sister and drew a neat line around both of Vicky's eyes, making them look even more exotic than they usually did.

'And will you do mine?'

'Of course. If we're going to make sure you get grabbed you need to look your best.'

The tip of Vicky's tongue stuck out between her lips as she concentrated on helping her sister make the most of her already pretty looks. She finished with the eyeliner and picked up the mascara wand from the shelf.

'The trouble with being ginger,' moaned Shania, 'is that you get rubbish eyelashes. Look at them.'

'Your eyelashes are just fine. Okay, they're pale but they're long and thick. There's nothing a good coat of mascara can't sort.'

'But I can't wear mascara in bed.'

'What do you mean?'

'When Mikey and I marry, he'll see me without it. What can I do, Vick, I look well rough without it.'

Vicky stopped coating her sister's eyelashes with glossy black mascara and stared straight into Shania's eyes. 'Don't be daft. When you're married he'll be so mad for you he'll never notice a thing.'

'Do you think?'

Vicky tutted. 'He'll think himself the luckiest man alive – and why shouldn't he?'

'Is that how Liam thinks of you?'

'Of course.' Vicky was utterly confident about this.

'And that's how you feel about him?'

'And why wouldn't I?' Except as she said that it was Jordan's face in her mind, not Liam's.

It was gone two by the time Johnnie got his three daughters and their mother all piled into the white saloon. Billy and Jon-Boy had gone ahead to the church on their bikes as, being boys, it didn't matter if they were out in public unescorted, but there was no way that a good gypsy family would let two unmarried daughters out in public without a chaperone. In any case, the church was across town and too far for the girls to walk in their heels.

Shania wriggled with excitement on the back seat. 'Do we know for certain Mikey is going to be there?' she whispered to her sister.

'I would think so. Why not?'

'I don't know. It'd be just my bad luck that he mightn't make it.'

'You'll find out soon enough. And if he's not, there'll be other occasions.'

'I know but what'll I do if he doesn't show?'

'I don't know. Try and get grabbed by someone else?' Vicky suggested.

'No! I only want Mikey.'

'Then you'd best hope he doesn't let you down.' Shania looked crestfallen so Vicky gave her a hug. 'But I'm sure he'll be there.'

They approached the church and could see that there was some degree of chaos outside it. The bride had already arrived and was busy posing for pictures with her entourage of bridesmaids. Theresa looked lovely in her huge puffball of a dress that was in the palest pink. The bodice was covered in little crystals that sparkled like diamonds in the bright summer sun. Her attendants were in deep cerise – a lovely contrast, thought Vicky.

Waving at Theresa and her bridesmaids the O'Rourke family made their way into the church, stopping to cross themselves with holy water and genuflect to the altar as they made their way to an empty pew. The boys, who had already arrived, joined them. Ahead she could see the groom standing nervously and self-consciously at the front of the nave, his best man by his side. The poor

55

lad looked scared witless. Staring at Seamus wasn't going to help his nerves so she turned her attention to the other traveller families in all their finery. It made her feel proud to think of the effort everyone had made to look their best to celebrate Theresa's wedding. Across the aisle sat Liam and his family. She gave him a warm smile. Vicky noticed with approval that he scrubbed up well in a shirt and tie. And there behind him was Mikey. Vicky nudged Shania.

'You're all right. He's here.'

'I know.' Her voice came out in a squeak she was so excited. Vicky couldn't help but smile.

A minute or so later the organ began to belt out the wedding march. The congregation stopped chatting and laughing and rose to watch Theresa and her bridesmaids make their grand entrance, their magnificent dresses filling the aisle with net and chiffon and the church with colour.

'It'll be you next,' Shania whispered to Vicky as Theresa reached the altar.

Vicky nodded, not wanting to speak. Was she really ready for this step?

The party afterwards was at a local hotel. The bride and groom set off ahead of their guests in a gaily decorated pony and trap while the rest of the traveller families got themselves sorted into cars and taxis. Billy and Jon-Boy careered after the carriage on their bikes, determined to get to the reception before their family, which, given the amount of time it took Johnnie and Mary-Rose to greet all their many friends as they came out of the church, wasn't going to be much of a challenge.

Finally Johnnie and his womenfolk were back in the car and ten minutes later they pulled up in the big car park of the local hotel. More photographs were being taken of the bride, the groom, the best man and the bridesmaids. Their parents and siblings were being rounded up to join in the group shots and the scene was one of cheerful chaos. Eventually, the photographer seemed to think he had enough pictures and the guests trooped into the banqueting suite ready for the party.

While the girls all began to dance to the music the DJ was playing, the mothers took the weight off their feet and the men and boys headed for the bar. The noise was immense as travellers who hadn't seen each other for months met and caught up with news of families and friends. Around the room disco lights flashed and sparkled and bounced off the glitter ball revolving from the ceiling and the sequins and crystals on the girls' dresses.

Suddenly the music was silenced and the DJ announced the entrance of the bride.

In walked Theresa, looking radiant and stunning. Everyone in the room got to their feet and applauded her as she made her way to the dance floor where her father, pink with pride, led her in the first dance before handing her over to her new husband.

Vicky noticed several of the mums around the room were dabbing their eyes and even she felt a small lump of emotion form in her throat. Theresa looked so utterly happy in Seamus's arms; surely this was a match that was meant to be.

Vicky glanced over to her Liam. Would she look just as ecstatic on her own wedding day? She knew she ought to but she couldn't help thinking that she wasn't ready to settle down just yet. Maybe in a year's time she'd feel differently, after all a year was a long time.

'Penny for them,' said her mother, who had moved to stand behind her daughter. 'I bet you're wishing that was you there already.'

*Oh God no*, thought Vicky. That had not been what she'd been thinking at all but there was simply no way she could admit that to her mother.

'I was admiring Theresa's dress.'

'It's a beauty and no mistake. Would it be something like that you'd be after for yourself?'

'Maybe. I haven't really thought yet.'

'It's about time you did, my girl. It'll be your turn before we know it. A girl can't start planning her wedding too early. I'd have thought your head would be filled with ideas for your own dress.'

'I've got loads of ideas for my bridesmaids' dresses,' admitted Vicky.

'And not your own?' Mary-Rose sounded horror-struck. 'When I was your age I'd known for years exactly how I wanted my big day. I'd been planning my wedding since I was about ten.'

*Bully for you*, thought Vicky rebelliously. She did want to marry Liam, she really did, but did it have to happen quite so soon? Would the earth stop revolving if she waited a few more years? She wasn't going to turn into an old woman on the day she hit eighteen. Blimey, there were gorgios who didn't get married and have kids till

58

they were nearly thirty – or even later. She wouldn't wait *that* long but couldn't she have just a bit longer before she had to settle down?

But instead of voicing her thoughts to her mother she smiled and said that she'd been sketching ideas, which she'd take to a dressmaker soon.

'That's grand, darlin'. And then when you're safely wed we can start planning Shania's.'

Which was going to be a doddle. Judging by the way Shania was throwing her slim body around the dance floor, swinging her hips and sticking out her bust, she was doing her level best to catch Mikey's eye. This was a girl who couldn't wait to get grabbed, engaged and married. *In fact*, thought Vicky, *if Shania could have the whole process all wrapped up in just a few days she'd be one happy kid*.

She sighed. So what was so wrong with her that she didn't hold the same ambition as every other unwed traveller girl in the room? It wasn't as if she had a problem with her fiancé – quite the reverse. Liam ticked all the boxes: handsome, kind, hardworking, thoughtful, funny, not a big drinker, talented . . . Oh God, what was wrong with her that she wasn't twisting his arm up his back and marching him up the aisle right this minute?

She was hauled out of her reverie by a shriek behind her. Shania was over Mikey's shoulder in a fireman's lift and was being rushed out of the room. Oh my God, her little sister's dream had come true and Mikey was carrying her off to steal a kiss. Vicky just hoped that it wasn't a big disappointment, although Shania didn't have anything to judge it by.

Vicky remembered the first time she'd been grabbed by Liam. Not that it had been a proper grabbing. It had been a slightly less physical affair as he'd caught her by the arm at a big travellers' party at Stow Horse Fair and just dragged her outside the tent. She had made a bit of a show of resisting – well, a girl couldn't look too easy, now could she? But Liam hadn't hurt her till she gave in, like she'd heard that some boys did; twisting arms or giving Chinese burns. Instead he'd just told her he thought she was beautiful, that he thought he loved her and would she do him the very great honour of letting him kiss her? With a chat-up like that what was a girl to say?

Vicky recalled how, as their lips had touched, the tingle that had shot down her back all the way to her toes, making them curl up in her shoes. Her insides had gone all squishy and a new and unknown feeling had left a pool of heat deep in her stomach. Dear God, it had been a powerful moment. And it had been similar on the other times they'd kissed. The trouble was their kisses always had to be snatched affairs, laden with guilt and keeping half an eye open for anyone catching them. Being with a boy unchaperoned, even when he was your fiancé, was frowned upon and so they couldn't revel in such moments of illicit intimacy like the heroines that she read about in steamy novels. If the descriptions of those fictional snogs were to be believed she was in for something else but in the meantime she and Liam would have had to make do with a few stolen kisses. Real, proper snogging would have to wait until she was married.

And now it was her little sister's turn. Well, not such a little sister now. Shania was fifteen, the same age as Vicky had been when she got engaged. But if Mikey asked Shania to marry him it would mean even more pressure on herself to get on with her own wedding. She was almost certain she could hold out for a year but there'd be no chance of pushing the date back beyond that once Shania got engaged.

Her mother had moseyed back to sit with the other mothers at a table near the enormous fairy-tale castle cake, the younger girls were dancing their socks off to impress the boys, Theresa was still draped over her new husband, and the boys and men were all crowded around the bar talking horses and cars and knocking back a few beers. It was going to be a while before the food was served and Vicky was suddenly fed up. She was too old to join in with the kids, she was too young to sit with the mothers and she was the wrong sex to go to the bar and be with Liam. Despite the jollity going on around her Vicky felt bored and more than a bit sorry for herself.

As if on cue her mobile rang. Kelly.

'Hiya, Kel. How's things?' At least chatting to Kelly on her mobile was a step up from being Norma No-Mates.

'Okay, what about you?'

'I'm at the Park Hotel. A mate of mine is getting wed.'

'No way, the Park? But I'm just down the road at the Boathouse. A gang of us from school got together this lunchtime for a drink to make the most of this weather and we're still here. It's gone from a few drinks to a picnic. We're all down on the riverbank enjoying the sunshine. Why don't you come along and join us?'

'Can't really. You know how it is for me about being out and about on my own.'

'Oh, come on, Vick. You're almost seventeen and it's broad daylight, what on earth could happen?'

On the one hand, Kelly was right about what could happen, but on the other, going out alone wasn't what traveller girls did. 'I don't know, Kel.'

'What if I came over to the hotel and got you?'

Now Vicky felt rather childish. Surely she was old enough and responsible enough to pop over to the Boathouse to hang out with a few mates for a little while? Although she would be a bit overdressed for a picnic. But hey, she was bunking off from a wedding. She'd hardly be likely to be wearing denim shorts, now would she? She glanced around the room. Liam was happy with his friends, her mum was gassing away, Shania – well, goodness knew what she was up to but she certainly wouldn't want her sister interfering – and her dad was well stuck into the beers. Realistically, would anyone even notice that she had gone? Vicky made up her mind.

'Okay, Kelly, but only for twenty minutes. It'd be bad manners not to be here when they cut the cake and everything.'

'See you soon then, babe.'

'Yeah, I'll be over in just a couple of minutes.'

Vicky slipped out of the big banqueting suite and headed for the loos. The instant she was sure no one was watching she slid through a side door and went towards the gates of the hotel. She hoped that, despite her short, pillar-box-red dress, no one would spot her disappearing over the road, through the park to the river.

As soon as she reached the park she slipped off her engagement ring like she always did when away from her own community and then she kicked off her high heels and ran barefoot across the grass. Heads turned at the sight of the extraordinarily pretty girl in a stunning dress as she flashed past picnickers and people taking advantage of the beautiful weather. Panting, she arrived at the Boathouse pub and instantly spotted Kelly and a gang from their school, all lounging around on the riverbank, glasses of cold drinks to hand, packets of crisps and a few leftover sandwiches on paper plates on the rug.

Vicky shouted hello as she approached and was suddenly cripplingly self-conscious of her clothes. All the others were in shorts and T-shirts, although a few of the girls were just sporting bikini tops with their denim cut-offs. And yet here was she, done up to the nines, more slap on her face than a circus clown, walking barefoot with her high heels in her hand.

'Cor you look posh,' said one of the girls.

'Just come from a wedding.'

'Not yours, I hope,' said some joker.

'Course not,' said Vicky, all the while wondering what on earth they'd say if she let on that this time next year it almost certainly *would* be her wedding. The novelty of her arrival quickly wore off; the kids went back to talking in groups and Vicky, despite her clothes, regained some anonymity. She chucked her shoes on the grass and flopped down on a rug spread out on the riverbank beside her friend.

'Love your dress,' said Kelly.

'Ta.'

'Did you make it?'

Vicky nodded.

'You're just so clever with a needle.'

'I dunno. I'm only following instructions. When I go to college I want to learn how to design my own stuff.'

'You'll be well good at it.'

'Not necessarily.'

'Yes you will. You've got style. You just know how to make clothes look good.'

Vicky shrugged, embarrassed by her friend's praise.

'I'll second that,' said a voice behind them.

Kelly looked up, shielding her eyes from the sun. 'And who asked your opinion, Jordan?'

Shit – Jordan. If Kelly had told her that Jordan was with this bunch of mates she'd have thought twice about coming. It was one thing sloping off to meet Kelly, it was something else entirely meeting Jordan. And meeting Jordan looking so hot. He was just wearing a pair of faded denims and a plain white T-shirt but the jeans were skin tight and his T-shirt emphasised not only how toned his body was but also his wonderful coffee-coloured skin.

Vicky shot a look at Kelly, which clearly blamed her of having engineered this rendezvous. Kelly returned the look and shook her head just slightly, the picture of someone wrongly accused. Vicky wasn't sure whether she believed Kelly hadn't had something to do with this meeting.

Jordan settled himself on the grass beside Vicky.

'Fancy seeing you here. It's not often you come out with us. In fact,' he said, 'you *never* come out with us. How come you've escaped from your ivory tower?'

'Don't be silly,' said Vicky. 'You make me sound like that girl with the long hair. Rapunzel?'

'And your point is? Anyway, it's part of your attraction – the fact that you're so mysterious. Let's face it, Vicky, you're not like other girls.'

Vicky snorted, he was right there. Not that she'd ever let on just how close to the truth he was. And she didn't like it that he was taking such an interest in her.

'Where's Chloe?' she asked pointedly.

'Won't be here till later. Got family commitments this afternoon.' Jordan seemed unfazed by her mention of his girlfriend.

'That's a shame. Aren't you feeling a bit lonely without her?'

'We're not joined at the hip, Vicky. We're just mates.'

'And there was me thinking you're boyfriend and girlfriend.'

'What you getting at? Just because we date doesn't mean I can't talk to anyone else.'

Vicky kept the fact that she didn't think that Chloe shared that opinion to herself, and anyway, what business was it of hers? The silence lengthened and Vicky basked in the warm sun while wondering, vaguely, about Jordan's apparent inability to commit.

'You haven't got anything to drink,' said Kelly, noticing.

''S'all right.'

'It's not all right. Jordy, be a gent and go and get Vicky a drink.'

'No, it's fine, honest,' insisted Vicky.

But Jordan was on his feet. 'What would you like?'

'Well, if you're sure, a Coke would be nice.'

'Just a Coke?'

Vicky nodded.

'Can't tempt you to a shot of Bacardi in it?'

'No – thanks,' she added, trying not to sound too shocked at being offered spirits.

'Suit yourself.'

Jordan wandered off to the pub on his errand and Vicky rolled over onto her stomach. 'So, Kelly, I hope you didn't get me here with any idea of setting me up with Jordan, because if you did, you and I are going to fall out.'

'As if,' said Kelly, her blue eyes wide and innocent.

'No? So it wasn't you who gave Jordan my mobile number?'

Kelly wrinkled her nose. 'You've got me bang to rights there. But only because he wouldn't shut up about it. He went on and on and eventually I just gave in. I reckoned you'd handle him though. I knew you'd tell him where to get off if he tried pestering you.'

'Yeah, well . . . but I wish you hadn't. Suppose Liam sees the number?'

'And what are you doing letting Liam snoop around your private life anyway? I think people who check out other people's mobiles are well out of order. It's like reading your email.'

'It's not like that.'

66

'Oh come off it, Vick. You're well under the thumb.'

'Am not.' Vicky glared at Kelly.

'Are too.'

'Am not. I'm here now, aren't I?'

'And hooray for that. But let's face it, this is a first. You could have knocked me down with a feather when you said you were going to come on over. So,' Kelly said, staring hard at her friend, 'what made you say yes this time?'

Vicky shrugged. 'I dunno.' She sighed and thought about her actions. 'To be honest, the wedding was a bit same-old, same-old. Know what I mean?'

'Not really. I've only been to one that I can remember. My cousin got married last year and it was a right laugh.'

'Well,' Vicky lowered her voice so the others in the group by the river wouldn't hear what she had to say. 'Well, us travellers, we have big families and there's a wedding just about every month in the summer. I've probably been to more weddings than you've had cooked breakfasts. And it's always the same.' She described the younger girls dancing to attract a boyfriend, the men getting stuck in at the bar and the mothers gossiping. 'And I felt left out. I don't belong to any of the groups right now – at least, that's how it feels.'

'Oh, babe. But what about Liam?'

Vicky sighed again. 'What about him? I mean, I know he loves me . . .'

'But?'

'But . . . I think sometimes I get taken for granted just a bit.' There, she'd said it. 'He's got me now – the rock

67

is on my finger,' she fingered 'the rock' on the chain around her neck as she said this and then added, 'and I'm his and that's it. I know he loves me, he really does and he's going to be a great husband, one of the best, but . . .'

'So he was ignoring you at the wedding, was that it? He was off with his mates, boozing at the bar and you felt all lonely.'

'That's it exactly, Kelly. How did you know?'

'Because, babe, that's men the world over. Once they've got you they think they can stop trying. Nothing special about your Liam there.'

'And who is Liam?' Jordan had arrived back with Vicky's Coke.

'Will you quit listening to other people's conversations,' said Vicky, rolling over and sitting up so she could give Jordan the full force of her irritation.

'I was just asking.' Jordan sounded defensive. 'Here's your Coke.' He held the glass out and some of the condensation that had collected on the chilled glass dripped off and ran down Vicky's arm. Jordan leaned down and wiped the trickle of water off with his forefinger. Vicky jumped like she'd been burned and slopped the drink, aggravating the problem.

'Now look,' she yelled, staring at the wet mark on her dress. But she was more fraught about the way her body had reacted to his touch. It had been like the moment when Liam had kissed her for the first time – but multiplied by ten.

'Sorry, Vick,' mumbled Jordan.

'And so you should be,' she yelled, using her anger to

68

try to push her body's treachery out of her mind.

'Look, I'll get this sorted.' Jordan sounded really apologetic. 'Come to the bar with me and we'll see if we can't rinse the Coke out somehow.'

'Don't be daft.'

'No, he's right, Vick. Let's go to the Ladies. If we get some water on the mark we can get the worst out. It'll soon dry in this sunshine and no one need know.'

'I suppose.' Vicky wasn't convinced but hey, it was worth a try. If all else failed she supposed she could pretend someone at the party at the hotel had spilt drink over her. No one need know the real truth.

The three teenagers made their way into the cool dark of the pub. Kelly managed to produce a tissue from her handbag and the two girls dived into the Ladies to try to repair the damage. Five minutes later they emerged. The mark was significantly better and they'd managed to almost get it dry with the help of the hand-drier.

'I'm sorry,' said Jordan, 'I shouldn't have made you jump like that. It was all my fault.'

'Nah, my fault for overreacting.' And what an over-reaction. Vicky pushed the memory of his touch back into a recess. She told herself he was right, that he'd just made her jump. The heat from his hand contrasting against the cold water off the glass had come as a shock. That had been all it was. And she wasn't going to think about it any more. Never. 'Come on, let's finish our drinks and then I must get going.'

'What is it with you?' asked Jordan as they made their way back into the sunshine. 'You're like Cinderella. I've

69

never known a girl who's so twitchy about being late. You need to learn how to chill.'

The three of them flopped down again on the big tartan rug. 'I'm not being funny, Jordan, but what is it with you and fairy tales today? Ivory towers? Cinderella?' Vicky laughed. 'The sunshine is making you all soft in the head.'

'It's not the sunshine making me soft in the head. It's you.'

Kelly cleared her throat. ''Scuse me, you two, but if you're going to carry on like this maybe you'd better get a room.'

Vicky's face flared bright red. To hide her embarrassment she necked the rest of her drink and leapt to her feet. 'Gotta go.'

Jordan reached up from where he was sitting and caught her hand. 'Don't go, not yet.'

Vicky jerked her hand out of his grasp as another jolt of desire surged through her so strongly she felt quite shaken. 'Let me go. I'm late. I'm going to be missed.' She grabbed her high heels off the grass and fled. 'Thanks for the drink,' she called over her shoulder and she caught sight of Jordan staring after her, looking utterly bewildered. As she ran she wondered if he'd felt the electricity too.

It was only a couple of minutes later that she arrived back at the hotel. She glanced at her watch. She'd only been gone about twenty minutes. Surely no one would have noticed. She sidled back into the hotel through the door by which she'd made her escape and from there to the main function room. As she entered the noise level that hit her was ear-splitting. She stood by the door taking in the scene. Shania wasn't to be seen. And shit, neither was Liam. *Oh God*, she thought in a panic, *he hasn't gone looking for me, has he?*

Trying to look casual, Vicky edged round the room, sticking by the wall, until she was standing behind a big gaggle of mothers. Maybe she could pretend that she'd been there all along. As the seconds ticked past she began to relax; the longer that Liam himself was out of the room, the longer she could pretend she had been back in it. And although she hated that she was about to lie to him, it was only a little white lie. What harm was there in going to meet Kelly down by the river?

Except, she knew that it wasn't really such a little white lie. It was, in fact, a great big fib because she hadn't just met Kelly, had she? And worse was the fact that she couldn't ignore how she'd felt on both the occasions when Jordan and she had touched.

One of the mothers sitting just in front of her turned.

'Were your ears burning just then, Vicky darlin'?'

Vicky felt her whole face burning – never mind her ears. Shit, what had they been saying about her? Her heart rate soared as her guilty conscience kicked in. She shook her head. 'No, should they have been?' She waited in anguish for the answer.

'We was just sayin' that it's got to be you next, sweetie. How long have you and Liam been engaged?'

Vicky nearly keeled over as the relief swept through her. Oh, dear God, was that all they'd been gossiping about? She mumbled something about the fact that it had been around two years and then made her excuses to escape. As she moved away from the mothers, Liam came crashing back through the main door.

'There you are,' he said as he caught up with her. 'Where on earth have you been?'

'Been?'

'You disappeared.'

Feigning a total lack of understanding, Vicky shrugged. 'Oh, I did pop to the Ladies.'

'For quarter of an hour?'

A flash of inspiration struck her. 'But I splashed water on my dress when I was washing my hands. It took a while to dry. Look, it left a mark.'

As she pointed out the still-damp place she could see the doubt clear from Liam's face. So, her big fat fib had just been accepted.

Liam, happy that he'd found his bride-to-be, returned to the bar and Vicky found herself a quiet corner so she could think about Liam, her future and Jordan, and try to get her head round all the complexities that had suddenly cropped up.

Suddenly life had just become a whole lot less simple.

# 4

'Don't you go doing anything that your mum wouldn't approve of,' said Johnnie as he dropped his daughter off a few hundred yards away from the gates of the college.

'Dad, as if I would.'

'I know, but this isn't like school.'

Vicky smiled at her father. Like he knew, bless him. He'd left any sort of education when he was only twelve. 'I know, Dad, and don't worry, I'll be fine. I won't let you down.'

'To be sure I know that, princess. Now off you go and work hard.'

Vicky jumped out of the car and set off to her first day at college. Vicky O'Rourke, college girl! How cool was that? She was almost pinching herself as she walked down the road, slipping off her engagement ring as had become her routine. Over her shoulder she wore a big knock-off Mulberry bag that her dad had got off a mate for her specially. She loved it, and it was the finishing touch to her outfit of leopard-print blouse and black pencil skirt. If she was going to be learning with a bunch of girls planning a career in the fashion industry she needed to be on trend. Turning up in the sort of kit she'd wear at home just wasn't going to cut it, and she'd lost the anonymity of a school uniform. But then, suppose all the other students turned up in jeans and T-shirts. Had she got it wrong? Too late to go home and change now. Her nerves got worse. The butterflies turned into great big vultures.

Vicky's step began to falter. What was she doing here? She was right out of her depth. What was she thinking of – a traveller girl going to sixth-form college? She stopped in the middle of the pavement as her confidence hit the ground.

'Hiya, Vick!' A shriek from across the road brought her to her senses.

'Hi, Kelly.' Oh shit, Kelly was wearing jeans.

Kelly dodged through the slow-moving rush-hour traffic to join her friend. 'You all right? You look all worried.'

Vicky laughed nervously. 'Worried? I'm shitting myself.'

'Me too,' admitted Kelly.

The girls linked arms as they headed for the gates and their first day.

'We're going to know a loads of kids here though, aren't we,' said Vicky.

Kelly nodded. 'Loads.'

'And it isn't as if we haven't got the grades to be here.'

'Keep talking.'

Vicky swallowed. 'I wish I could. That's all I can think of.'

'We're going to be okay. We've got each other.'

'Yeah, but not in classes.'

'We'll have to arrange to meet. Lunchtime would be good.'

The two girls got to the gates. 'Here we go,' said Vicky.

'Shit or bust,' Kelly said with a grimace.

They walked across the car park and into the huge airy atrium. It was packed with teenagers and Vicky was relieved to see that her clothes were not out of place. Obviously she wasn't the only one who didn't have a clue what to wear on the first day. And she could also see that lots of the students looked just as nervous as she felt, although there were a few who managed to look cool and sophisticated. Kelly followed her gaze to one group that looked particularly underwhelmed.

'Huh, they may look like they don't care but check out the front of that guy's trousers.'

'Kelly? What are you like?'

'Not *that* bit of his trousers. You have a filthy mind, Miss O'Rourke. No, look at his knees. You can see they're shaking through the material.'

Vicky giggled. 'They are too.' Instantly she felt so much better; it was immensely reassuring to know that being nervous was normal. She looked about her and saw that everyone else either seemed to be clutching information packs or were queuing up at the registration desks.

'I suppose we'd better register. Make it official that we're here.'

The two girls made their way over to a desk staffed by

a team of administrators and gave in their names and their subject choices. They were then directed to different areas of the college to meet their tutors and fellow students.

'I'll see you in the canteen at lunch,' said Kelly as they parted.

Vicky made her way over to the art and design faculty where the textiles department was based. She was busy looking at the signs on the doors when she almost cannoned into someone. Chloe.

'Vicky. So you decided to turn up. Bit out of your league, isn't it?'

Vicky was taken aback; what had brought that on? She felt her jaw slacken before she pulled herself together. She wasn't going to take that sort of bitching, not from the likes of Chloe. Vicky wasn't normally aggressive, but she was scared enough without Chloe making it worse.

'Oh yeah? I'd say that was a case of pots and kettles, wouldn't you? So what are you studying? A-level spite?'

Chloe sniffed. 'Just the sort of response I'd expect from the likes of you.'

'And what do you mean by that?' Vicky was putting on a show of bravado but she was bricking it that Chloe had sussed out her background. Surely not?

'I mean the sort of girl who tries to muscle in on other people's blokes.'

'Jordan? You are joking me. I mean, he's a nice bloke and all that but I'm not interested. Really I'm not.' She thought about dragging out her engagement ring to prove her point but decided against it. 'I've got my own man, Liam.'

'Really?' Chloe didn't sound convinced.

'Really.'

Chloe frowned and sighed. 'So you weren't trying to get off with him down by the river a couple of weeks ago?'

'No. I went to meet Kelly. I had no idea who else was there and I certainly didn't go there to see Jordan.'

'Good. And see that it stays like that.'

Chloe swept off, leaving Vicky feeling shaken. 'Bloody hell,' she muttered as she stared after her. But she couldn't help wondering whether Chloe's accusation had come from a sense of insecurity. Jordan's reputation wasn't brilliant as far as his previous girlfriends were concerned and maybe his and Chloe's relationship was starting to crack. Well, if it did fall apart it wasn't going to be because of anything Vicky did, that was for certain, whatever Chloe thought.

By lunchtime, when she and Kelly met, Vicky had put Chloe's unprovoked attack to the back of her mind. Instead she and Kelly discussed their timetables, their new classmates and their tutors.

'Oh, and Kelly, you should see the facilities, all the machines and wonderful worktables. And some of the other students' work on the wall. Kelly, if I can ever make stuff like that I'd be well pleased.'

'I know what you mean. It's like that where I am. We work in a proper salon some of the time, with all the products and proper massage tables and . . . oh Vick, it's just lovely.'

'I am so glad we made it here. I can't wait to start working on projects and stuff.'

'Like your bridesmaids' dresses?'

'Going to have to pull my finger out on those. Did I tell you that Shania is engaged?'

'Shania? No, get away. But she's only little.'

'She's fifteen, same age as I was when Liam asked me.'

'I suppose.' Kelly blinked. 'It's just . . . no, forget it.'

Vicky put her hand across the table and took Kelly's. 'It's our way, Kel. It's how it works in my world.'

'Yeah,' Kelly smiled. 'None of my business.'

'It's not that, it's just we do things differently.'

Kelly nodded.

'There is just one problem about it, though,' admitted Vicky.

'What's that?'

'Shania can't wait to get hitched. She wants to marry as soon as she's sixteen but Mum won't let her till she's got my wedding out of the way.'

'But you're not having second thoughts, are you?'

'No, course not. But . . . but I was hoping to do the full two years here and, well, if I get married next summer I'll have to leave.'

'I don't follow. There's no rule that says you can't study here if you're married.'

'Not here, no. But traveller wives stay at home.'

'But Liam wouldn't mind, would he?'

'It wouldn't be right. It'd make him look less of a man.'

Kelly shook her head. 'How?'

'As I said, different world, Kel, different world.'

'Then that's a bugger, ain't it.'

A chair scraped back at their table. 'Hiya, girls.'

Jordan sat down next to Vicky. 'You both look down. College not coming up to expectations?'

Vicky sighed heavily. What was it with Jordan? Why was he always turning up in her life? And why on earth was her heart racing? She suddenly felt a kick of anger – anger that she reacted to his presence like this. What was the matter with her? She turned her irritation on him. 'Are you trying to cause trouble, Jordan?'

'Why, what've I said?' Jordan was genuinely bewildered.

'Not you, Chloe. Your girlfriend had a right go at me this morning, accused me of deliberately meeting you in the park that day.'

'Chloe?'

'Yes, Chloe. She thinks I fancy you.'

'And don't you?' A smile played across Jordan's lips.

'No I don't. So listen to me, I think it would be doing everyone a favour if you kept away.' Vicky stood up. 'Now I've got stuff to do. See you later, Kel.' She picked up her tray and left.

Jordan stared after her.

'She might not fancy you but I wouldn't kick you out of bed,' said Kelly hopefully.

Jordan shook his head. 'Darling, from what I've heard you don't kick *anyone* out of bed.'

'Bastard!' And giving him an evil look Kelly left too.

The first few days shot past in a blur of getting used to the new routine of college, making new friends and finding her feet. As the first week came to an end, Vicky realised that she was happier than she could ever remember. It was as if she'd just found a perfect niche that fitted her exactly. Everything that Mrs Mead her tutor said, every new skill she was starting to learn, just made sense. It was almost as if she'd always known this stuff but that it was buried deep inside and now she had the keys to unlock it.

And, as far as Vicky was concerned, Mrs Mead was the perfect person to be teaching textiles. Her dress sense was bizarre and bohemian but wonderfully original and she managed to mix modern fashion with some amazing retro accessories, which meant that Vicky thought she was a walking style icon. Every morning, when Vicky got to college, she found that part of the pleasure of being there was seeing what Mrs Mead would have on that day.

As Vicky was only taking the one subject at college she had plenty of free time between classes but instead of going back home she spent her time in the art and design faculty working on her pieces. She was fascinated by the new techniques she was learning, really understanding for the first time what she could do with fabrics, how they worked, how she could get different textiles to interact together to achieve knock-out effects that made each garment look unique. And with everything she was beginning to learn she could see better possibilities for the big project that she knew she had to tackle very soon.

She was sitting at one of the big worktables in the textiles room when her tutor, Mrs Mead, came over.

'You are allowed time off, Vicky,' she said gently.

Vicky looked up and smiled. 'I know, but I wanted to

get this finished.' She held up the piece of hessian that she was threading through with other types of fabric to make a wall hanging.

'That's really lovely, Vicky. I can't believe you've managed to achieve such a brilliant piece of work in such a short space of time.'

'Thank you, miss.'

'You've got real talent. Are you planning a career in fashion? You could, you know.'

'Not really.'

'No? Look, Vicky, I don't say this to my pupils very often and certainly not so early on in a course, but you have something special. Really you do and if you waste this God-given talent it would be criminal.'

Vicky felt stunned. Talent? Real talent? She knew she was neat-fingered, she knew she could sew pretty well, but talent? 'Thank you,' she said in a shaky voice.

'You see, I think you've got a real chance of getting into a top fashion college. Somewhere like Central St Martins. Your eye for colour is astounding and you just seem to have this intuitive feeling for what you can do with fabric. Just look at this.' She pointed to the hanging Vicky was working on. 'The way you are mixing all these different textures is wonderful. This is the sort of standard I'd expect from my second-year students, not from someone who has only just started.'

'Thank you,' repeated Vicky.

'So you'll promise me you'll think seriously about your future?'

Vicky nodded even though she knew that what Mrs Mead was saying was hopeless. But maybe this was a moment to broach the subject of making her brides-maids' dresses. Although she knew she was going to have to tell a bit of a fib.

'Actually, there's something I'd like to ask.'

'Yes?'

'I've got a friend who is getting wed. She's asked me to help her make her bridesmaids' dresses.'

'Oh yes? Sensible girl. She obviously knows she's going to get someone who'll do a fantastic job.'

'Yes, well, I was wondering if I could use the machines here for some of the work.'

'I don't have a problem with that.'

'It's mainly for doing some of the embroidery work.'

'That's fine. What sort of design are you going to be using?'

'Can I show you?'

'Of course.'

Vicky put down her hanging and took a notebook out of her big Mulberry bag. She grabbed a pencil and began to draw. 'I was planning on doing something quite traditional.' She quickly sketched a dress with a small waist and a big flouncy skirt. 'Ballerina length is flattering for most shapes, and I'm going to give the girls boned bodices.'

Mrs Mead smiled when she saw the design that Vicky sketched out using a few elegant lines. 'That's lovely. Have you found a pattern for that sort of dress?'

'I was hoping to just use my own design. I was wondering if you could help me in that way, with the pattern cutting.'

'Of course. We'll need the measurements for the dresses. How many are you making?'

'Seven.'

'Seven! Crikey, this is going to be some wedding.'

*It certainly is,* thought Vicky.

Vicky quickly settled into a routine and as September drifted, along with the falling leaves and the scent of wood smoke, into October she finally got going with her task of making the dresses. She decided that as the skirts were relatively simple — just yards and yards of green silk scattered with dozens and dozens of crystals – she'd make only the bodices at college. The cut and fit would be critical and the boning and embroidery would involve skills that she would have to learn. Still, she might be able to help other traveller friends with dresses in the future. If she didn't take money she was sure she'd be able to carry on dressmaking. It was the idea that the man wasn't the only breadwinner in the family that travellers couldn't cope with. Surely dressmaking for love, not money, would be acceptable.

Unlike Vicky, Kelly wasn't quite such a committed student. Sure, she loved her course and being a beautician was a big ambition of hers but unlike her best friend she was more than happy to only roll into college for her lessons and then shoot off again as soon as they finished. Consequently her path didn't cross with Vicky's that often but the two friends always made a point of lunching together every Wednesday.

'You're going to have to come along with me to the textiles department when you've eaten. I need to get your vital statistics.'

'Ooh, this is quite exciting. I'm longing to know what I'm going to be wearing on your big day.'

'Ssshh,' said Vicky in a low voice. 'Don't go yelling all over the place that it's *my* wedding.'

'Sorry.'

'I've told Mrs Mead that I'm making the frocks for a friend.'

'Okay. And don't look now but Jordan and Chloe are heading our way.'

'Oh shit.'

Vicky looked up and saw that Chloe was, as usual, glued to Jordan. 'Hi, you two.'

'Hello,' said Jordan with a warm smile. Chloe remained impassive and silent. 'I'm having a party at the weekend – on Saturday night. It's my birthday and I'd like it if you two could come along.' Judging by the look on Chloe's face she was no way as keen as Jordan.

'Love to,' said Kelly. 'Where's it at?'

'Mine.'

'Cool. What about you, Vicky?'

Vicky shot Kelly a look. Like Kelly didn't already know the answer. 'Sorry, no. Got something else on.'

'That's a shame. You'll be missing out on a good night. Still, maybe next time, yeah?' Jordan replied.

He and Chloe wandered off again, presumably to issue more invites to the party.

'Thanks a bunch, Kel.'

'What have I done now?'

'Rubbing it in like that. There's no way I'm ever going to be allowed to go out partying with you or Jordan or anyone and you know it.'

'Yes I do. But I could hardly say,' Kelly lowered her voice, 'that old Vick here isn't allowed out, ever, so you're wasting your breath asking her.'

'No, I suppose not,' she conceded grudgingly.

'It's well unfair.'

Vicky shrugged. 'You get used to it. I could go if I took a whole bunch of my girlfriends from the site but I can just imagine how that would go down with the likes of Chloe. If there was ever a quicker way to start a cat fight I can't think of one.'

'On the other hand it might be worth it to see that stuck-up bitch's face.'

Vicky laughed.

'Supposing you stayed over at mine?'

'That's not going to work either,' said Vicky. 'There's no way I'd be able to stay a night away from home, even if it was with a girlfriend on the site.'

'You mean you've never had a sleepover?'

Vicky shrugged. 'No.'

'You know,' said Kelly. 'I reckon there's nuns with more exciting social lives than yours.'

'I get to have fun,' Vicky said defensively.

'Yeah?'

'We have lots of parties. Any excuse and one'll happen. It's just . . . it's just . . .'

'It's just what?'

'No booze.'

'What, none?' Kelly was aghast.

'Oh, the men and boys can drink. And you can drink when you're married but us girls can't.'

'You've never had a drink?'

'I have.'

'What?'

'Communion wine.'

Kelly laughed so hard at this that heads turned in the canteen. 'Vicky, Vicky,' she said, wiping her eyes. 'You have so missed out.'

'I don't think so,' said Vicky defensively. 'I don't see anything in getting drunk.'

'Says someone who's never tried it.'

'No, well . . .' Vicky sighed. Had she really missed out on a life experience? Maybe it'd be fun to try once. Not that it was going to happen so she might as well forget that idea. She looked at her watch. Lunchtime was almost up and besides, sitting around gossiping to Kelly wasn't going to get those wretched dresses made.

'I'm going back to the classroom. And you can get off your arse and come with me so I can measure you. And once I've done that you had better not put on any weight as I've only just got time to make all these blooming dresses. I haven't got time to go altering them later.'

The following Wednesday the two girls met again for lunch.

'Don't you go stuffing your face,' warned Vicky. 'I want you to try the bodice of your dress on.'

'Is it finished already? You're a wonder.'

'It's not finished but it's getting there. So, how was Jordan's party?'

'It was great. Although Chloe got off her face and was sick in the rose bushes and I wasn't much better. I had the hangover from hell on Sunday.'

'It doesn't sound that great to me.'

'Maybe you had to be there. Anyway, Jordan got all arsey about you *not* being there, which got on Chloe's tits no end, I can tell you. But then he had a few drinks and kept banging on about it all adding to your mystique. I mean, *mystique*! Shit, if he only knew!'

Even Vicky had to admit it was funny. 'I bet that's the first time a gyppo has ever been described like that.'

The two girls swiftly ate their lunch and then raced off to the textiles department. Vicky was keen to show Kelly her work and Kelly was longing to see what her dress was going to be like. Vicky hauled a huge carrier bag onto the worktable and pulled out the half-made bodice.

'Oh my God, Vick, that's fantastic.'

'Like it?'

'Like it? It's gorgeous.' Kelly fingered the dark green silk almost reverently.

'Well, get your kit off and try it on. There's a screen over there, you can change behind that.'

Kelly nipped behind the screen and Vicky could hear the rustle of clothing. A couple of minutes passed.

'You're going to have to give me a hand here, I can't get the zip done up.' Kelly emerged holding her bodice to her chest.

Deftly Vicky zipped up the top. 'Breathe in,' she

ordered as she tried to connect the hook and eye at the top. 'Turn around. Let's see what it looks like.'

Kelly spun around and looked down at her figure, trapped inside the heavily boned bodice. 'Bloody hell, Vick. Look what you've done to my tits. It's like a dead heat in a Zeppelin race.'

Vicky snorted with laughter. 'No it isn't. You look very sexy. Look in the mirror.'

Kelly walked over to the full-length one. 'I see what you mean. It's given me a well tiny waist. I've got proper curves.'

'You've always had proper curves, just this sort of support makes them dead obvious.'

'I love it.'

'Good.' Vicky walked around Kelly checking the fit. 'It's not too tight?'

'Meaning, *can I breathe*? Just about.'

'Try sitting down.'

Kelly hooked a chair over with her toe and plumped down on it. 'Well, I won't be slouching. There's no way you can do anything but sit up straight in this outfit.'

'And the boning doesn't dig in anywhere? I don't want you ending up injured.'

'No.' Kelly twisted and moved a bit. 'No, it seems fine, but whether I'll feel the same way after I've been in it for half a day I don't know.'

'You can change back now, if you like.'

Kelly took a last lingering look at her new-found figure in the mirror, as Vicky unhooked the bodice and dragged the zip down, before her friend disappeared behind the screen again.

'Can I ask a question?' Kelly's voice drifted over the screen.

'Depends on the question.'

'Just why can't you go out and have a good time?' Kelly emerged back in her street clothes and handed over the bodice.

Vicky sighed. 'I can. I do.' She shrugged. 'I'm allowed out as long as I go with friends, other travellers. It's just . . .' Her brow furrowed as she tried to find the words to explain to Kelly what the restrictions on her were all about. 'In my world, Kel, a girl's reputation is everything, so it's dead important that no one can ever say that you might have done something wrong, like being alone with a boy. Because if you were alone, you might get up to anything – or even if you didn't, people might say that you did.'

'Like saying you'd had sex?'

Vicky nodded. 'So if you always have your mates or your mother with you, you're safe. No one can say anything bad about you.'

'But I'm not a good-enough mate, am I? People in your world wouldn't take my word for it if I said I'd look after you and make sure you didn't get into trouble.'

Vicky nodded. 'That's about it.'

'That's harsh. I mean I don't lie or nothing, do I? Why wouldn't they trust me?'

It was hard being honest, but she owed it to Kel to tell her the truth about her world. 'It's because you're not one of us.'

'But they trust me enough to let me be a bridesmaid at your wedding.'

Vicky remained silent.

'You have told your folks, haven't you?' said Kelly, her eyes narrowing.

Vicky shook her head. 'But they'll be okay with it.'

'Oh yeah?' Kelly looked even more sceptical. 'And what if they're not?'

'I'll talk them round.'

'Like you could talk them round into being allowed to come out with me?'

'That's different, Kel, and you know it.'

Kelly shook her head. 'It's not. This is all about you being right under the thumb.'

'I am not.'

Kelly raised an eyebrow.

'It's about being looked after,' said Vicky. 'It's because they care.'

'And you're saying my parents don't.'

'No. No – it's just . . . different.'

'It certainly is,' said Kelly. She glanced at her watch. 'Look, I hear what you're saying and I know your life and mine are miles apart so let's not fall out.' She gave her friend a quick hug and a kiss on the cheek. 'I just think it's a crying shame that you're about to get married and you've never really lived.' She shrugged. 'But if you're happy about it . . .' she shrugged again. 'Why don't you ask if you can come round mine one evening? Your dad could drop you off and pick you up. Tell him that I won't let you get into any mischief – Scout's honour. What about it?' She smiled at Vicky. 'My parents are nice – they're not pissheads or druggies. They're not going to let us have an orgy or anything. What do you say?'

Vicky still looked uncertain. She really fancied going over to Kelly's; it would be fun and why not? What would be so wrong with two school friends hanging out together, except that she had this awful feeling, deep down, that even asking wasn't going to go down well with her father.

'Why don't you just ask?' insisted Kelly.

Vicky shrugged. 'I suppose. Asking can't do no harm, can it?' As the words came out of her mouth, she knew she sounded more confident than she felt.

'Good, make sure you do. If your folks say yes we can fix a date another time. Now I've got a lesson to get to.' She left and Vicky stared after her, wondering if she might be allowed the freedom to spend an evening with a girlfriend on the other side of town. Was it so much to ask? It was hardly an outrageous request but what were the chances of her parents agreeing?

Disconsolately she fingered the bodice. Like she'd said to Kelly, her world and Kelly's world were so very different. She could sew like a professional, she had talent and she had her whole life in front of her, so what was to stop her from making something of herself?

Vicky sat down on one of the chairs in the classroom and tried to put her thoughts in order. Could she really make a living from sewing or was that just a pipe dream? If she had any chance of finding out, she'd have to move off the site. No way could a traveller girl have a career. If she didn't move off, she'd be run off. And if she moved off the site would she ever be accepted in the non-traveller world? The site meant safety and tradition – and marriage to Liam. Striking out on her own would mean uncertainty and loneliness. But it might also mean a whole mass of possibilities.

Oh God, she was at an awfully big crossroads and she didn't have a clue as to which way she should go.

'What,' yelled her dad, 'don't you get about *no*?'

'But I'd only be at Kelly's. She only lives across town. You could take me there and back,' Vicky pleaded.

'No. For a start anyone else might be there.'

'Who? Her parents? Yes, very likely.'

'Don't get cheeky with me, my girl, you know very well what I mean.'

'But there won't be. It's just going to be me and Kel. We're just going to chat, maybe watch a DVD—'

'—get pissed, smoke.'

'No! As if I would.'

'Then what's wrong with staying here? You can talk to this Kelly girl on the phone. You see her at college all week.' Johnnie turned away, exasperated.

'Your dad says no,' said Mary-Rose. 'Leave it at that.'

Vicky felt like crying. Was her request so unreasonable? She was seventeen: old enough to be wed, old enough to have a baby but evidently not old enough to be trusted. Kelly had been allowed to walk to school on her own since she was eleven but Vicky still wasn't allowed to go anywhere off the site without a gaggle of friends or relations around her. Was she so untrustworthy? Apparently so.

Vicky flounced outside and walked to the edge of the site to where she could look over the countryside. The view calmed her. She climbed onto a gate that led into an adjoining field and felt her bout of sulkiness ebb away. She wasn't untrustworthy and her dad didn't think that, not at all. The barriers and boundaries were there to protect her because her parents loved her and just wanted to keep her safe. *The trouble is*, thought Vicky, feeling hugely disloyal, *that sometimes I wish they just cared for me a little bit less.*

# 5

It was one of those perfect late autumnal days. The early morning chill had given way to clear blue sky and in sheltered spots the sunshine was warm. Russet leaves were clinging to the trees, waiting for November gales to tear them off. The long grass in the meadow beyond the trailer park had turned brown and yellow and the countryside beyond the main road looked tired, but the late afternoon sun gilded the windows of some cottages in the half-distance making bursts of fire that glinted and shimmered.

Vicky sat outside the family trailer hand-stitching gold braid around Kelly's bodice. It was the last job to do on it and then she could start on finishing off the other six. She was well on course with her self-imposed workload, although she hadn't yet given any proper thought to her wedding dress itself. She secured the needle and laid the bodice in her lap. She really needed to start on that, mapping out some ideas for the dressmaker at the very least. Her mother was getting anxious and was nagging her, reminding her constantly about clocks ticking.

'We've got to get this wedding off the ground,' her mother had said over breakfast. 'If you don't pull your finger out, I'll go to the dressmaker and order something, *anything*, so I will.' Mary-Rose had stood at the table, her hand on her hip and had dared Vicky to contradict her.

'I know, Mammy, but it's only the one dress. A professional dressmaker will be able to run something up in a few weeks.'

'And organising the fittings? Are you going to take time off your precious college course, or are we going to have to fit them in at weekends? And as for your bottom drawer . . .' she shook her head in exasperation.

'Oh, Mammy, I won't have to get that much. It'll only be me and Liam for a while.'

'But once the babies start to arrive you won't get the chance to get out often.'

'So we'll go to that big Sunday market. We could go tomorrow if this weather holds.'

Mary-Rose nodded, pleased that her daughter seemed to be talking sense at last. 'I think that'd be for the best.'

Placated, Mammy had gone off to put the family wash on in the laundry block, leaving Vicky to start cleaning the trailer and to think about what her mother had said.

All day she mulled over the conversation. Deep down she knew her mother was right, that she really did need to make a start with planning her wedding properly, but even deeper down Vicky knew that she was stalling for time. The longer she left everything the better her chances of getting at least one year of her course completed. She longed to get both years under her belt but even she realised that was going to be impossible. If she dragged her feet just a little she could hold out till June, maybe even July, but that was the absolute best she could hope for.

These thoughts had filled her head as she'd cleaned the family home and now as she sewed the bodice of Kelly's dress. It was time, she realised, to start making a mental list of things she ought to buy at the Sunday market. She turned her thoughts to that.

'Hiya, babe.' It was Liam.

Vicky looked up and smiled, genuinely pleased to see him. Her heart gave a little skip of pleasure.

'Slacking?' he asked.

Vicky looked at her sewing, which had been ignored for some time now as it lay untouched in her lap. 'Enjoying the sunshine and thinking about my bottom drawer. What have you been up to today?'

'This and that.'

'Mammy and I are going to the big market tomorrow – the one on that disused airfield. I need to start getting stuff together for our own home. Do you want to come along with us?'

'You and your mammy don't want me there, do you?'

'Why not? Don't you want to keep a check on what I might choose?'

'You'll choose lovely things, I just know it. Here.' He hauled out a big bundle of notes from his pocket and pulled off a fat wedge from the roll. 'Buy something nice.'

'Liam, I can't take all this,' Vicky said, surprised at his generosity.

'Why not? Just don't get mugged.'

The next morning dawned like the day before: a hint of frost on the ground and a sky of robin's egg blue while on the eastern horizon the rising sun had tinged it with shades of gold, apricot and peach. After breakfast had been cleared away Vicky got herself ready to go out with her mum.

'You ready yet?' she called through to her mother's bedroom next door.

'Not quite, but there's no hurry. Shania's got to get the baby ready yet and then we're waiting on Mikey and his mum. And I think his sisters are coming along too.'

Vicky put her hairbrush down and went into her mother's room.

'So how many of us are going to the market?'

'I don't know, love. A few. Why not? It's a lovely day, we've all got things to get. I thought we could make a big party of it and spend the day there. Shania wants to start looking for things for her bottom drawer too. You're not the only one engaged now, remember.'

Vicky leaned against the door. So not only was her mother giving her a big fat reminder that Shania couldn't wait to be wed – as if anyone could forget – but her jaunt out with her mother had turned into a great big traveller day out. Which wasn't what she'd been looking forward to.

It seemed to take for ever to get the whole party organised. It wasn't just a question of rounding up the various participants it was also a question of organising the transport, getting the toddlers sorted, the buggies and prams found and shoved into car boots or the backs of vans. It was nearing eleven o'clock before the caravan of cars and vans finally set off from the site and on the twenty-mile journey to the Sunday market.

By the time they arrived Vicky was out of sorts. If it had just been her and her mother they'd have been there hours ago but now all the best bargains would have gone, there were bound to be further delays on the way home because half of the families would want to stop and eat and besides she'd been looking forward to having some time with her mammy alone, and now she was going to be sharing it with Shania and Kylie and half a dozen cousins.

She climbed out of the car and shrugged into her coat. The sun was warm but there was a chill breeze that gave an edge to the temperature. It took some minutes for the buggies and prams to be extricated and the babies strapped in, and all the while Vicky's temper was getting shorter and shorter. By the time they began to cross the bumpy grass of the car park to the entrance she was heartily fed up by the whole proceedings.

'And what's up with you?' asked Mary-Rose.

'Nothing,' scowled Vicky.

'It looks like it. You know, sometimes, my girl, I just can't make you out. You've been given a heap of money by your lovely man to shop with, the weather is perfect, you're surrounded by friends . . . I just don't know why you can't count your blessings like any other normal girl.'

'Oh, Mammy, I do count my blessings.'

'It doesn't look like it from here. And why you couldn't dress up a bit I don't know. Look at the effort Shania's put into her outfit. Anyone would think you didn't have any decent clothes in your wardrobe.'

And in truth, Shania did look lovely in a sparkly top that she wore under her coat which she'd left open so as not to hide the full impact of the plunging neckline and the gorgeous pink colour that enhanced the creaminess of her skin. Her bottom half was clad in a pair of skin-tight purple leather trousers with sequins running down both legs to pink cowboy boots. In contrast Vicky was in a simple pair of jeans and a dark sweater. And lots of her cousins were dressed more like Shania than herself and even the babies and toddlers were in frilly frocks or dear little suits and dicky bows.

'I was afraid of feeling cold, Mammy.' But in truth Vicky had got used to being careful about what she wore to college so as not to attract any attention and her low-key dress-sense had now become a habit.

'Were you now,' said her mother in the sort of tone that left Vicky in no doubt that her mother didn't really believe her.

They had barely got into the market proper when they began to meet all manner of people they knew. Many of the market traders were friends or relations and other traveller families had also come along to shop for clothes, or housewares. Within an hour there were several large groups of traveller families in various parts of the market exchanging news and gossip noisily and attracting stares from non-travellers because of their colourful clothes and the men's tattoos.

As Vicky became swept up in the traveller scene her bad humour began to give way and people she hadn't seen for an age congratulated her on her impending wedding or offered her discounts on china and glass-ware for her bottom drawer, 'As a wedding present, me darlin'.'

By two o'clock she had her bed linen sorted, a dozen crystal wine glasses, a load of saucepans, frying pans and casseroles, a bone-china dinner service and a tea set. She and her mother had made the trek back to the car park on several occasions to dump purchases in the car and the roll of twenties that Liam had given her was almost spent.

'I can't think why you like this tea set so much,' her mother grumbled as they returned to the car a fourth time, this time to offload the box of tea things. 'The one covered in pink roses was so much prettier. And what about the one Shania bought? That was lovely. And it had a matching cake-stand.'

'But I like the plain one, Mammy. I like things that are simple.'

'I don't know what's the matter with you. It doesn't look expensive like the patterned one does. We could take it back and change it. If you're worried about the extra cost I'll pay the difference.'

'But I don't want the patterned one.'

Mary-Rose shook her head. She didn't understand her daughter at all and her trailer was going to look awfully bare and drab if she didn't have nice knick-knacks and lots of ornaments round and about. No matter how she encouraged her daughter to buy various

100

bits and pieces Vicky had remained stubbornly obstinate about not wanting 'clutter'. It was just as well, thought Mary-Rose, that she'd managed to raise one daughter who was normal and liked things on the fancy side.

They returned to the market for a last look around and met up with Shania, Mikey and his family. It was a big, exuberant and colourful group that pretty much filled one of the walkways between the various stalls.

'For God's sake,' a loud angry voice said, cutting through the travellers' laughter. 'Bloody pikeys, blocking everything.'

Vicky spun round before she could help herself; she recognised that voice.

'Chloe.'

'Vicky! What the hell . . .'

'Don't you dare call us that,' screeched Shania, not realising that Vicky was already trying to manage the situation.

Chloe turned her attention to Shania. Her bravado was buoyed up by the fact that she was also in a big group of girls, some of whom Vicky recognised from college. '*Us? Us?!*' screeched Chloe in shocked amusement. '*How dare you call us that,*' she said, mimicking Shania. 'If the cap fits . . .' She leaned towards Shania and said 'pikey', right into her face.

'Don't you dare talk like that to my sister,' said Vicky.

'Your sister?' crowed Chloe. 'Oh my God. I don't believe it. This gets better and better. A whole family of pikeys and they're all Vicky's relations.'

There was a disturbance as Kelly forced her way through to stand beside Chloe.

101

'Vicky. Oh my God, I am so sorry.'

'What have you got to be sorry for, Kelly?' said Chloe, her voice like acid. 'It's not your fault that your mate's a pikey.' Then the penny dropped when she saw the look on Kelly's face. 'You knew. You knew, didn't you? All along you've known Vicky's dirty little secret. And now you're feeling sorry for her because we've found out the truth.'

The other travellers hadn't really spotted what was going on at the edge of their group, they were too busy chatting and catching up. But a mother's sixth sense alerted Mary-Rose to the quarrel and she waded through the crowd of friends and relations to be beside her daughters.

She was a big woman with forearms like cooked hams and as soon as she clocked what was going on she acted, moving forward to stand squarely in front of Chloe.

'And just who do you think you're talking to,' she said, her bulk dwarfing Chloe's slim frame.

Chloe quailed but stood her ground. 'I was talking to Vicky here.'

'You mean my daughter.' Mary-Rose's eyes narrowed and she thrust her face aggressively towards Chloe. 'And what right do you have to talk to her like that?'

Chloe drew on her last reserves of courage and fought back using spite as a weapon. 'Every right,' she spat back, 'because she keeps making eyes at my boyfriend.'

'I doubt that,' roared Mammy. 'Vicky's a respectable girl who's engaged to be wed and there's no way she'd ever look at another man. Maybe it's your boyfriend

102

who's making the eyes, and why wouldn't he want to look at my Vicky in preference to you, you whey-faced trollop.'

Chloe was dumbfounded by the insult and, lost for words, knew she was beaten. She wasn't going to take on this belligerent Irish woman, not if she didn't want a good thrashing, so she turned and walked away with as much pride as she could muster, followed by her entourage. Only Kelly didn't follow her.

'Kelly?' said Vicky, not understanding why her best mate now seemed to be siding with the enemy. 'But you hate Chloe, don't you?'

'I do,' Kelly said with conviction. 'I didn't know she'd tag along too when a gang of us fixed up this trip. If I'd known . . . If I'd imagined for a minute . . . Oh Vick,' said Kelly with a shaky voice. 'I can't believe what's happened.'

'It's not your fault,' said Vicky. She sighed with relief that her friend was still true. 'You were nowhere around when she started on me. If you'd realised I was here, I know you'd have done everything to make sure our paths didn't cross. You'd have warned me or something and I could have kept a look out for her. It was just one of those things. I think my background was bound to come out eventually.'

'But what,' said Mary-Rose with a steely edge in her voice, 'was all this business about you making eyes at another boy?' Whatever anger Mary-Rose had felt towards Chloe was now being focused on Vicky and the possibility that her daughter had behaved inappropriately.

103

'Mammy, I swear I haven't. Honest. May I burn in hell if I'm lying.'

'She hasn't, Mrs O'Rourke. What Vicky's saying is true.'

Mary-Rose swivelled round to face Kelly. 'And just who might you be?'

'I'm Kelly. Vicky and I have been friends since year seven. Chloe's just a nasty piece of work and her boyfriend makes eyes at anything in a skirt. But Vicky's always just ignored him. Honest.'

'Is that so?' Mary-Rose didn't sound at all convinced.

'Yes it is, Mammy. I wouldn't lie to you. Never.'

'It'd better be so, my girl. If your daddy thought you were behaving in a way that would shame the family he'd never get over it. And you could forget Liam. He wouldn't want you. Frankly, no one would.'

'I know, Mammy, I do.' Vicky's face was pale and earnest with worry at the consequences of Chloe's allegations if no one believed her side of the story.

Mary-Rose sighed. 'Then I'll take your word for it. But don't ever, *ever* let me hear anything like this again.'

Vicky felt quite shaky as her mother left her with Shania and Kelly and returned to the main group of her friends.

'So *were* you making eyes at that girl's fella?' asked Shania, hopping with curiosity. The thought that her sister might have done something quite so terrible was deeply exciting. 'That was that Chloe, wasn't it? Isn't she the one you told me was going out with Jordan?'

Vicky nodded.

'The bloke you think is fit, even if his dad is from Africa?'

Vicky nodded again.

'So did you make eyes at him? I mean, he is a looker, isn't he.'

'No, I didn't.' Vicky's voice was almost shrill with indignation. 'You're as bad as Mammy. As if I would.'

'Well, I don't know. You're the one who thinks Jordan is fit; you're the one wanting to do college instead of getting married; you're the one who has to be pushed into everything to do with your wedding.' Shania shrugged. 'Strikes me that if you really, *really* loved Liam you'd have done it by now. And then *I* wouldn't be hanging around waiting for *you* to get on with it and you wouldn't be seeing Jordan behind Liam's back.'

Vicky was trying hard not to lose her temper with her sister. 'But I'm not.'

'Chloe seems to think you are.'

'We all go to college together. I see a lot of people there but just because I do doesn't mean there's anything else going on. And just because I want to learn how to make dresses properly doesn't mean I don't want to get married.'

'Huh.' Shania didn't even try to keep the sceptical note from her voice.

'Well, I can tell you,' interrupted Kelly, 'that your big sister always behaves totally properly. You remember how she was at school? She hasn't changed just because there's no other travellers to keep an eye on her.'

Shania didn't look convinced. 'Well, *I* think if she

really wanted Liam she'd have wed by now. For God's sake, she's been engaged for over two years now.'

*That's what the problem really is,* thought Vicky wearily. If her mammy wasn't so set on the idea that her daughters had to get married in age order the heat would be right off her. And Shania wouldn't be snapping at her heels like an angry Jack Russell.

Kelly shook her head, not understanding travellers' ways. Vicky was only a teenager so she was hardly over the hill, was she? She said goodbye to Vicky and Shania and headed back home.

'So what did you get for your bottom drawer?' asked Liam as soon as Vicky had got out of the car. He'd been waiting for her return outside his own parents' trailer.

'Take a look.' Vicky popped the boot of her father's car to reveal her haul. 'And it would be a real favour to me if we could store this in your daddy's workshop.'

'I've got a better plan than that,' said Liam with a smile.

'Oh?'

'I've got a surprise,' he said, the grin spreading over his face.

'Oh, what?'

'Never you mind. Close your eyes.'

'Why? What's the surprise, Liam?'

'Just shut your eyes.'

Vicky closed her eyes and allowed herself to be led by Liam by the hand. They seemed to go for miles. At one point Liam slipped his arm around her waist and pulled her close to him to make her steps less hesitant. Vicky could feel the warmth of his body, even through her sweater. A delicious shiver ran through her.

'Don't worry, babe, I won't let you walk into anything,' said Liam, clearly thinking it was a shiver of nerves, not desire. 'Almost there, now. You're not peeking, are you?'

'Promise,' said Vicky, squeezing her eyes tighter shut still, fighting the urge to open them.

Liam stopped. 'Okay, take a look.' Ahead of them was a brand-spanking-new trailer. 'You're not the only one who's been shopping.'

Vicky didn't know what to say. It was perfect.

'Take a look inside,' said Liam, opening the door.

Vicky peered into the pristine interior. There was plastic down to protect the soft furnishings and the carpets and it had that wonderful fresh smell that was a mixture of wax polish and unused fabrics, the sort of smell that you only got with new trailers or cars. The bunks were covered in cream leather and the curtains at the windows were pale yellow. Everything was light and bright and just perfect as a new home. Excitedly Vicky stepped up and in through the door and slipped off her shoes. No way was she going to have any mess being trampled into this fabulous caravan.

Liam jumped in behind her. 'We'll need to get a step,' he said as he did.

Excitedly he showed Vicky round all the cunning features that hid other cunning features so not a square inch of space was wasted. 'So you can move all the things you bought today right on in here.'

Vicky turned to him with shining eyes. Her own trailer. Her very own home. And what Liam had chosen was exactly what she'd have chosen herself. *He's so wonderful*, she thought. *I couldn't be happier than I am right at this minute*.

'I'm going to be living in it from now on. I'm over twenty, I think it's time I did, but Ma and my sisters are going to keep it nice so it'll still be perfect for when you move in.'

A tiny bit of Vicky resented that she wouldn't be the first person to cook or clean in the place but it was just as much Liam's trailer as hers – more really; he'd paid for it when all was said and done.

'But I'm not going to sleep in the double bed till we're wed. I want to save it for when I can share it with you. I want my first time in that bed to be so special.'

Vicky felt her eyes welling with tears. 'Oh Liam, that's wonderful. I do love you so.'

Vicky spent the rest of the afternoon ferrying her new possessions into the caravan, watched by Shania, who did little to hide her jealousy.

'You're just jammy, you are,' her little sister grumbled. 'Your own trailer waiting and ready for you and a fiancé who can't wait to get you into it.'

Vicky put down the stack of plates she was about to carry over to her new home and put her hands on her hips.

'Yes, I am lucky but it isn't as if I don't appreciate it. And Mammy bought you a load of nice stuff today, to be sure. It isn't as if things are that unfair for you.'

Shania just gave her a look that clearly showed her

disbelief, which Vicky, not wanting a row to spoil things, ignored.

'Why don't you help me carry this lot over? I've got to wash all these plates and glasses before I put them away. I could do with a hand. Please,' she added hopefully.

'I suppose.'

Vicky gave her a warm smile that Shania returned. 'It'll be your turn soon,' Vicky assured her, 'and I know Mikey will make sure your trailer will be just as nice. Better maybe.'

Shania, placated by the thought of one day having a nicer trailer than her sister's, began to help.

Together the girls finished lugging Vicky's stuff over to the new trailer. Shania managed to put her envy aside long enough to admit it was 'very nice' and then in a better frame of mind she and Vicky got on with the business of washing all the crockery and glasses before they stored them. Vicky washed and Shania wiped, sometimes chatting, sometimes in friendly silence. Dusk fell as the girls finished.

'I think we deserve a cup of tea,' said Vicky as she surveyed the shelves stacked neatly with her new possessions.

'We could christen the tea set.'

'Why not. You get the tea and milk and I'll put the kettle on.'

While Shania was gone Liam popped in to see why the lights were on.

'You've been busy,' he said, admiring the neat stacks of china and the ranks of glasses lined up with military precision.

Vicky wiped her hands on a tea towel before polishing the kitchen counter with it. 'Just putting stuff away. Shania helped. We're about to have tea, fancy a cup?'

'That'd be wonderful.'

Vicky lifted down the teapot and three cups and saucers from the cupboard over the sink.

'Oh,' said Liam. 'Is this what you got?'

'What do you mean?' Vicky was on guard; Liam didn't sound thrilled.

'Nothing.'

'No, it's not *nothing*. Don't you like our tea service?'

Liam swallowed.

'You don't, do you. You hate it.'

'I don't hate it. It's just – it's just a bit ordinary, isn't it?'

Vicky felt deflated. That was exactly what her mammy had said. 'I thought it looked classy.'

'Classy? What do the likes of us want with *classy*?'

'I'll go back next week and change it. I've kept the box it came in so I can pack it back up.'

'No, I don't want you to do that. Not if you really like it.'

Vicky looked at her tea set and wondered if she really did.

Shania returned with the teabags and milk. 'I brought sugar too,' she said, dumping the paper bag on the table. As she did so she picked up on the atmosphere between Liam and Vick. She glanced from one to the other.

'Make up your mind,' said Vicky. 'I can't take it back if we've used it.'

'Take what back?' asked Shania.

'The tea set. Liam doesn't like it.'

'I never said that. I said it was ordinary. There's a difference. And I'm getting used to it. Anyway, you like it, which is all that matters to me, so we'll keep it.'

'Are you sure?' asked Vicky doubtfully. Maybe it *was* too plain.

'You don't want to go back to the Sunday market,' said Shania. 'You might run into that horrible Chloe girl again.'

'What's this?' asked Liam.

'Nothing,' said Vicky quickly, shooting a warning look at Shania. But Shania missed it as she was busy popping teabags into the new pot.

'Some girl from college was there. Called Vicky and me pikeys and then accused Vicky of wanting to steal her boyfriend.'

'Vicky?' Liam sounded horrified.

Vicky sighed. *Thanks a bunch, Shania.* 'It was nothing. The stupid cow was making a mountain out of a mole-hill. Her bloke plays around behind her back so she's jealous of everyone. And she's a troublemaker. I swear, I've never even given him the time of day. Besides, I hardly see him. I'm doing textiles, Liam, there isn't a single boy in my class, let alone Jordan.'

'Yeah, well, I suppose dressmaking isn't the sort of thing a bloke would do,' said Liam with a grin.

'Exactly.'

'But I wish you weren't mixing with gorgios. I worry about you, Vicky. I don't like you being somewhere I can't protect you. Supposing she gets others to gang up

111

on you? I couldn't bear it if that happened, it would break my heart if you got hurt.'

'I don't have a choice, Liam. There aren't any colleges for travellers, are there. If I want to learn proper dressmaking this is my only chance. I'll be fine, though. Trust me.'

But as he was drinking his tea Vicky caught him glancing at her once or twice with a worried expression. It almost seemed to her that he was trying to figure her out. Well, good luck to him because she couldn't even figure herself out, so she didn't think anyone else stood a chance.

# 6

When she and Shania got back to the family trailer her mum was making supper for the whole family. Her kid brothers were watching re-runs of *Top Gear* with her dad in the sitting area and Kylie was in her high chair banging an upturned plastic bowl with a wooden spoon.

'What's for tea, Mammy?' asked Shania, 'I'm famished.'

'Stew and dumplings. But I want some carrots peeling. You can make yourself useful and do that for me, so you can.'

Shania dragged a big bag of carrots out of the cupboard in the corner of the kitchen and got busy.

'And you, young lady, can lay the table,' she told Vicky.

It was a scene of domestic harmony: the girls busy in the kitchen helping their mother and the boys enjoying TV with their daddy. Vicky looked at it as she worked and wondered if her own trailer would be as contented as this when she had a family of her own.

'So,' said her mammy as she stirred the stew, 'is

that new trailer Liam's bought you everything you dreamed?'

'It's lovely.' Vicky's eyes shone as she spoke.

'I've had such a job keeping that piece of news to myself. He's been asking me so many questions about what you would or wouldn't want. What colours you like, what arrangements you'd like.'

'So you knew about it all along?'

'To be sure I did. That's one of the reasons we had to get you away off the park today so you wouldn't see it being delivered. So now you're getting your bottom drawer sorted and you've a home to put it in we need to get you over to the dressmaker for your dress. No more excuses, miss. You've got everything now to get wed, except a date and a dress.'

For a second Vicky felt trapped. Her mother was right, there really was no excuse now. She totted up the months till the summer – seven till June. Eight if she could hang on till July. That would be another few weeks' grace, a few more textile lessons squeezed in, a few more skills learned.

'You need to get married in May or June,' chipped in Shania. 'Then I can wed Mikey in August. I'll be sixteen by then and I don't want to wait a minute longer.'

'Mammy? Two weddings in one year?' Vicky was aghast. 'You couldn't manage that, surely?'

'Why not? Shania doesn't want to do anything daft like you and make her own dresses.' Mary-Rose stopped stirring the stew and faced Vicky. 'And once we've found a place for your wedding breakfast we can use it again for hers. In fact, Shania's wedding will be easy to

114

sort as we'll know what we're doing by the time we fix hers.'

'But June?'

'And what's wrong with that?' Mammy waved her spoon at her daughter. 'You said you wanted a summer wedding. June's summer, so what's your problem?'

'Nothing, Mammy.' She went to her room, shut the door and lay down on her bed. Through the thin partition she could hear the sounds of family life carrying on, the soundtrack that she'd known since birth. As she listened she realised it wasn't just family life she was hearing but a way of life. Getting married was her destiny. It was what she'd been brought up to do. *Really*, she told herself sternly, *just pull yourself together and get on with it*. But maybe she could get the family to let her wait till the summer term finished in July. Would that be such a compromise?

'So what's this your mammy told me about a row at the market?' asked her dad through a mouthful of beef stew.

'It was something and nothing, Dad,' said Vicky. *Jesus, does everyone in the world need to know about the row I had with Chloe?* She recounted the unpleasant meeting for the second time that day, leaving out the bit about what Chloe had said about her and Jordan. Her dad really didn't need to know about that because she just knew it would lead to another row, only her dad mightn't be so easy to convince as Liam that it was just a storm in a teacup.

'So everyone at college is going to know who you are now.' Johnnie made the statement flatly.

'Not necessarily.'

Johnnie snorted. 'Like this girl is going to keep this information to herself. If she's as spiteful as you say she's going to just love spreading around that you're a traveller.'

'Maybe not.'

Johnnie forked up another big mouthful. 'Trust me, gorgios never cut a traveller an inch of slack. She'll make life miserable for you, mark my words. If I were you I'd cut college. Give it up, darlin'. Your little sister gave up school two years ago and it hasn't done her any harm. I just don't understand why you're so hell-bent on carrying on. It's not worth the heartache. I've never met a non-traveller that I've liked and I don't suppose I ever will, and I've no doubt that if you go back to college on Monday you're going to find out the truth of that for yourself the hard way.'

Vicky sighed. The trouble was that she knew her dad was right. She hadn't got to the grand old age of seventeen without experiencing endless petty discrimination. She'd had friends whose wedding receptions had been cancelled at the last minute because the hotel had found out who the guests were. At the Appleby Horse Fair and at the one at Stow she'd seen gypsies being spat at, being turned away from pubs and picked on by the police for doing nothing more than just standing on a corner. She knew with a sinking feeling of dread that college wasn't going to be any different. Chloe would see to that. Chloe would make sure she was stared at, singled out, bullied and discriminated against. Much as she wanted to be a proper dressmaker, maybe she ought to just cut her losses. Maybe her dad was right and she should sack her ambition. Her dream seemed to be fading and Vicky felt like crying.

On the Monday morning, after she'd helped her mother clean their own trailer, Vicky went over to Liam's new trailer to help Bridget, his mother, clean that one. Why not, she reasoned, as she wasn't going to college when all was said and done? Although how she'd finish all the bridesmaids' dresses without the college's fancy machines she didn't know. Hand sew them, she supposed, or give in and let a professional dressmaker finish them. Another dream down the pan.

'You not at college?' Bridget asked.

Vicky was still feeling hideously raw about her decision to quit but managed to bite back a slightly snarky remark that unless she could be in two places at once then, fairly obviously, she wasn't.

'No. Giving it a miss for a while.'

Although more realistically it was for ever. But she wasn't going to tell anyone that just yet. If she breathed a word of her decision it would be round the site in less time than it would take to say 'please don't tell a soul'.

'Is this to do with the trouble at the market?'

Was there no one on the trailer park who didn't know? *That's the trouble with this place*, thought Vicky, *no one can mind their own business, not for one second*. She nodded.

'It's for the best,' said Bridget. 'Things always happen for a reason. If you've given up learning then there's no reason for you and Liam not to get wed real soon.'

Vicky gave her a thin smile and set about cleaning the

117

already sparkling windows. Thankfully, despite the fact that the trailer was new, they both had more than enough chores to do to keep the caravan up to their own exacting standards and silence fell. Then Vicky's phone bing-bonged.

She took it from the back pocket of her jeans and checked to see who the message was from. Kelly. *Well, there's a surprise.* Vicky could just guess what this message was going to be about. She flicked her phone open and wandered out of the trailer to read the message away from Bridget and her curiosity.

'Where r u.'

Just as she thought. 'Home.'

'Y.'

'Guess.'

There was silence for a few seconds and then her phone rang.

'Is this all about Chloe?' Kelly said, without bothering with a greeting.

'Hello to you too, Kelly. And yes, thanks for asking, I'm fine.'

'Never mind the crap. Is this all about that bitch Chloe? Is that why you're not in college today?'

'What is it to you? It's no skin off your nose if I cut classes.'

'Don't be a dumbass, Vicky. If you don't come back it means Chloe has won. You can't let her get the better of you.'

'It's not just that, Kel. It's all right for you. You don't have to put up with the sort of shit me and my family have to on a daily basis.'

'So don't let her win. If you stand up to her she'll stop picking on you.'

'But it won't just be just her, will it?'

There was silence for a few seconds. Then Kelly said, 'I can't talk to you properly over the phone. Can we meet?'

'You know the rules about me going out on my own.'

'Then can I come to you?'

'Here?'

'Don't sound so shocked, Vick. You only live on the edge of town. The 68 bus passes the trailer park. If I hop on that I can be with you in thirty minutes.'

'But . . .'

'But *what*? But *I won't be welcome*? Is that it? I'm your mate, Vick, why can't I come and see you if you can't come and see me? I'm going to be your bridesmaid, ain't I? Isn't it about time I met some of your family because if I don't soon, it's going to be bloody awkward on your big day.'

'I suppose.'

'Meet me at the gate to the trailer park. I'll ring you again when I'm five minutes away.'

Vicky's phone went dead. Shit, Kelly coming to the caravan site might cause real problems, but then Kelly had a real point. If Kelly was going to be her bridesmaid she had to break it to her parents at some time. And this was probably as good a time as any. But they weren't going to like it. And on top of that, she had to face a talking to from Kelly about college as well. Just wonderful.

Vicky tried to imagine how the meeting with her

119

parents might go. Would it be awful? Given what her father had said about non-travellers only the night before she wasn't terribly hopeful. On the other hand, maybe Kelly coming to the trailer park wouldn't be so bad. She and her mum had already run into each other at the market, although the circumstances hadn't been brilliant. And Kel already knew Shania a bit from school. So it was just her dad and Liam really that Kelly had yet to meet.

Except that was the problem. Her dad hated gorgios, and while it wasn't in Liam's nature to truly hate anyone, neither of them trusted non-travellers and her recent spat with Chloe was only going to make things worse. All that had done was to reinforce their view that all gorgios were bad, not to be tangled with and avoided at all costs.

*What a sodding mess*, she thought as she returned to Liam's trailer and carried on with the windows.

She'd just about finished when her phone chirruped again with another text from Kelly.

'With u in 5.'

Vicky excused herself from Bridget's company and walked towards the main entrance to the park. She'd pretty much arrived when she saw Kelly walking between the gates and heading towards her. Vicky quickened her pace. She didn't want Kelly getting a load of abuse from any of the traveller men. It wasn't just her fiancé and father who mistrusted non-travellers, almost everyone on the park felt the same. And generally, the arrival of any outsiders meant trouble: some busybody from the council, someone from the planning department out to cause trouble, social workers checking up on the kids or some other nosy parker interfering where they weren't wanted.

'Hi, Kelly,' she said, giving her friend a quick hug. She linked her arm through Kelly's and led her towards her family trailer. This was it: shit or bust, as Kelly liked to say. Had she made the right decision by not warning anyone that she was bringing Kelly home, least of all her father? She'd decided that, on balance, it would be better to present him with a done deal than risk him refusing to allow Kelly near his family or even on the park. She'd learned enough from life to realise that you should never ask a question if the answer 'no' was unacceptable. She'd certainly learned it a few weeks back when she'd asked her dad if she could go over to Kelly's house. But she knew it was a risky strategy. What if he went off on one? It was tricky enough when he lost his temper with only his family to witness it but what if he lost it with Kelly? Swallowing nervously and putting on a brave face to hide her fears, Vicky led Kelly to the door of their trailer.

She motioned Kelly to go in. 'And take your shoes off on the mat, please,' she said as she stepped in after her.

'Cor, this is lovely,' said Kelly as she toed her pumps off.

'What did you expect?' asked Vicky defensively.

'I don't know. I didn't really think about it but it's just like a real home, innit?'

Mary-Rose came out of the main bedroom at the rear of the trailer. And stopped dead when she saw Kelly, her eyes widening.

'Mum, this is Kelly,' Vicky said quickly. 'You met her at the market.'

'With Chloe.' There was an edge to her mammy's voice.

'Sort of,' said Kelly, stepping forward. 'But we're not friends. Not like Vick and me are,' she added. 'Vick and me go back to our first day at King John's.'

'Is that a fact?' Mary-Rose still sounded wary.

'I thought Kelly might have a cup of tea with us,' suggested Vicky.

'Tea?' Mary-Rose's eyebrows nearly hit her hairline. 'Kelly has come all the way over here for tea?'

'And a chat with me,' said Vicky.

'A chat?'

Jesus, was her mother going to repeat every bloody word? But Vicky decided to plough on and broach the subject that needed addressing. 'And to try on her bridesmaid's dress.'

Mary-Rose leaned against a counter to steady herself but to give her her due, she didn't shout. She just nodded slowly as she took in the information. 'Ah, so Kelly is to be one of your bridesmaids?'

'Yes Mammy, along with Shania, Kylie, Liam's two sisters and Auntie Colleen's two, like we agreed.'

'That's . . . nice. Have you told your daddy?'

Vicky swallowed. 'I'm about to.'

'Then we'd better have tea first. Take a seat, Kelly.' Vicky could see that her mother was as apprehensive about Johnnie's reaction as she was.

Mary-Rose went to the sink and filled the kettle while Kelly perched on the bunk under the window and looked around at the spotless trailer and took in all Mary-Rose's china ornaments.

'You've a great collection of Doulton figurines,' she said.

Mary-Rose turned round and gave her a surprised but broad smile as she plugged the kettle in. 'And how do you know about Royal Doulton? I didn't think kids your age were into stuff like that.'

'My granny's got a collection. Not as nice as yours, though.'

Vicky could have kissed Kelly. Vicky didn't think her friend could have made a more perfect comment even if she'd been coached. And as a way of getting Mary-Rose onside it couldn't have been bettered. She could see her mammy preening and purring over the compliment. Vicky flashed a smile of gratitude to Kelly, who just shrugged, obviously not really understanding the importance of the breakthrough she'd just inadvertently made.

'Where's Daddy?' asked Vicky.

'Gone to see a man about a horse.'

'Any idea when he'll be back?'

'Lunchtime, he said.' Mary-Rose glanced at the clock on the wall. 'He'll be about another hour. Kelly, will you stay and have a bite with us? It's only bread and cheese and pickles but you'd be welcome to join us.'

Vicky just managed to prevent a little squeal of delight from escaping. If Mammy was inviting Kelly to eat with them then that was half the battle won. Her mother's approval of Kelly was of paramount importance in winning her dad round. Okay, an offer of lunch wasn't in quite the same league as agreeing to let Kelly attend the wedding as a bridesmaid but it looked very hopeful. And frankly, given how shit Vicky felt about a lot of things at the moment, it was nice that just one thing looked as if it might work out. If her mother had decided that Kelly wasn't an enemy and wasn't set against her attending her eldest daughter's wedding, then she didn't think her father would be nearly so likely to argue against it, either.

'Then while we're waiting for lunch we can get you into your dress,' said Vicky.

The two girls went into Vicky and Shania's bedroom where Vicky got the half-made dress out of the cupboard above the bed.

'I've just got to finish the petticoats,' explained Vicky, 'but the bodice and the skirt are done. Try it on.' She handed the dress to Kelly and left her to get on with it. As she went, she added, 'Call me if you need me to zip you up.'

'Will do,' answered Kelly from behind the shut door.

'Your friend seems nice,' said Mary-Rose in a quiet voice.

'She is, really nice,' said Vicky.

'Not like that other girl I met.'

'No, well, she's a cow.'

'Like most gorgios.'

Vicky couldn't be bothered to argue that Chloe was a one-off when it came to bitchiness and that most of her acquaintances at college were pretty normal. Not especially nice but not complete cows either. But, of course, things might change if they now knew her background.

'Zip me up, Vick,' yelled Kelly from the bedroom.

Vicky went in and caught her breath. Kelly looked stunning in the dark green. Even just holding the bodice to her chest the dress was a triumph. Vicky zipped it up and then dragged Kelly out of the room.

'Look, Mammy.'

Mary-Rose turned round and then clapped her hands in delight. 'Oh my, oh my, to be sure that's a beautiful dress. Give us a twirl, darlin'.'

Kelly obediently spun round.

'And just think what it'll look like with petticoats,' said Vicky. She bent down and fluffed up the skirt to give an impression of the puffball shape it would reach with proper support.

'That's a piece of work and no mistake,' boomed Johnnie from the door of the caravan. Then the look on his face made it clear that he had just realised that he didn't recognise the girl modelling the outfit. She wasn't a relation and she wasn't from the trailer park so who the hell was this stranger in his home? He looked from Vicky to Mary-Rose for an answer.

'This is Vicky's friend, Kelly,' said Mary-Rose.

'Kelly?'

'Yes,' said Vicky. Wanting to add *the Kelly you won't let me visit* but she bottled out.

'She's going to be taking a bit of lunch with us,' said Mary-Rose. 'That's okay isn't it, darlin'?'

Johnnie looked sceptical but if Mary-Rose was happy to have a stranger at her table it wasn't really up to him to contradict her. 'As you wish,' he said. 'And she's to be a bridesmaid too, I see. You're not from round here, are you, Kelly?'

125

'No, Mr O'Rourke. I live on the other side of town.'

'Ah, that Kelly.' The penny had obviously dropped. His brow furrowed deeply and he did not look happy.

'Her gran collects Royal Doulton,' said Mary-Rose, as if that conferred honorary gypsy status on Kelly.

'Only I was telling your wife that Granny's collection isn't a patch on this one here,' said Kelly.

'Really,' said Johnnie. What Kelly's gran did cut no ice with him although, when it came to ice, his own voice was so cold it was almost sub-zero.

'She's been Vicky's friend from the start at King John's,' added Mary-Rose. 'Her best friend.'

'Has she now.' Johnnie sighed heavily then turned and left the trailer. It was only once he'd gone that Vicky realised she'd been holding her breath.

Kelly looked from Mary-Rose to Vicky. 'Would it be easier if I didn't stay for lunch?'

'Absolutely not,' said Mary-Rose, forcefully. 'Johnnie'll come round, it'll just take him a while. We don't mix with . . . we don't usually . . .'

'As you know we don't get out much,' said Vicky, 'so Dad isn't good with non-travellers.'

She reasoned that to put it like that was more polite than to say he thought they were the scum of the earth. Kelly mightn't appreciate it.

When Johnnie returned for his lunch Kelly was back in her street clothes and chatting to Mary-Rose like they'd known each other for years. Vicky was making a few alterations to the fit of the skirt and Shania was feeding Kylie with a sandwich.

Johnnie grunted hello to the women and then sat at

the table, flicking on the TV with the remote as he did so.

Mary-Rose put a plate of bread and cheese in front of him and then passed over a tray with jars of pickles and a big pat of butter on it.

'Why do you want to be one of Vicky's bridesmaids?' said Johnnie with no preamble.

'She's my best mate,' said Kelly, looking him square in the eye. 'She and I have been through a lot together.'

'Have you now. So what do you know about the sort of things the likes of Vicky has to cope with?'

'I don't. Doesn't mean I can't see it's hard for her. Doesn't mean I don't hate others for making life miserable for her, does it?'

Johnnie wasn't used to having a woman stand up to him quite like this. 'I suppose,' he conceded.

'Sure, she and I are different, but only in some ways. Deep down we still want the same things.'

Johnnie raised his eyebrows. What on earth would Kelly want that his daughter might too? 'Like what?'

'A nice husband, a family, a home.'

'Oh.' Johnnie carried on eating in silence.

'Talking of homes,' said Vicky, desperate for a chance to talk to Kelly in private, 'can I take Kelly to see the trailer Liam bought for us?'

'You'd better ask Liam about that,' said Mary-Rose. 'If he says yes, then I won't object.' She looked at Johnnie, who nodded his agreement.

'Come on,' said Vicky, grabbing Kelly with one hand, their coats with another and dragging her out of the trailer and into the cold November air. She slammed the door behind them and giggled. 'I thought we'd never get the chance to talk on our own. But you made a hit with Mammy. You were so cool spouting all that nonsense about your gran and those figures.'

'But it's not nonsense, it's true.'

'Never!'

'Honest.'

'But I thought it was only the likes of us that filled our homes with that stuff.'

'Nah. And when Gran dies she's promised them to me. I like them.'

'You want them?'

'Of course, they're lovely.'

Vicky shook her head in disbelief. 'You know, Kelly, I sometimes think you and me ought to swap places.'

'Except I don't want to get married for a few years yet.'

'Sometimes I don't think I do either.' There, she'd said it.

Out loud.

They reached Liam's workshop and Vicky pushed open the door. There was the love of her life busy turning a chair leg on a lathe. 'Hi, Liam,' she shouted over the high-pitched whirring.

He flicked the switch and the noise slowly wound down.

'Hi, babe,' he said with a smile.

'I've brought someone to meet you. Mum and Dad said I could,' she added. 'This is Kelly, she's going to be one of our bridesmaids.' Vicky pulled Kelly right through the door to stand in the light where Liam could see her properly.

Liam wiped his hands on his trousers before holding one out to Vicky's friend. 'Pleased to meet you,' he said.

'Kelly's a mate from college,' said Vicky. 'Mum loves her because she knows all about Royal Doulton.'

Despite her carefully planted signals that her parents almost approved of Kelly, or approved of her as much as they were capable of, a wary shuttered look formed on Liam's face.

'Is that so,' was all he said.

'I want to show Kelly the trailer you bought for us.'

'Do you now.'

'Please, Liam.'

'I suppose,' he said grudgingly.

'Thanks, babe.' Vicky dragged Kelly out of the workshop before he could change his mind.

She whirled Kelly through the park, ignoring the curious stares from her traveller friends and relations, till they got to the pitch where her new trailer was parked.

'Shoes off,' she ordered again as she opened the door and pulled herself up the high step.

Once again Kelly toed off her shoes and followed. 'So this is going to be home sweet home.'

'That's the plan. What do you think?'

'Lovely.' Kelly wrinkled her nose. 'Is it just me or does everywhere around here smell of polish?'

'That's because everywhere does. We like things just so.'

'I can see. My mum's house looks like a right shithole compared to these places.'

Vicky shrugged. 'We're very house proud. I know people call us all sorts of names but it's not fair.'

129

'People like Chloe.'

Vicky nodded.

'So because of her, one nasty little cow, you're going to give up college, is that it?' said Kelly, settling herself on the bunk by the big window at the end.

'But it won't be just one nasty little cow once she's told everyone just who I am, will it? Everyone will be against me. You know full well what people in the town think about us here on the park. That we're dirty, thieving gypsies. Layabouts and good-for-nothings, benefit cheats and scroungers.'

'So they're wrong. I know that.'

'You're the only one,' said Vicky, bleakly.

'Don't you think that all the people at college, all the kids who were at King John's and who know you as Vicky O'Rourke, not Vicky the Gypsy, will stick by you?'

Vicky looked her friend in the eye. 'No, no I don't.'

'I think you're wrong.'

'Says someone who's never suffered from discrimination.'

'You didn't at King John's,' said Kelly reasonably.

'Because I spent half my time there working out how to fit in. I was so careful never to let anyone know. I was terrified when you guessed; I thought if you did, everyone would.'

'You mean you thought if someone as dim as me could do it, then so would all the bright kids.'

Vicky laughed. 'No I didn't! And you're so not dim. But, you know, I thought I must've given something away.'

'I think,' said Kelly, 'I guessed because you were so

130

private. You never said anything ever about your home or your folks. I wondered if you were in care or something. Then the penny just sort of dropped. But by that time we were best mates so I never let anything I heard about travellers worry me.'

'Didn't work like that for Shania. She wasn't so careful, that's why she got bullied and left school a couple of years back. But, to be honest, that's why I avoided her in school. I didn't want everyone to realise she and I were sisters.'

'Harsh.'

Vicky shrugged. 'I know it sounds that way, but Shan understood – she didn't really care and bunked off school all the time anyway. But she knew school was important to me, so we just didn't hang out. It sounds worse than it actually was.'

'So after all that, you're going to throw everything away.'

'I don't want to.'

'Then don't.'

Vicky stared at her hands, twiddling her engagement ring around. 'It's just, is it worth it? Is it worth all the hassle and heartache just to make a point, a point that won't matter in the long run because I'll be married?'

'So why does being married make a difference?'

'Traveller wives don't work.'

'Oh, I remember now, you said. But couldn't you bend the rules. College isn't like working, is it. Not properly, not for cash.'

'Not a chance. And why go for a qualification I can never really use.'

131

'Shit, Vicky, that's not fair.'

'Fair or not it's how it is.'

'But dressmaking isn't proper work, is it. Not if you just make stuff for yourself and your family. If you do that it's just a hobby, like collecting Royal Doulton.'

'That's what I've been telling myself but who am I kidding?'

Kelly leaned forward and took Vicky's hands. 'Look, this is your life, and you have to have faith in your skill. That dress I tried on is a work of art, Vicky. You can't let talent like that go to waste. And you're not married yet so whatever life has to be like for you once you *are*, you have to make the most of everything beforehand. Come back to college, please. Show Chloe that you're better than she is by not running scared, by not giving in to her bullying tactics. Because that's what you're doing.'

'Maybe you're right.'

'I am. And I'll stick by you and I bet Jordan will too. You'll see.'

After Kelly had gone Vicky went back to Liam's workshop.

'Thanks for letting me show Kelly our trailer.'

'It's okay. Don't know why she came here to nose about, though.'

'She wasn't *nosing* about. She came to try on her bridesmaid's dress and to have a chat to me. She's my friend, Liam.'

'She's a gorgio. She'll never be a real friend to you, she can't be. Gorgios are all the same; they hate us. And I don't know why you want her at our wedding,' he grumbled. 'Because I know I don't.'

132

students standing around were staring and whispering.

'Don't be daft,' said Kelly. 'It's like this every day. People are just chatting. No one is giving you a second look, honest. You're just paranoid.'

*Am I?* Vicky wondered. She looked about her. Did some of the girls glance away as soon as they made eye contact? Were students giggling behind their hands? Or was Kelly right that they were just chatting and laughing like they always did?

Kelly gave her arm another little squeeze. 'Stick with me, hon, there's nothing to worry about.'

Yeah, Vicky decided, Kelly was right, there was nothing to worry about. She held her head high and squared her shoulders. She had as much right to be there as anyone and her background just didn't matter. She'd be fine.

They were going through the double doors that led to the courtyard between the main building and the arts block when Jordan came banging out of the cloakroom and ran up to them.

'Hi, girls,' he said. 'Are you OK?'

Instantly Vicky was aware of three feelings: firstly was fear that Chloe would spot them. Instinctively Vicky looked around for her. Much as she didn't care whether she upset the bitch or not, she didn't want to court trouble. And chatting to Jordan was doing exactly that. Secondly she felt her insides flip and flutter. What was it about Jordan that did this to her? It was so wrong. It was Liam she loved, it was Liam she was marrying and her body had no reason to behave so treacherously. Which explained her third feeling: one of huge guilt.

'Okay, thanks. Can't talk, late for lessons,' she replied as she hurried on, leaving Jordan looking bemused and a little irritated. He wasn't the sort of lad who got ignored by girls he took an interest in.

'Whoa,' said Kelly as they went back out into the fresh air. 'Jordan's done nothing wrong.'

'Chloe accused me of trying to steal him off her *in front of my family*. Have you any idea how bad that made me look to them?'

'But it wasn't true.'

'No, and it can't ever be true, not if I want to keep Liam.'

'So?'

'So I can't be seen talking to him.'

'But no one from your family would know.'

'*I'd* know.'

'So what?' Kelly felt she was losing the plot. 'He's just a mate. Chatting to him is no different from chatting to me.'

But Vicky couldn't admit, even to herself, that chatting to Jordan wasn't a bit like chatting to Kelly. For a start, after she'd spent time chatting to Kelly she didn't constantly find her thoughts straying back to her – which is what always seemed to happen with Jordan. And when she chatted to Kelly her insides didn't turn cartwheels.

They hadn't seen a sign of Chloe when Kelly dropped Vicky off at the textiles room, much to Vicky's relief.

'I'll meet you back here at twelve thirty,' said Kelly as she turned to go.

Feeling a lot less nervous now she was on her own

territory and in a place where Chloe wasn't going to appear, Vicky opened the door and walked inside. Instantly the four girls already gathered there stopped talking. An awkward silence followed. Vicky just knew they'd been talking about her.

'Carry on, don't mind me,' she said pointedly as she put her bag and carrier containing her work on the side, where she always left her stuff. Behind her she heard scuffling and some quiet thuds. She turned round to find her classmates were all, equally pointedly, shoving their handbags and kit into the lockers provided. In the weeks that Vicky had been at the college she had never once seen anyone use the lockers. With a sick feeling she knew exactly what had brought this on.

'So you've heard,' she said defiantly. 'Word gets around fast, doesn't it?'

The four girls looked uncomfortable but didn't reply.

'You think I'm going to steal your stuff, don't you? Obviously, because I'm a gypsy it means that I'm a lying, thieving piece of scum, doesn't it? Even though you thought I was okay until this morning.'

'Maybe,' admitted Leah, who had, on a previous occasion, borrowed Vicky's notes when she'd lost her own and who, until this moment, Vicky had considered a friend.

'So how much of your stuff went missing when you knew nothing about me?'

'None,' Leah conceded.

'So what's the difference now?' The answer was silence. 'Suit yourselves,' said Vicky, her head held high. *You're not to cry*, she told herself sternly. *They're not worth it.* But inside she felt as if she'd just been knifed.

When Mrs Mead, their textiles teacher, entered she made a swift appraisal of the room. On one side, all alone, sat Vicky looking proud and defiant but upset; on the other side of the room sat the other ten girls in her group. She sighed. She'd known that Vicky's background, which she'd been aware of since she'd seen Vicky's application form and its give-away address, was bound to come out sooner or later, but she'd fervently hoped it would be later rather than sooner. And if she was honest with herself, she'd had huge doubts as to the girl's suitability for her course – that was, until she'd seen Vicky's incredible talent and instinct for the subject.

So now, did she say anything, or ignore the situation? This was a first for Mrs Mead, never having taught an Irish traveller before, and would saying something make the situation better or worse? She decided, on balance, not to make an issue of things and carried on with her lesson on the use of the felting machine as if nothing had happened. She demonstrated how it could be used for distressing fabrics, meshing them together or punching strips of one fabric into another to make random and unusual textures.

'Right, Vicky,' she said when she'd finished going through the various possibilities, 'why don't you have a go on the machine and see what you can produce.'

On cue the other girls chuntered about it being unfair that she should have first go but Mrs Mead silenced them with a sharp stare and told them to get on with their work on fabric collages.

'It isn't as if any of you is so far ahead with your work that you can afford to waste any time chatting, either.'

The other girls took the hint and silence fell over the classroom, punctuated only by the whirr of some of the sewing machines and the snip of scissors.

At the end of the long morning session Vicky was packing up her work when Mrs Mead signalled to her that she'd like her to stay behind. *Great*, thought Vicky, *she's heard too and is about to tell me she doesn't want to teach a pikey.*

'What's going on, Vicky?' Mrs Mead said as soon as the heavy fire door had closed behind the last of the other girls.

'I don't know what you mean, miss.'

'Don't treat me like an idiot.'

'I'm not.'

Mrs Mead raised her eyebrows. 'Is this about where you live?'

Vicky nodded.

'So they've found out.'

Vicky nodded again.

'Which is why you didn't come to college yesterday.'

'Yes.'

'Well, I'm glad you changed your mind.'

'Thank you.'

'Of course, they're jealous of you, which also doesn't help. You're far and away the best student in the class. I suppose they feel that with all their so-called advantages it should be the other way round.'

'Maybe,' Vicky conceded.

'You mustn't let them grind you down. You mustn't even think about dropping out just because of some stupid attitude towards you.'

'It's easy for you to say.'

'I agree. I've never had to deal with anything of the sort and I have no idea what it's like for you. All I can say is that you mustn't let them win.'

'That's what Kelly said.'

'Kelly? Is she a traveller too?'

'No, she my best mate since school. She's doing beauty therapy. She told me to come back today.'

'Then you should listen to Kelly. She's dead right. And if you've got an ally here things should be easier, shouldn't they?'

'Dunno. If people want to make life difficult they totally can, even if you have a couple of mates.'

The door to the classroom creaked open.

'Talk of the devil,' said Vicky.

'Kelly?' asked Mrs Mead.

'You all right, Vick?' asked Kelly.

'Fine. Mrs Mead's just giving me a pep talk.'

Mrs Mead laughed. 'A talk Vicky probably doesn't need with a good friend like you to gee her up.'

'Thanks. Sorry to interrupt but I promised Vicky I'd come and get her and when I saw all the other girls go off for lunch I wondered if everything was all right. I was afraid she might've given up and gone home early.'

'No,' said Vicky. 'What do you take me for – some sort of coward?'

'Never,' said Mrs Mead and Kelly in unison.

140

\*

Vicky was still smiling at the faith her tutor and her best mate had in her when she entered the canteen for lunch. The smile was wiped off her face, though, when the hubbub of chatter and the clatter of cutlery and crockery diminished, silence fell and all the faces turned to look at her. If Kelly hadn't been standing right behind her and blocking her escape route she would have turned and fled.

'Chin up,' whispered Kelly. 'Don't let them win.'

But Vicky was frozen with fear and embarrassment.

'Hi, girls,' said Jordan, standing up at a table across the room. 'Join me?'

A murmur ran round the room. Kelly gave Vicky a sharp shove in the small of her back, propelling her forward.

'We can't,' squeaked Vicky over her shoulder to Kelly. 'What about Chloe?'

'She's not here.' Kelly caught hold of Vicky's arm and dragged her into the canteen. After a couple of steps Vicky shook her off. If she was going to face these people down she needed to do it on her own. Yes, it was great to have Kelly there but this was a battle she had to fight herself.

She slid into a seat beside Jordan. 'You like living dangerously or something?'

'Not really,' he replied as Kelly sat down opposite the pair of them.

'So what'll Chloe say when she hears about this?'

'Hears about what?'

'Come off it, Jordan, don't play dumb,' said Vicky.

'Chloe hates me, she thinks I fancy you and she's the one who's told everyone I'm a pikey.'

'So?'

'*So*?'

'It doesn't change who you are, the person a lot of people liked until yesterday. Remember, you aren't the only one who has ever been discriminated against. Think what it was like for my dad when he was growing up and the shit he had to cope with. You can hide your background but he couldn't hide his skin colour. Compared to him, I reckon you've got it easy.'

'Yeah, well . . .' Vicky couldn't argue against that. 'But whatever you say, they don't like me now.'

'It'll blow over.'

'Maybe. In the meantime I need to get some food.' Vicky and Kelly stood up and went over to the serving counter to get their lunch. The noise in the canteen had returned to normal levels, although Vicky was conscious of glances being cast in her direction now and again.

'Come on, Kelly,' she said, stuffing the baguette she'd just paid for in her bag. 'Let's go and eat somewhere else.'

'What's wrong with sitting with Jordan?'

Vicky shook her head. 'You don't get it, do you? I *can't*. Not after everything.'

'You're mad,' said Kelly. 'He wants to look after you too, you know.'

Vicky knew that it should be Liam who was her knight in shining armour, not Jordan. But Liam couldn't protect her at college.

*

As the autumn term drifted towards Christmas, Vicky wasn't sure if she was getting used to the cuts and taunts or whether they were getting less frequent. Either way, the attitude of her fellow students bothered her less. Her work in the textiles department continued to be outstanding and she managed to finish the third of the seven bridesmaids' dresses. But best of all was that Chloe seemed to have given up her own personal hate campaign, now choosing to totally ignore Vicky. If, thought Vicky, Chloe reckoned she'd be upset by this treatment, she couldn't be more wrong. Frankly, as far as Vicky was concerned, being ignored by Chloe was a huge bonus. But as the days ticked past Vicky was increasingly conscious that her wedding day was getting ever closer.

'I've fixed for you to see the dressmaker on Saturday,' Mary-Rose said when Vicky returned from college one evening.

'Saturday?'

'And what's wrong with that?'

'Nothing,' said Vicky.

'You have decided how you want your dress now, haven't you?'

Vicky nodded vigorously, although she'd only given the matter the most basic of thoughts: lots of petticoats, white or cream, obviously, and a train. She'd been telling her mother for weeks, months now, that she had an idea of what she wanted but it was an out-and-out lie. Truth was, she didn't really have a clue. She went to her room and was glad to see that Shania wasn't there already. Dumping her college bags on the bed she extracted her sketchbook and sat down. What exactly did she want to look like on her wedding day? The phrase 'fairy-tale princess' popped into her head. Well, duh? What else did any traveller girl want to look like? Except that Vicky wanted her dress to be not just about the big skirt and the frills. She wanted something else, something original, something classy, something . . . more.

She began to sketch out some ideas. No, that wouldn't do. She ripped out the page and crumpled it up. She tried again. No. And again. No. Vicky sighed and sucked the end of her pencil. She got up and went through into the living area. Under one of the bunks was a drawer which contained Shania's stash of wedding magazines. Unlike her big sister, Shania had been obsessing about her big day since she'd been about ten. Vicky hauled out a couple and returned to her room. Idly she flicked the pages, trying to get some sort of inspiration that would satisfy her mother's idea of an ideal traveller's wedding dress and her own ideas about style and individuality.

The door crashed open and Vicky jumped, guiltily trying to hide the magazine – she didn't really want to give her sister the satisfaction of being able to crow – but Shania was too quick for her.

'Hallelujah,' said her little sister, grabbing the magazine out of Vicky's hands and brandishing it. 'I don't believe it. You're finally going ahead and doing something about your blooming wedding.'

'Well, yes, but as I've managed to make three brides-maids' dresses already I don't think I can be accused of slacking.'

'Says you, but I know you're just dragging your heels.'

'Jeez, give over, Shan. I've heard it all before and, for your information, I'm going as fast as I can.'

'What's this?' Shania lit upon one of the crumpled balls of paper.

'Nothing. Gimme.' Vicky lunged to rescue it.

But it was too late. Shania had already jumped forward and scooped it off the floor before her sister could get to it. Whirling away she smoothed it out. 'Gross,' she said. 'You're not really thinking of wearing this to your wedding.'

'Obviously not,' said Vicky, 'considering I'd chucked it.' But she was stung by Shania's words.

'You ought to go for something like this.' Shania dropped the discarded design and opened the bridal magazine. 'Here.' She thrust the open page under her sister's nose. It was a picture of a classic 'meringue' wedding dress. Very pretty, yes, but deeply unoriginal. There was nothing wrong with it and yet there was nothing right with it either. But Vicky knew that if she didn't come up with an idea of her own soon she'd end up wearing something almost exactly like it.

Maybe, she conceded to herself, she'd put off thinking about her own dress for just a little too long, because if she didn't get a design nailed before Saturday she'd be stuck with one of the dressmaker's ideas and Vicky could imagine what that would be like.

The next day, at college, while she was supposed to be working on a project using carded wool, she was doodling in her sketchbook.

'This isn't like you,' said Mrs Mead.

Vicky jumped guiltily and tried to slide her pad out of sight. 'Sorry, miss.' She began to apply herself to her work.

'What's this?' Mrs Mead had pulled the pad round so she could look at the sketch. 'You going to a ball or something?'

'No.'

'But this is lovely. Is this just an idea for a dress?'

'Sort of.'

'You're not planning on making it up?'

'Not really.'

'That's a shame, it'd look lovely on you.'

'Thank you.'

After Mrs Mead had gone to check on the work of some other students Vicky drew the pad back towards her. Was the dress really any good? Did she trust her teacher to give her the absolute truth? What if she explained to Mrs Mead what the dress was really for, might she be able to make some suggestions?

After class she hung back, ignoring the snide comment from Leah about being teacher's pet. She approached Mrs Mead's desk.

'Have you a problem, Vicky? Are the girls still giving you a hard time?'

'Yes, no . . . it's not about the others,' Vicky said.

'Okay. So what's up?'

'It's about that dress I was sketching.'

Mrs Mead nodded.

'The dress is for me.'

'And?'

146

I was wondering if you could help me a bit with it.'

Mrs Mead smiled broadly, flattered to have the trust of this girl. 'I'll help in any way I can.'

'It's just . . . it's my wedding dress.'

'*Wedding*?' blurted out Mrs Mead in shock before she could stop herself.

'Us travellers get wed young. Mine's next summer.'

'But you're only a child!'

'I'm seventeen, and I'll be almost eighteen by then,' said Vicky defensively.

'I know but . . .' Mrs Mead sighed and shook her head. '. . . it's none of my business.'

'It's all right, miss. I know our ways seem strange. My mate Kelly doesn't get it either but we're happy as we are.'

'Are you?'

'Of course.'

Mrs Mead didn't look convinced but she let the matter drop. 'So all those bridesmaids' dresses you've been making are for your own wedding, not a friend's.'

Vicky nodded.

'And they are quite remarkable. Really very accomplished.' She paused. 'Look, Vicky, I am *not* going to nag you but I really, *really* want you to consider your future.'

'I know what you're on about, but it's not going to happen.'

'What?'

'Me – having a career. After I'm wed I keep house, I have kids and I don't work.'

'That's criminal. Not that you shouldn't want to be a

147

good wife, but it's criminal that you're going to waste your ability. Surely your parents would be proud of you if you made something of yourself.'

Vicky shook her head. 'I don't think so. And I don't think I'd be happy going out on a limb like that. I once had a dream of having my own shop. I saw *My Fair Lady* a couple of years ago and I thought Eliza Doolittle had a great idea, wanting her own shop and all. But if people knew it was a shop run by a pikey I just know no one would come to it.'

'You don't know that.'

'Come off it, miss. You saw how the girls were when they found out.'

'But when people see the sort of designs you do, the quality of the work . . .'

'I'd still be a pikey, though, wouldn't I?'

'That is so unfair.'

'Trust me, when you come from travelling stock one of the very first lessons you ever learn in life is that nothing is fair.'

'You sound very cynical for someone so young,' Mrs Mead said sadly. 'I can't imagine what it's like for you – but I do sympathise. So,' she said, her tone becoming brisk as she changed the subject, 'how would you like me to help with this dress of yours?'

'I want something special, obviously, but traveller girls always go for the Disney princess look. I want something different.'

Mrs Mead nodded. 'Okay. So rather than copy a cartoon princess, why not copy a real one.'

'What – like Eugenie or Beatrice?' Vicky didn't think

either girl had enough style to be some sort of role model.

'No, not them. An historical princess. How about looking at pictures of people like Queen Victoria when she was young, or Queen Elizabeth the First? And given that your bridesmaids' dresses are in such a classic style and dark green, if you did your dress in ivory it would look amazing. I've got some pictures, would you like to see if those give you any ideas?'

And as Mrs Mead brought up the images on her laptop an idea for a dress, a dress that Vicky found was really exciting her, began to form in her mind.

When Mary-Rose, Vicky and Shania got to the dressmaker's shop on Saturday, Vicky was astounded at the range of fabrics, trimmings and patterns that were kept on the premises. To someone interested in textiles, the shop was a total Aladdin's cave. Wide-eyed, Vicky wandered around the bolts of fabrics, chiffons, tulles, satins, silks and polyesters that all came in rainbow colours, fingering the various textures and qualities, admiring the sequins, crystals and embroidery that ornamented many of them. If there was a heaven on earth, she felt she'd just found it. Shania, meanwhile, was leafing through the pattern books and the albums of photographs of other dresses that had been ordered by previous traveller brides.

'Oh my God,' she exclaimed, 'butterflies. I love them. I want butterflies.'

'We'll do your dress another time,' said Mary-Rose. 'Let's just concentrate on Vicky's right now.'

149

Shania looked thunderously sulky but she had the sense not to argue and continued to flip through the pictures.

From the back of the workshop swept a woman with improbably red hair and over-plucked eyebrows, which gave her a permanently astonished expression.

'Welcome. I'm Paulette,' she said in a heavy Brummie accent, 'and which one of you beautiful ladies is the bride to be?'

Mary-Rose giggled. 'It's my eldest, Vicky. Not me, naturally.'

*Puh-lease*, thought Vicky as she came forward to shake Paulette's hand.

'So, what theme are you having for your wedding? Tropical paradise? Sleeping Beauty? Cinderella?'

Vicky shook her head. 'I've been making the bridesmaids' dresses . . .'

Paulette's eyebrows went even higher. 'You?'

Vicky shrugged rather diffidently. 'I'm doing textiles at college.'

Paulette still looked unconvinced. 'Can you show me what you've done so far?' Her tone of voice seemed to convey, in that one short sentence, her personal belief that everything would have to be unpicked and re-worked.

Vicky went over to where she'd dumped her stuff and hauled over a massive carrier bag. 'This is one of them,' she said, pulling out the dark green satin bodice and skirt. 'I haven't done the underskirts yet. Maybe you have something we could use to give the effect of how it'll look when I have.'

150

Paulette pulled over a dressmaker's dummy. 'Put it on that so I can see it properly.' She still sounded underwhelmed. While Vicky was busy arranging the bodice on the hessian-covered body form, Paulette went to another part of the workshop and pulled a net underskirt off a hanger.

'This'll give us an idea, although I imagine you'll want something much bigger. This petticoat isn't really right but it'll do for now.'

Once that was in place the two manoeuvred the main part of the dress over it and attached it to the bodice.

'There,' said Vicky, pushing a lock of hair off her face and standing back to admire her dress. It was the first time she'd seen it at its best with the net underskirt giving it some of the volume and shape she'd wanted. As she looked at it she reckoned that it would need about double the fabric and maybe a crinoline. She'd have to think about that when it was time to make them. She pushed the issue of the size of the petticoats to the back of her mind as it wasn't a matter that needed dealing with then and there and watched Paulette as she wandered round the green dress, examining it from all angles.

'Quite nice,' conceded Paulette finally, fingering the gold braid trim and the intricate embroidery. 'So what have you got in mind for yours? Only, as a general rule, we do things the other way round here. We get the bride's dress sorted and then the bridesmaids' dresses are designed to fit with that.'

'I know but I think my idea will work.'

Paulette looked sceptical.

Vicky produced her sketchbook and flipped open a page. 'You see, other girls want to be a fairy-tale princess, but I want to be a real one. And as I'm called Vicky – well, Victoria – I thought I'd base my idea on a dress she wore before she became queen, when she was Princess Victoria. But then I found this.' She unclipped a postcard-sized reproduction of an oil painting. 'This is one of Queen Victoria's daughters in her own wedding dress, and I love it. So I've sketched an idea for a dress based on it.' She flipped to another page in her sketchbook and held out her drawing to Paulette.

'Oh, yeah.' But despite the lack of enthusiasm in Paulette's voice Vicky noticed she was peering closely at her sketch.

'And if we made it in ivory silk with dark green trim and gold embroidery I think it would look really stunning.

'Maybe.' But there was a hint of a thaw in Paulette's voice.

'Let me see,' said Mary-Rose. She turned the pad so she could look. 'Oh, Vicky. I take it all back, that's a lovely dress.'

'And I'd want a plain, diamanté tiara and a really simple veil.'

'With a dress like this you don't want anything too fussy,' agreed Paulette. She turned away from the sketch and went over to the ranks and ranks of fabric. At the end of one row she pulled out a huge roll of ivory damask. 'I think something like this would work,' she said.

Vicky could tell from the tone of her voice that

Paulette had been won over. And what with her mother on side as well, Vicky knew that her design had been accepted. She just wished that this dress and the bridesmaids' frocks weren't going to be the sum total of her creative output. Despite the words of encouragement from Mrs Mead earlier that week, Vicky couldn't see how she could possibly make a commercial success of her skills like Paulette obviously had. She didn't think she had the strength to fight the two battles that would be required: the battle needed to flout travellers' attitudes towards working women and the battle against the public attitude towards travellers. One might be possible but both? No chance.

On the Monday Vicky sought Kelly out as soon as she got to college.

'I thought you'd like to see this.' She got out her mobile and showed Kelly a picture she'd taken of the dress, complete with its underskirt.

Despite the fact that Kelly already knew what the dress looked like she was blown away to see the dress brought into its proper shape by the addition of petticoats. 'Oh my God, Vicky. That is just the most beautiful thing I've ever seen. You are so talented. You really should take it up professionally.' Vicky was about to tell Kelly that the petticoats were a fraction of the proper size when they were joined by Mrs Mead, who took the phone from Kelly so she could have a good look too.

'That's what I keep telling her. Yes, stunning. Just as good as anything a proper bridal house could come up with.'

'Thank you,' mumbled Vicky, embarrassed by such praise.

'I'll see you in class in a minute, Vicky,' said Mrs Mead, moving away. 'You can tell me all about your design for your own dress and how you got on, then.'

Kelly glanced at her watch. 'We've time for a quick coffee in the canteen if you want one.'

Vicky nodded. 'Yeah, we've got fifteen minutes.'

'So,' said Kelly, as they stood in the queue waiting to get served. 'What's the low-down?'

'The dressmaker was quite nice about my design.'

'*Quite* nice – is that the best she could do? It's stunning and you know it.'

The girls grabbed their coffees and took them over to a table.

'Yeah, well,' said Vicky as they sat down opposite each other, 'I don't think she liked the fact that I wasn't using one of hers.'

'Tough. Doesn't she like the competition?'

'I don't know. Maybe she doesn't like the fact she's not getting the gig to make all the bridesmaids' dresses. That would have been worth a bit of cash to her.'

'So you should think about getting paid for your work like she does.'

'You don't listen, do you?' said Vicky. 'It's all right for you; you'll finish here, go off to a salon somewhere and get a job. But me . . .' She stopped, unable to continue, awash with self-pity.

'Oh come on, hon,' said Kelly, reaching across the table and taking Vicky's hand. 'There has to be a way round this for you. Really there does. Getting married

154

can't be an end to everything.'

But Vicky knew differently. She was going to be like a pop-singer with a one-hit wonder. As far as the world of fashion was concerned, her bridesmaids' dresses were going to be her debut and her swan song, all rolled into one.

# 8

Back in the classroom, her eyes dried and her head held high, Vicky sat down in her customary place. The other girls drifted in and, as usual, made a show of locking away their bags and purses before sitting as far away from her as they could. Although Vicky was used to it now, it still hurt and as she was already feeling raw, today it was doubly unpleasant. What had she ever done to deserve this sort of attitude? She'd never said anything mean or spiteful, she'd never lashed out at any of them, despite some nasty provocation, she hadn't lied or cheated to get them in trouble – although she'd been tempted. She'd had quite enough shit come her way over the past weeks to justify some tit-for-tat.

Leah said something behind her hand and several of the other girls snickered, looking at Vicky as they did so. She felt the tears well up again. What was the matter with her? She was the girl who hardly ever cried, the girl who knew all about hard knocks, the girl who could find the good in even the worst of situations but now . . . now she seemed to be a basket case.

Well, she wasn't going to give these bitches the

satisfaction of seeing they'd got to her. Picking up her handbag she swung it onto her shoulder and walked out of the room, praying her tears didn't roll down her cheeks before she escaped. She ran into Mrs Mead at the door.

'Just need the loo, miss,' she said. She knew, from the way her tutor's eyes widened, that Mrs Mead had spotted that she was about to cry but thankfully she didn't say anything.

'Of course, dear,' was all she said, offering her a smile of sympathy. 'Come back when you're ready,' she added in a low voice. 'No hurry.'

Vicky fled, praying she didn't run into anyone else before she found sanctuary.

Once in the Ladies she ran into an empty cubicle and slammed the door. Even now she'd found somewhere private she didn't dare let her sobs overwhelm her. If she howled someone was bound to come in and get all nosy. Instead she stifled them with a wodge of tissues from her bag as she sat on the loo, leaning against the cistern.

Miserably she blew her nose and dabbed her face.

Maybe she was tired, working so hard at college and grafting at home on those dresses. She knew she shouldn't be like this, after all she was marrying a wonderful man. Any other traveller girl in her place would be over the moon. Her dad had told her not to worry about the cost of anything and whatever she wanted for her big day she was to have. How many kids of her age could have whatever they wanted and not have parents bitching about the cost? As she thought

157

about all the good things in her life she stopped crying and slowly brought herself under control. She blew her nose more vigorously and pulled herself together. She was being a spoilt little cow, worrying about something that really didn't matter. No one was going to die, she told herself sternly, if she didn't have a future in dressmaking. There were probably thousands, millions, of girls who would give their back teeth not to have to spend their lives grafting, juggling jobs and childcare, and she was lucky not to ever have to worry about anything like that. She was going to have the life of Riley, being a kept woman.

And as for those stupid girls in her textiles class – she'd show them. She'd prove that they couldn't get her down. She decided that if they were going to be horrid to her she'd be the very opposite to them. Instead of taking their cruelty to heart, she'd just smile sweetly back. Vicky reckoned it would be very difficult to maintain a hate campaign if she was relentlessly nice.

Exiting the loo she took a look at herself in the mirror. Crap. Her eyes were all pink and piggy from crying and her face was blotchy. Running cold water into a basin she splashed her face to reduce the puffiness and calm her cheeks. Then she got her make-up out of her handbag and re-touched her mascara and eye shadow. Satisfied that she didn't look like a complete dog she left the loos and made her way back to the classroom.

'Hiya, Vick,' called a familiar voice.

Fuck – Jordan. Not only was he the last person she wanted to see right now, he was the last person she

158

wanted to see at any time around college. And this time the corridors around her were all empty and she didn't have the safety net of having Kelly with her. Double fuck.

'Hi, Jordan,' she replied, keeping walking. 'Can't stop. Late for my lesson.' She heard footsteps running behind her and then a hand on her shoulder.

'Are you avoiding me?' Jordan asked.

She could hardly talk to him with her back turned. She swivelled round to face him, hoping her repair work on her face stood up to close scrutiny. 'Not really, just busy, you know. Besides, we're not likely to see each other in class – you doing computer studies an' all, and me doing textiles.'

'You've been crying,' said Jordan.

Vicky shook her head. 'Don't be silly. What on earth gave you that idea?'

Jordan reached forward and traced a tear track down Vicky's cheek. It was like there were sparks in his fingertips; her whole cheek tingled. She leapt backwards, overwhelmed by confusion and remembering the last time he'd touched her, down by the river. What was it with her that she reacted like that whenever he got too close? Was it because he was a gorgio, someone she could never have, or was it her guilty conscience? Not that it mattered either way, it was wrong.

Jordan smiled knowingly. Had he experienced that pulse of intense feeling too? But all he said was, 'You didn't quite do a good-enough job covering up the traces.'

Vicky knew she was blushing frantically and the last

159

thing she needed right now was for Jordan to be all sympathetic and kind. She decided to play down how upset she'd been only a short while previously. Besides, it would make her look pathetic that the other girls had got to her. 'Yeah, well, it was nothing. I was just being stupid.'

'Oh yeah. Like Chloe hasn't set most of the girls at college against you. It's about that, isn't it?'

'What would you know?'

'I've got eyes, Vicky. I see how you get treated in the canteen. That's why I always made a point of inviting you to sit with me.'

'Thanks a bunch but I don't need charity. I can look after myself.'

'Really? It doesn't look like it from where I stand.'

'And what would you know?'

'Come off it, Vick, just because it hasn't happened to me personally doesn't mean I can't sympathise.'

'Yeah? Well, you and your family have got laws against racism on your side but no one gives a stuff about travellers. Or pikeys. Or gyppos.' She spat the last words out. 'If I called you a nigger I'd get run in. Call me a pikey and no one turns a hair.' And for the third time that day Vicky felt tears of self-pity stream down her face. Mortified, angry and confused she fled once again to the sanctuary and privacy of the Ladies.

Jordan was waiting for her when she came out.

'What are you doing?' she said grumpily. 'You should be in your lesson.'

'That can wait. I wanted to make sure you're all right.'

'Won't your tutor mind?'

'I'll think of some excuse. He'll be cool. But what about you? There seem to be two of us bunking off right now.'

'I got excused. Mrs Mead didn't want me making her classroom damp.' She gave Jordan a watery smile.

'I didn't mean to upset you again,' he said. 'But I am on your side, honest. I don't care about what Chloe says.'

'Well, you should. She's your girlfriend, isn't she?'

'Just because we're seeing each other doesn't mean I agree with everything she thinks and says. In fact, she and I had a row over you.'

'You shouldn't've. I'm not worth it. I'm trailer trash, remember.'

'Stop putting yourself down,' said Jordan crossly. 'You are so not.'

'Then you're the only one in this crappy college that thinks like that.'

'And Kelly? And your textiles teacher?'

'Maybe not them. But that's still only three of you. There's hundreds of others here.'

'And hundreds who don't know you, don't care and certainly don't listen to Chloe.'

Vicky shrugged, unconvinced. 'You're not very loyal to her, are you?'

'Chloe? Sometimes she just doesn't deserve it. There's a lot of great things about Chloe, things I really like, but I can't take how she picks on you. I'm hoping to convince her to leave off but . . . well, we'll see.'

The bell rang. 'I've got to go,' said Vicky. 'I've missed a whole period. But thanks, Jordan, thanks for caring.'

161

Jordan took her hand as they heard the sound of classroom doors banging open and the noise of students on the move. Swiftly he leaned in and gave her a brief kiss on the lips. 'Be brave,' he said as he let her hand go and moved away.

As students swirled around Vicky she stood there like a rock in a river as she watched Jordan disappear down a corridor, then she put her hand to her mouth as if that could take away the burning and tingling she felt.

The first term at college ended and Christmas was upon Vicky before she knew it.

'Your last one as a single girl,' Mary-Rose reminded her daughter over breakfast on the first day of the holiday. 'Best you pay attention to how to cook the turkey this year. You'll be doing it for your man next Christmas.'

As if Vicky needed reminding. *Only six months to go now*, she thought. Only six months and three dresses still to make plus more fittings for her own. And the cake to order, the reception to organise, the limo to arrange . . . She sighed. So much to do. She glanced across the table at her sister and wished she was brimming with excitement at the prospect like Shania. Shania's one and only topic of conversation was her wedding, planned for late August, just two months after Vicky's own. In fact, given that her wedding was further away, it was far further forward in terms of planning than her big sister's.

'And me,' said Shania with a smirk.

'Och, you're better in the kitchen than Vicky, to be sure,' said Mary-Rose. 'You won't be needing any help in that department.'

Shania preened with pride at her mother's words. 'My Mikey won't starve and that's for sure,' she said smugly. 'You'd have been better off not bothering with college and learning some proper skills.'

'Oh shut up,' said Vicky.

'Stop that,' said Mary-Rose, casting an anxious glance at Johnnie, who was watching breakfast TV.

'But really, why do you bother?' Shania picked at the argument like a child with a scab.

'In case you haven't noticed, I've been making bridesmaids' dresses till they're coming out my ears.'

'If it's such a chore I don't see why you didn't get Paulette to make yours like she's making mine.'

'It's not a chore, I like doing it and the machines at college make it a whole lot easier.'

'Suit yourself.' Shania paused and flicked over some pages of a glossy magazine. 'And have you thought about a cake? You can't have a fairy-tale castle because that's what I'm having and as your wedding is first I'm not having people say I copied you.'

'No, I don't want a fairy-tale castle,' said Vicky.

'So what *do* you want?'

'I don't know.' Couldn't Shania talk about anything other than bloody weddings? 'It's ages yet. I don't have to get that sorted till just before. It's not like a dress, it won't keep for ever, so it can't be made until the last minute.'

'Just saying.'

'Well don't.'

And before her mother could have a go at her for rowing with her sister, Vicky flounced out.

163

She ran across the frosty grass to Liam's place but it was empty. He must have gone to his workshop so she wandered over there. She could hear the sound of sawing as she approached. Through the open door she could see Liam working, sawdust falling at his feet as he cut the wood with rhythmic, even strokes. The scent of pine filled the air with resiny sweetness.

'Hiya, babe,' she called softly from the door.

He turned and a smile beamed from him. 'Hello, darling.'

'What you making?'

'Just a door for a house someone I know is renovating.'

'A traveller?'

'No, someone in the building trade. He puts work my way now and again.'

'That's nice.'

'Unusual, more like. You know how gorgios think of us.'

Didn't she just. Not that she'd told anyone on the site about the difficulties she'd faced at college. If word got round, either her dad would insist that she gave up or worse, some of her relations might rock in to college and cause trouble. That was the last thing she wanted. Better everyone thought that it was all plain sailing for her.

'What brings you round here?' asked Liam.

'Is it suddenly against the law for a girl to want to see her fiancé?'

Liam put his saw down on the workbench and walked across the shed to her. 'Of course not, hon.' He took her in his arms and gave her a peck on the lips. 'And isn't my day brighter for seeing you.'

Vicky rested her head on his shoulder, feeling the warmth of his body through her thin jacket. She felt safe with him, secure, but where was that spark that she'd felt when Jordan had kissed her? She breathed in the woody smell that always surrounded Liam and told herself that there was no electric jolt because she didn't feel guilty about him touching her. It was guilt that brought that on, pure and simple. It was nothing to do with animal attraction, it was just a plain old-fashioned feeling of sinfulness.

She snuggled closer to Liam. This was how life would be all the time once she was married. She wouldn't have to worry about stupid spiteful girls like Chloe ever again. She wouldn't need to rely on guys like Jordan riding shotgun on her behalf. She wouldn't have to leave the safety and security of the trailer park every day and face bullies alone. But she wouldn't have college. She wouldn't have Kelly. She wouldn't have Jordan. With a jolt she realised that once she left college she'd probably never see Jordan again. That'd be awful.

She pushed herself away from Liam.

'What's the matter?' he asked.

'Nothing,' she lied, riddled with guilt. What was she doing thinking about Jordan when she was in the arms of her future husband? What was she on? And of course she wouldn't miss Jordan. No way. He meant nothing to her. But she knew she was lying to herself.

'Then come here,' said Liam, wrapping his arms around her yet again. 'Just think, another couple of weeks and we'll be able to say that we're getting married *this* year. I can't wait.' He squeezed her tighter. 'I don't think any man could be happier than me.' He smiled down at her. 'Oh, Vicky, just six months and you and I are going to be man and wife. I can hardly believe my luck.'

Vicky longed to be able to say the same, but though she loved Liam, she just couldn't bring herself to reply. Instead, she reached up and kissed him on the cheek.

The spring term at college began on a wet, miserable January day. If Vicky thought that the girls in her class might have changed their attitude over Christmas she was mistaken.

'So much for the season of goodwill to all men,' she mumbled under her breath as once again she sat alone on one side of the textiles room while the others crowded together on the other.

Mrs Mead went around the room handing back work that had been given in at the end of last term before letting the girls get on with their course work, which had to be finished for assessment later that week. She stopped by Vicky as she was sorting out some bits of scrap velvet she was planning on incorporating into a collage.

'How was your Christmas?' she asked.

'Nice, thanks. Mum and Dad gave me a new sewing machine which is a huge improvement on my old treadle one.'

'That's fantastic.'

'I'll be able to get on with those dresses I'm making at

home now. I won't be in your hair as much, cluttering up your room.'

'You're never in the way. And don't feel you have to work at home. It can't be easy in a caravan – not a lot of space, I imagine.'

'Well, you do have to be organised. And it is easier here. I can spread out and these tables are a better height to work at than the table at home.'

'How many have you left to do?'

'I've started the fifth so I'm almost there, but there's a lot of other stuff happening and my sister—' Vicky stopped and glanced across the room to see if any of the others was eavesdropping but they were all chatting with each other as they worked. 'My sister is getting married too this summer so I've got my mum's wedding outfits to make as well. Then there's fittings for my dress and my exams coming up in a few months. I don't have much spare time. Mind you, that'll all change when I'm wed.'

'Does it have to?'

Vicky nodded. 'Lady of leisure then.' She shrugged to make light of her impending situation.

'Well, you know what I think about that,' said Mrs Mead. She went off to supervise the other girls in their practical work.

When the bell went Vicky went to the big foyer to meet Kelly as they had arranged by text message the night before.

'How's tricks?' asked Kelly.

'Same old, same old. You?'

'Met this great guy over Christmas. We've been out a couple of times.'

'Oh yes? Did you go anywhere nice?'

'Just the pub and the flicks but it was good. He keeps ringing me too. I think he's keen.'

'Sounds it.

'He's called Alex.'

'Is he at college?'

'No, he's got a job. He stacks shelves in Tesco.'

'Wow.'

The note of irony in Vicky's voice didn't go unnoticed. 'Don't knock it, at least he's *got* a job, which is more than a lot of people can say, and because he works early mornings he's free every night.'

Someone bumped into Vicky, knocking her bag off her shoulder and nearly sending her flying.

'Oi!' She spun round.

'Watch where you're going,' said Chloe.

'But . . . but . . .'

'But what?'

'But you knocked into *me*.'

'Oh yeah?' The girls with Chloe giggled and Chloe gave Vicky a cold stare, daring her to take her on.

Kelly took Vicky's arm. 'Don't mind her, she's not worth it.'

The two girls walked off together with Vicky shooting evil looks over her shoulder at her tormentor.

'Seems like she's back to her old ways again. Even she's managed to work out that just ignoring me was a shit plan.'

As they walked away they heard a scuffle behind them. Vicky whirled around, sure it was Chloe coming to launch another attack.

'You can't talk to me like that,' shrieked Chloe at Jordan, who had her by the arm. Chloe was trying to shake him off but from the whiteness of his knuckles his grip was firm.

'I just have,' he replied.

'What is it with you?' Chloe's face was contorted with anger and her voice was shrill. It carried right across the foyer. 'Why do you want to defend that tramp?'

'She's not a tramp.'

Chloe snorted. 'Oh yeah? Of course she is. Everyone knows what girls like her are like.' She looked directly at Vicky.

'Don't react,' warned Kelly quietly in her ear.

'If you say anything like that again,' said Jordan in a low but dangerous voice, 'you and I are finished. Understand?'

Chloe paled. 'You don't mean that?'

'Try me.'

Chloe shot Vicky a look of pure venom as if to say that it was all *her* fault that Jordan was angry before she stormed off.

Jordan came over to join the two girls.

'Sorry,' he said.

'Don't apologise for her,' said Vicky. 'It's not your fault she's a cow.'

'I mean it, though, if she has another go at you I'll dump her.'

'Don't break up with her on my account.'

'I won't. I mean – I don't want to go out with someone who behaves like that. I'll give her one more chance, and then . . .' He shrugged and turned away.

'I don't know if that has made things better or worse,' said Vicky to Kelly in a low voice.

'We'll find out soon enough,' said Kelly.

And although Vicky loved Kelly for her solidarity she couldn't help feeling there wasn't much 'we' about the situation. Vicky reckoned that the only person who would really be finding out how Chloe was going to react to that little showdown was just her.

Over the next days and weeks Vicky was increasingly busy, what with her course work and her efforts to get the last few of the bridesmaids' dresses finished. Once she'd done that she would have to start on the seven huge underskirts but she was leaving that task till the very last minute as storing them was going to be a problem. Kelly had suggested that she might be able to put them in her parents' loft – which, if they agreed, would be a terrific solution. Although quite how Kelly was going to explain to her mum and dad that she was being a bridesmaid at a traveller girl's wedding was a bridge neither of them knew how to cross.

As dull, gloomy January morphed into a bitterly cold and wet February, it sometimes seemed to Vicky that she had no spare time for herself. When she wasn't finishing off course work, she was making her bridesmaids' dresses, and when she wasn't doing either of those things she had her chores around the home to be getting on with. The dank weather made keeping the trailer spotless an uphill battle as the family weren't inclined to spend more time outside in the cold than was absolutely necessary and the mud they tramped in, coupled with the fact that her brothers were frequently underfoot, made all the housework take twice as long as it seemed to in the summer. Spare moments for going out and enjoying herself with her traveller friends and relations were rare indeed and even rarer were the few snatched moments she got to share with Liam. It was almost as if they were living in different countries, not on different sides of the trailer park.

On one of the rare occasions when they managed to get together Liam had presented her with a little jewellery box that he'd made himself.

'I made it so when you look at it in the morning, you think about me,' he'd told her with a smile.

Vicky was so touched by the gesture she almost cried, and he was right: whenever she used the box, she always thought of him, and often felt a little jab of guilt if they hadn't met up that day.

What with one thing and another Vicky found herself on the go from the moment she woke up each day till the moment when she flopped, shattered, into bed. As a result, she sometimes found herself wishing that her wedding day would hurry up and arrive – at least when she was married she would just have to look after Liam and everything else that made her life so crowded now would cease to exist.

Really, she thought as she cleaned the windows, her life after June would be a breeze compared to what she was trying to squeeze in now. Of course she'd miss college, Kelly and Jordan, but she wouldn't miss coping with the petty bullying that she had to put up with there. And she'd miss learning the skills that Mrs Mead taught her but she wouldn't miss sewing bridesmaids' dresses. Frankly, if she never saw another piece of green silk again in her life she'd be happy. And she'd miss sharing a room with Shania and a home with her family but there was no denying the thrill that coursed through her every time she thought about sharing a trailer – and a bed – with Liam.

A bed – with Liam.

'What's it like?' she asked Kelly over lunch one day.

'What?'

'Sex,' whispered Vicky.

Kelly giggled. 'It depends,' she replied. 'My first time was rubbish. And it hurt.' Vicky was amazed by Kelly's frankness and lack of embarrassment but also reassured. It was great that she could talk to Kelly about anything – even sex. 'The bloke I was with – Bradley – didn't have a clue and neither did I. All that stuff about your first time being special is a load of bollocks. It took him about five seconds to come and left me feeling as if I'd completely missed out. What a let-down.'

'Oh.' This wasn't what Vicky wanted to hear.

'But then I went with another bloke, Nick, and he knew what he was doing. That was okay.'

'Okay?' *Okay* didn't seem to suggest the sort of mind-blowing experience she'd read about.

'Well, pretty good really.'

Getting better. 'So what's an orgasm like?'

'Oooh, lovely. It makes you feel all warm and sort of shaky.' Kelly looked at her. 'Haven't you – you know,' she grinned naughtily, 'done a DIY job?'

Vicky felt her face flaming. 'My God no! It's a mortal sin.'

'Crap,' said Kelly robustly. 'And it doesn't make you blind neither. Blimey, if it did I'd be needing a Labrador and a white stick.'

'Kelly!'

'Well, I would,' she said with another cheeky smile. 'Anyway, this isn't about me. You ought to have a go. At least then you'd know what you ought to be aiming for. If you know what you're doing you can help him press the right buttons. In my experience, men don't have a clue.'

Which made sense, but all of Vicky's Catholic upbringing told her she shouldn't. *It would be*, she thought, *as sinful as sex before marriage and that is never going to happen either*. She and Liam would just have to take their chances on their wedding night. *At least*, she reasoned, *if it's rubbish to start with, I'll be having rubbish sex with lovely Liam so that won't be so bad*.

The pressure to get her course work finished meant that Vicky spent more and more time in the textiles room. Her new sewing machine at home was fabulous and she loved it but it still wasn't up to the standard of the ones in college. The downside of this was that she had less time to spend in the college canteen chatting with Kelly over cups of coffee but the upside was her path crossed Chloe's much less frequently. When they did meet it seemed Chloe never missed an opportunity to give her the evils but, as Vicky told herself, a filthy look never hurt anyone. But Chloe was never able to do more than that because it seemed that Jordan was

173

always hovering nearby, ready to distract Chloe or to keep an eye on her. Vicky did wonder once or twice if Jordan was looking out for her on purpose but dismissed it straight away. Why would he? If he was always there when Chloe pitched up it was because he was Chloe's boyfriend, that was all. Of course, he'd be hanging around with her. But, nevertheless, there was something in the way he looked at Vicky, almost apologetic, which didn't quite make sense to her. Not that she had time to worry about Jordan and Chloe, no way. She had far too much to be getting on with.

What she also didn't notice, however, was the fact that the more she ignored Chloe the more it riled her tormentor. She couldn't have found a better way of irritating Chloe if she'd planned it especially.

It was about a week after her little chat with Kelly about sex that a particularly vile sick bug swept through the college. Half the students seemed to be absent with it and many of the staff. Lessons were cancelled and rescheduled as the administrators tried to minimise the disruption but with the timetables no longer being stuck to students were forced to check out the temporary arrangements every morning when they arrived. No longer could Vicky come in and cruise straight over to her class, instead, like everyone else, she had to check the notice boards which were on the wall down a side corridor.

She was standing in front of it, checking where she was supposed to be and at what time, when she felt a sharp jab in the ribs. She didn't need to turn round to see who it was.

'I don't know why you're here,' said Chloe. 'Pretending you can read and everything. Everyone knows that pikeys are as thick as pig shit.'

Vicky wasn't going to get into an argument with her. She sighed and went to move away, but Chloe grabbed her shoulder and spun her round.

'Don't you ignore me,' hissed Chloe. 'Who do you think you are?'

She gave Vicky a shove, which propelled her into one of Chloe's gang.

'Watch where you're going,' sneered the girl and gave her another push, which made her cannon into someone behind her. Vicky realised that she was surrounded by Chloe's mates and suddenly felt completely intimidated. Then one of the girls lashed out and kicked her shin. The pain was awful and Vicky felt tears well up.

'Ooh, the gyppo's crying,' said another gang member.

Vicky looked over the girls' shoulders for help. Where was a member of staff when you needed one – or Jordan? If he were here he wouldn't let this happen. Maybe he was off sick. Maybe this was why Chloe had grabbed the opportunity to really have a go at her.

Then someone pulled her hair.

'Ouch,' she screeched. 'Get off me.' She swung her bag and caught one of the girls in the chest with it. In return she got another kick on the shins.

Her tears really began to flow, partly from the pain but also out of sheer fear. Unless someone else came along she was at the mercy of these girls.

'Your mate Kelly's not here to look out for you, is she,' taunted Chloe.

'If Jordan knew you were doing this he'd have something to say,' said Vicky with a bravado she certainly didn't feel.

'Well, he doesn't and you ain't going to tell him, neither. Not if you know what's good for you. Otherwise you'll really get a slap.' And to back up her words Chloe landed the flat of her hand on Vicky's cheek. The crack rang down the corridor

'Stop that!'

Chloe spun round, her face suddenly ashen. 'Jordan!'

Vicky felt saggy with relief. The girls around her moved away and she took a step back so she could lean against the wall. Her knees were quivering so much she wasn't sure if they'd hold her up.

'What the fuck are you doing, Chloe?' he stormed, his dark eyes blazing with anger.

'Nothing. Just having a bit of fun, weren't we, Vicky?' Chloe tossed her hair defiantly. 'That's right, ain't it?'

'Fun?' thundered Jordan. 'I don't think so. That's your handprint on Vicky's cheek.'

Vicky's own hand flew to her cheek, which was wet with her streaming tears. It was still stinging.

'I warned you, Chloe, I told you what I'd do if I caught you bullying Vicky. Well, you've gone too far this time. I did my best to keep you out of her way to save you from yourself but you just didn't get the hint, did you. And the one time I'm not around you have a go. You're sick, Chloe, and I want nothing more to do with you.'

'You can go and fuck yourself, Jordan. You know what – I don't know what I ever saw in you. You're a loser. And you don't dump me, you bastard, no one dumps me.'

She turned on her heel and stamped off, her gang of friends trailing after her all looking shamefaced.

Jordan turned his attention to Vicky. 'You all right, babe?'

She nodded, still feeling shocked by the brutality and awfulness of Chloe's attack.

'Come here,' said Jordan. He opened his arms and Vicky moved towards him. He enveloped her in a big comforting hug. She rested her head on his chest and felt her tears subside as she drew strength from him.

'Did you really try to keep Chloe away from me?' Her voice was muffled by his thick jersey.

'Yeah, but I didn't do a very good job, did I. Cocked up today and no mistake.'

'Thank you.'

'She really hates you, I don't know why. Jealousy, maybe.'

'That's rich.' Vicky turned her face upwards to look at Jordan. 'What's she got to be jealous of?'

'Your looks.' Jordan wiped away a tear on Vicky's face with the ball of his thumb. 'You're beautiful.'

And then he kissed her. Not just a peck on the cheek, not a brushing of the lips, but a deep intense kiss, with his tongue at first gently probing her mouth and then growing in intensity. Vicky felt as if she was standing too close to an open fire as a wave of heat swept through her, pooling in her groin, and sensations she had never experienced before shook her. She felt herself melt against him and a tide of desire course through every

177

vein and artery, down every nerve, leaving a wake of electric tingling throughout her body. Dear God, she'd never felt like this before. Even that first kiss from Liam when he'd asked her to marry him hadn't been like this, hadn't made her feel like this. Liam had just pressed his lips to hers, which had been nice, but this was something entirely different. This was just heaven.

## 9

'Vicky?' Kelly's shriek from the end of the corridor brought Vicky back to reality.

Dear God, what was she doing, what was she thinking of? 'No!' She tore herself away from Jordan's grip and stared at him, her eyes wide with shock as she realised just how badly she was behaving. She shouldn't be kissing Jordan like this. This was almost like having sex with him. If word ever got back to Liam . . . 'No!'

Kelly ran the ten yards to get to Vicky and confront her, but then she saw Vicky's tear-stained face. 'Vicky? What the hell . . .?'

'Chill out, Kelly,' said Jordan. 'It was only a kiss. And anyway, what's it to you?'

'It wasn't *only a kiss*, though, was it?' said Kelly. 'I saw the pair of you. You were practically shagging. And Vicky's crying her eyes out. What the hell is going on?'

'Chloe and a gang of her mates attacked Vick,' explained Jordan. 'She was really upset.'

'So you thought that it would make her feel better if you tried to suck her face off.' Kelly stood with her hands on her hips and glared at him.

Vicky glanced from one to the other, her face red with guilt.

Kelly turned her attention to her friend. 'And you have every right to look as guilty as sin. What about your precious Liam?'

'Liam? Who's Liam?' asked Jordan.

'Her fiancé,' Kelly replied.

'Fiancé?'

'She's engaged, Jordan. She's getting married in a few months' time.'

Jordan turned to Vicky. 'Married? You didn't tell me.'

'I . . . it's . . .'

Jordan caught up her left hand. 'You don't even wear a ring,' he said accusingly.

Silently Vicky pulled out the chain from under her blouse and showed him the diamond ring threaded on to it.

'So why don't you wear it? Are you ashamed or something?'

'No, it's . . . I got engaged when I was fifteen. I didn't want awkward questions when I was at school so I only put the ring on at home. It's sort of a habit now.'

'Sounds more like a lie to me,' said Jordan angrily. 'All these years you've known me, all this time we've been friends, and you didn't think you could trust me. All those times I've stood by you, tried to keep Chloe and her mates off your back, stuck up for you . . .' He stared at her, confused, angry and upset. 'I thought . . . I thought . . .'

'You thought what, Jordan? That you were in with a

180

chance with me? That I'd be so grateful I'd let you get off with me?'

'No, nothing like that.'

'Oh no, Jordan?' chipped in Kelly. 'I've seen the way you look at Vick. You've always fancied her rotten.'

'Maybe I have, who wouldn't, she's a lovely girl.'

Kelly sighed. 'But she's not *your* lovely girl. She's Liam's.'

'And I'm not taking her away from Liam. It was just a kiss. So what?'

*But*, thought Vicky, *it wasn't* just *a kiss*. It had been something far more mind-blowing than 'just' a kiss. That talk she'd had with Kelly, the way Kelly had described an orgasm, that warm and shaky feeling she'd been told about, was exactly what she'd experienced. *Is it possible*, she wondered, *to have an orgasm just by kissing?* Whatever, that kiss had been out of this world and she'd bet her last penny that Jordan had felt the same way.

'Just a kiss, my arse,' said Kelly with obvious disbelief.

Jordan, fed up with Kelly's hostility, began to slope off. 'And,' he said, stopping after a couple of paces and turning, 'if this is all the thanks I get, I'll let Chloe carry on next time.'

'Don't, Jordan. I am grateful, really I am,' said Vicky. 'It was my fault too that it got out of hand.' She turned to Kelly. 'You're right, Kelly, we shouldn't have kissed. I was wrong.' She took a step towards Jordan. 'Thank you. I don't know what would have happened if you hadn't been around. I owe you.'

Jordan shrugged. 'Yeah, well. I'd keep out of Chloe's way for a bit if I were you.'

'Don't worry, I will. She's not going to be happy though, is she?'

'You could report her for assault. I was a witness.'

Vicky gave an ironic laugh. 'Oh yeah? Chloe and her mates would all swear I was lying and who would believe me – a pikey – against a bunch of nice middle-class college girls? Even with you on my side, it ain't going to happen. Do me a favour.'

Jordan seemed to think about Vicky's words, before saying, 'I'll warn Chloe that if she ever has another go at you I'll make her name mud around the college. She isn't the only one with a gang of mates, I've got friends too.'

'Thanks, Jordan, but maybe it's better to let it drop.'

'If that's what you want.'

Vicky nodded.

After Jordan had gone Kelly checked out the temporary timetable. 'I don't have a lesson till after the break. What about you?'

Vicky nodded. 'The same.'

'Fancy a coffee then? I need filling in on what Chloe did.'

The two girls made their way to the canteen and as they walked there Vicky told Kelly all about the attack.

'The cow. How's the cheek?'

Vicky rubbed it. 'Still a bit sore. She didn't half belt me.'

Kelly rolled her eyes and sighed. 'I know what you said but that was a proper assault. Maybe you should see the principal about this.'

'I don't know. If I get Chloe into trouble she'll just come after me again.'

'If she hears about you kissing her boyfriend—'

'Her ex-boyfriend,' corrected Vicky. 'Jordan dumped her on the spot. And she won't hear anything about that though, will she. You won't tell on me and I can't see Jordan telling either.'

'But still. She's obviously a bit of a nutter. She really hates you.'

By now the girls had reached the canteen where they ordered two coffees and went to sit at a table by the window.

'Kelly,' said Vicky. 'Can I ask you something?'

'Depends.'

'When your boyfriend kisses you, how do you feel?'

'How do you mean?'

'Do your insides go all jiggly?' Vicky gave an embarrassed little laugh.

'Sort of mushy like?'

'Yes, that's it.'

Kelly nodded. 'Why you asking? Now, I mean.'

Vicky's face coloured.

'Oh, I get it.' Kelly paused. 'That kiss with Jordan. This is what it's all about, isn't it?'

Vicky nodded.

Kelly narrowed her eyes as she stared at Vicky. 'But you and Liam . . . I mean, you've kissed *him*, haven't you?'

Vicky shook her head slowly. 'Not like that, not with . . . tongues.'

Kelly's jaw sagged. 'You're joking me. I mean, I know you can't go with him – not all the way – but you haven't

. . . you've never . . . shit, Vick, how on earth do you know that your marriage is going to work? If you've never even kissed him properly how do you know that you love him?'

'I do love him, I'm sure I do, and marriages aren't all about kissing and sex, you know.'

Kelly raised an eyebrow. 'Oh no? There may be other things going on in a marriage but if you two can't get it together successfully I reckon you're going to have a pretty poor time of it. I can't believe you're not even allowed to kiss your fiancé. That's awful.'

Vicky sighed. 'Kissing is allowed, just not much. When a boy takes a fancy to you he's allowed to grab you.'

'What? Grab? Nope, you've lost me.'

'It's the way we get courted.'

'Grabbing – doesn't sound like much fun to me.'

'When a lad fancies you he grabs you and runs off with you. Takes you away somewhere private and kisses you.'

'What if you don't fancy him? What if you don't want to be kissed?'

'He'll kiss you anyway. If you fight he might hurt you so it's best to give in.'

'You're kidding. But ain't that against the law? If a bloke did that to me I'd have him for assault. It's got to be sexual harassment at the very least.'

'It's our way, Kelly.'

'A bloody awful way, if you ask me.'

'Well, I didn't.' Vicky's eyes blazed with a flash of anger. Just because the gypsy way wasn't Kelly's way didn't mean it was wrong. And who was Kelly to criticise? She was hardly Little Miss Perfect herself, not judging by the way she'd slept around.

'Sorry,' said Kelly, realising she'd strayed into dodgy territory. 'Anyway, it still doesn't explain how come you've never really kissed Liam.'

'Because he never had to grab me.'

'You mean you just gave in without a fight.'

'Not really. Liam and I have known each other all our lives, we're next-door neighbours. It was sort of a done deal that we'd wind up marrying.'

'An arranged marriage?' Kelly was horrified – this was getting worse and worse.

'No, not really but neither of us was looking for anyone else. When he asked me to marry him I just said yes.'

'But didn't you kiss him then?'

'Yes, but it wasn't like when Jordan kissed me. It was lovely, but . . .' Vicky felt her face flaring. Kelly might be happy to tell the world every detail of her private life but Vicky found it appallingly embarrassing to go into any sort of detail.

'Like you said, no tongues with Liam,' said Kelly baldly.

Vicky blushed even deeper scarlet and shook her head.

'You do know that the way Jordan kissed you is the norm, don't you? It's how boys kiss you when they really fancy you.'

Vicky nodded. 'I'm not completely dim. I do know about the facts of life.'

Kelly raised an eyebrow. 'Yeah, it sounds like it. If I may remind you, *you've* just been asking *me* about kissing.'

'So I don't know everything, but I've read books.'

Kelly's forehead wrinkled. 'What? How-to guides?'

'No, Mills & Boon.'

Kelly giggled. 'What are you like?'

'Only they're novels and the authors make up stuff. So I don't know whether the sexy bits are accurate. They always seem a bit over the top. You can't really feel like that, can you?'

'Maybe. How do they describe the heroines when they've been kissed senseless by the hero? Do they feel what you felt?'

Vicky nodded.

'So there you go. At least you know you're normal.'

'Normal for a pikey?'

'Normal for a girl.'

'But I'm not normal like you, am I? I mean, I reckon I'm about the only girl in college who's still a virgin, I've only had one proper kiss, and I'm going to be married in a few months to a bloke who's never kissed me. Well not . . .'

'With tongues,' Kelly added helpfully.

'No, not like that.' Vicky sounded glum.

'It's not that bad.'

'Maybe.'

'And you love Liam.'

Vicky nodded.

'Then get him to kiss you properly. For fuck's sake, Vicky, the sky won't fall in if he does and then at least

186

you'll know how it feels with him, rather than with Jordan.'

Vicky nodded. Kelly had a point. And apart from anything else, Vicky knew that she had to find a way of banishing the memory of snogging Jordan because what had just happened with him had shaken her to her roots, and getting a proper kiss from Liam seemed the only way to get rid of the guilt.

On the way back home in her dad's car, Vicky wondered how she could engineer a situation to get Liam to kiss her like Jordan had done.

'You're very quiet,' said her dad, glancing across at her.

'Am I?'

'Something wrong?'

'No,' she lied. Nothing at all was wrong, apart from getting beaten up and kissing Jordan.

Her father drove into the trailer park and as the car drew to a halt the familiarity and sense of security of being home almost overwhelmed her. Here she was safe from all the people who didn't understand and who didn't *want* to understand her life. Chloe certainly fell into that category and she thought that sometimes even Kelly did. Her way of life wasn't wrong, it was just different, but sometimes the way Kelly spoke about her wedding made it seem sinful. She hadn't been pushed into it; she'd got engaged to Liam out of her own free will – hadn't she? And at least she was going to go up the aisle a virgin and wearing white with a clear conscience, which was more than could be said for most of the non-traveller girls whose wearing of white was a complete farce.

Besides, one thing that had been brought home to her today was how much some gorgios hated travellers. And the idea that she could ever have any sort of business where she depended on trade from non-travellers was just pie in the sky. Eliza Doolittle might be able to dream of owning a shop but she never could. The likes of Chloe would make sure everyone knew where she came from, and it wouldn't matter how good her designs were or how talented she was with a needle, she'd be boycotted by all and sundry.

As she got out of the car she spotted her mother and Liam's mother, Bridget, chatting by the washing line at the back of their trailer.

'Hello, darlin',' her mother called across to her as she unpegged a sheet. 'Me and Biddy here were discussing your wedding.'

'I was asking how the dress is coming along,' said Liam's mum.

'I've got another fitting next weekend.'

'I bet it's lovely.'

'I like it,' admitted Vicky.

'Of course you do. To be sure, it's every girl's dream to have a wonderful dress on her big day. And you make sure the dressmaker doesn't make it too tight. Your wedding day is a long day, isn't it just, Mary-Rose? You want to be as comfortable as you can be, even with a big heavy dress on. You don't want to have bruises and sore places when Liam gets you out of it.'

*Oh my God*, thought Vicky. *How can these two discuss*

*their own two children going to bed with each other? How tacky is that!*

'Don't you look so shocked, missy,' said Mary-Rose. 'It's only a few months till you'll be in your marriage bed with Liam. You'd better get used to the idea.'

'And given how close it's getting I don't know why you're still bothering with being educated,' grumbled Bridget. 'Your mother needs a hand with this wedding, given that Shania's is going to happen right after. It's not fair that you're not around. What's the point of this course? It's just a waste of time, if you ask me. Liam won't want you working. Just think the shame he'd feel if you felt you couldn't rely on him to provide for you. Couldn't you make dresses perfectly well before?'

Not that old argument again. *What a shit day this is turning out to be,* thought Vicky. First getting thumped by Chloe, then getting it in the neck from Kelly about that kiss and now being given a dressing down by Bridget about being educated. Well, thank God Biddy and Mary-Rose didn't have a clue about what had gone on at college. It didn't bear thinking about what Bridget and her mother would have had to say about that.

Guilt washed over her for the umpteenth time that day. Suddenly she needed to see Liam. She had to get Jordan out of her head. She didn't love him; she loved Liam.

'I've got to go and see Liam about something,' she told the two women as she sped away. She ran across the trailer park to Liam's shed, over in the far corner. The door was ajar when she got there so she peeped round.

189

He was working on another door, chiselling out the space for the locking mechanism. Every now and again he'd put down the mallet and chisel and measure his progress then he'd chip away some more, being a perfectionist, taking his time.

He chewed his lip as he eyed up the brass handle and lock and the hole he was carving out of the side of the door. Vicky thought about kissing that lip; how it would taste, how it would feel. Would it be very different from Jordan?

No! She wasn't going to think about Jordan. She was going to get him out of her mind. If she could scrub her brain to erase the memory she would.

Liam was so busy concentrating on his work he didn't see his fiancée watching him, so Vicky was able to observe the way he moved, the way his muscles rippled beneath his shirt, the curve of his buttocks when he bent over the workbench and the way his hands caressed the wood. She'd seen him often enough working in just a pair of shorts in the summer to know what he'd look like undressed – well, mostly undressed.

She began to wonder what he would look like completely naked and realised that the thought was almost as stirring as Jordan's kiss. Was it a sin, she wondered, to want to be married and to find out about sex? To find out about sex with the man she was betrothed to? And for the first time in her life she looked at Liam as something completely other than her friend. This was her marriage partner, this was the man she was going to sleep with for the rest of her life, the man she was going to undress in front of in just a few months' time. She

190

realised with a shock that even the thought of Liam seeing her naked made her feel quite embarrassed. Wait till she told Kelly that!

Maybe she moved but Liam suddenly spun round. Her train of thought was broken.

'Jeez, but you gave me a shock,' he said.

'Sorry, babe. I was just watching you work. I love to do that.'

'It's nothing special, just a door fitting.'

'The way you make it, makes it seem special.'

'Don't be daft, it's just carpentry.'

'It's a skill, like dressmaking.'

'I thought all you girls could sew.'

For some reason Vicky felt cut that he didn't recognise that she had a real talent. 'Don't be daft,' she said, trying to make light of his comment. 'Mammy couldn't sew on a button if her life depended on it and I don't think Shania could even thread a needle.'

'Of course they could.'

'Like Billy and Jon-Boy would know how to make a proper joint or put a chair together?'

'Of course not, they'd need to be taught.'

'Exactly. But it takes more than just knowing the basics. You care about what you do, like I care about my dresses.'

'I suppose. Still,' Liam added, 'you won't have to worry about that soon. Come June you can put that all behind you.'

'Maybe I don't want to.'

'Don't be silly,' said Liam, missing the point. 'It isn't as if you have to make Shania's wedding dress

191

or anything. Just think, no more having to get up a the crack to traipse off to college. Won't that be nice?'

Vicky forced a smile. 'Lovely.'

'Come here and give me a hug,' said Liam.

Vicky walked across the shed and allowed herself to be enveloped by Liam. She hid her face in his shoulder, not wanting him to see how fed up she felt. Why couldn't he see how important her dressmaking was? How would he feel if she went around saying that what he did was nothing special and that all he did was cut wood or bash nails in with a hammer? Wouldn't he be hurt? Surely, if he loved her, he'd pick up on her feelings.

Like Jordan had.

Liam unwrapped his arms from around her body. 'I've got something to show you,' he said. 'I thought about waiting till our wedding night but . . . well, I want you to see it now.

Vicky pushed down a filthy thought that had popped into her head. Of course he wasn't going to show her anything like *that*!

'Come with me and I'll show you.'

Intrigued, Vicky followed her fiancé. He led her over to his trailer.

'Close your eyes,' he instructed her.

'What's all this about?' Vicky said with a giggle, her earlier smutty thought bouncing back into her mind.

'Shut your eyes and you'll find out.'

Vicky did as she was told. She heard the creak of the door as he opened it and then she felt Liam take her hand. With faltering steps she followed him as he guided her up the step and into his home. She could tell from the way they turned right that he was leading her towards the back of the caravan, where the bedroom that they would one day share was.

'You can open your eyes now.'

And in front of her was a bed, a beautiful bed made of deep, rich red, cherry wood. The headboard was carved with a design of birds and butterflies surrounding a big heart in the middle with their initials intertwined in the centre. Each of the bedposts was carved with wreaths of flowers winding up them and there were more butterflies and birds on the footboard. The carving was so careful and intricate that Vicky could actually identify the different species.

'Oh my God, Liam, it's beautiful.'

'I made it for you.'

'For us, Liam, for us.'

'I thought that if you were going to all the trouble of making the bridesmaids' dresses I ought to do something for us too.'

Vicky ran her hand over the footboard of the bed, feeling the silky smooth wood under her fingers, gently touching the wings of a red admiral and then a peacock butterfly. 'This is so special, Liam. It'll make our wedding night special, too.'

Liam blushed at the thought of sharing the bed with his fiancée. 'I am so glad you like it.'

'Like it? I love it. Was this what I caught you making back in the summer?'

Liam nodded. 'I've been bricking it that you'd find out or guess before I'd finished it.'

'No, I never imagined . . .' Vicky stopped. 'I mean I know you're skilled but this is *really* beautiful.'

'I'm not just a chippy. I want to do more of this sort of stuff.'

'Furniture making?'

Liam nodded. 'I know it's a crazy dream but I have this idea I could do it properly.'

'A business?'

'Yeah.' He gave an embarrassed laugh. 'But what would I know about business? I can hardly even write my name.'

'But I could help. I can do maths and everything.'

Liam shook his head. 'But it wouldn't be right now, would it? Isn't it my job to bring home the bacon? If you helped me run the business, tongues would wag, you know that, don't you?'

'But it's my role to look after you. What would be wrong about me doing something other than cleaning and cooking? Wouldn't *me* making sure *you* were getting the right price for your work be a help? I could work out how much your materials cost and what your time is worth and then add in a profit. What would be wrong with that?'

Liam looked troubled. Vicky's argument made complete sense but generations of built-in tradition tore him against the logic.

'Well, as I said, it's just a dream.'

'No, Liam, it isn't *just a dream*. It really, *really*, could be a reality.'

'But what if the reality was too much for you? Knowing how to add up isn't the same as knowing how to run a business. If you've got kids to look after and a home to run and you're sorting out stuff for me – well . . .' He shook his head. 'It might get too much for you. I know how talented and clever you are but . . . I don't want you to end up being ground down by stuff you shouldn't have been dealing with in the first place.'

Vicky sighed. Why couldn't he trust her to do something hundreds of other women did every day? If she was given a chance she was sure she could do it. And she was sure that Jordan wouldn't have worried about her coping.

God, why was Jordan getting into her thoughts again? What was it with her that she kept comparing Liam to Jordan? Racked with guilt she turned to leave.

'Vicky, don't go! I didn't mean it like that. Really, I didn't.' He caught her hand. 'I truly didn't. Honest. Forgive me Vicky, please.'

She nodded. Vicky could tell that Liam was distraught. She knew he hadn't meant to hurt her feelings it was just that the thought that she might want to do something other than the norm had upset him. 'Oh, Liam, I know you didn't. You're right: I know nothing about running a business. Let's face it, I only know about making a home.'

'And making dresses.'

She nodded. 'And that.'

Perhaps this was the moment to kiss him properly. They'd had a tiff and made up, they were on their own . . . She leaned into him. 'Liam,' she whispered.

The door to the trailer banged open.

195

'Only me,' said Biddy, hauling herself up the step. 'Oh,' she said, seeing Vicky. 'You're here.'

Vicky sighed. The moment was gone.

'You look tired, darlin',' said Mary-Rose over supper the next evening.

'I'm fine.'

'She's frying her brain with all that college work,' said Shania, unhelpfully.

'Am not,' snapped back Vicky. 'At least I've got a brain to fry.'

'Girls, stop it,' said Johnnie. 'I won't have you bickering.'

Vicky was tempted to snipe that Shania had started it, as usual, but was too knackered to argue. She'd hardly slept the night before and had spent most of her time in bed going over and over events of the previous day.

Could she really face having another run-in with Chloe? Could she risk ever being alone with Jordan again? Did she really love Liam or was she marrying him because it was what was expected of her? Was she going to be happy after her wedding day? And what if she wasn't, what then?

She'd lain there, in the dark, listening to Shania's quiet, peaceful breathing, wishing that she was without a care in the world like her sister, as the problems circled round her brain like vultures over a corpse.

If she didn't like her lot, what was the alternative? Run away from home? And go where? If she ran away she'd have to leave the caravan site and then what? Go to Kelly's? Sleep rough? She'd never even had a sleepover in another trailer. The prospect of moving in with Liam was scary enough, and that was hardly a leap into the unknown.

If only she had someone to talk to. Kelly was no good. She loved her best friend to bits, of course she did, but Kelly couldn't see the problems from her point of view. Kelly would simply tell her to get out and get a job. Vicky was sure that Kelly thought that being a traveller was some sort of lifestyle choice, like whether or not to dye your hair. Kelly just didn't get that it went deeper than that, that it was a part of her, like skin colour. She couldn't talk to her sister or her parents; they'd just tell her she had cold feet about getting wed. Liam wouldn't understand. He'd take it as a personal slight that she might want to work. Which left . . . effectively no one.

So what if she just lit out? If she ran away from her roots, would she be an outcast for ever? Would she be seen as betraying everything that her family believed in?

Vicky had tossed and turned, unable to get comfortable, unable to stop the thoughts batting around, unable to find peace, until she'd heard the alarm clock go off in her mother's room. It had been with relief she staggered out of bed to face the day. At least being busy at college would stop her problems going round and round in her head – which it had. But now she was facing another night and she was no nearer to solving anything.

After supper, Vicky and Shania got on with clearing up the supper things, wiping down the kitchen till it shone and making up the bunks for the boys. Their mam and Johnnie had gone off to Bridget and Jimmy

Connelly's trailer next door to share a few drinks, leaving their eldest girls to settle the children.

'Are you going to get Kylie bathed or am I?' said Shania.

'Would you be a love,' said Vicky. 'I'm so tired – didn't get a wink of sleep last night.'

'As I said, you're messing with your brain.'

Wearily, Vicky shook her head. 'It's nothing like that.'

'Then get Paulette to make the last of the dresses. God knows we could do with getting shot of them. There's little enough spare space in this place without all those frocks cluttering up the cupboards.'

'There's only two here. I've stored the rest at Liam's.'

'Well, it seems like more,' grumbled Shania. 'I just don't get why you have to be different.'

'Neither do I,' admitted Vicky.

'What is it you're trying to prove?'

Vicky shrugged.

Shania folded a tea towel and hung it neatly over the rail. 'You know, people round here are talking about you. About you going to college and everything. They think you're setting yourself up to be better than everyone else, just because you've got GCSEs. They think you're turning your back on your roots and they don't like it. They don't say anything to your face but it's what they're saying behind your back.'

'But I'm not. Just because I like textiles doesn't mean I want to be something I'm not.' Vicky was stung by the accusation. For fuck's sake, she was hated at college for being pikey and now she was hated at home for being a gorgio. This was so unfair.

'Just saying,' said Shania. 'Give it up, sack it.' She shrugged. 'It isn't as if you can stay on to get the A level, Liam won't let you, so what's the point?'

'Can I have a word, Mrs Mead?' Vicky had been standing outside the staffroom for ten minutes hoping to catch her tutor.

'Here?' Mrs Mead asked. The corridor outside the staffroom was always busy with students wanting to see tutors or visiting one of the cloakrooms nearby.

'We could go to the foyer.'

Mrs Mead nodded and followed Vicky into the huge space. There was always room there to find a quiet spot.

'I've decided to give up the course,' she said bleakly.

Mrs Mead looked poleaxed. 'No, you can't possibly. I won't allow it.'

'You can't stop me. I'm over sixteen, I don't have to be here.'

'But why?'

'It's not working out.'

'Don't be daft, you're doing splendidly.'

'It's not working out because there's no point in me carrying on.'

Mrs Mead perched on a nearby window ledge. 'Now you listen to me, you have endless talent, you can't waste it.'

'Why? It isn't as if I can go to fashion college, like you want.'

'Why can't you? I really don't understand this. Why can't you postpone your wedding for a few years, what would be so bad about that? Really, Vicky, before the year is out you'll be eighteen and an adult and you can do as you please.'

Vicky could see that Mrs Mead was close to losing her temper. 'I'm sorry but that's how it is.'

'Then at least stay till May and take the exam. It's only a few weeks, Vicky. You won't get this chance again with your education, not if everything you've told me is true.'

'But I just don't see the point.'

'Maybe, when your parents see your grade, they'll think again.'

Vicky snorted. 'They won't care. What matters for them is that I know how to look after my husband properly.'

Mrs Mead sighed. 'Surely that can't be the sole direction your life is going to take.'

It was Vicky's turn to sigh. 'Look, miss, I know you mean well but you're like my mate Kelly. You don't understand what it's like so you shouldn't judge.'

Mrs Mead put her hands up in surrender. 'Okay, Vicky, have it your way, leave. Leave before you take your exam, leave before you find out that I'm not the only person who thinks you have an extraordinary talent. Leave before you've got any chance of convincing your family and friends that maybe, just maybe, you could go places. But if you do, I just hope you never regret it.' She stood up and stamped back towards the staffroom.

Vicky felt completely bewildered. Couldn't she do anything right? If she stayed on at college she'd get it in the neck from her friends and family and if she left Mrs

Mead was going to hate her. She was sure that whatever she decided it was going to be wrong. What was she supposed to do now?

# 10

'There,' Vicky said, biting off a thread and giving a small sigh of satisfaction coupled with relief, 'that's them all made.' She'd made all the dresses, she'd almost done her end-of-year exams, she'd got through everything and she felt she had every right to feel pretty satisfied with herself.

'All of them? Give us a hug, darlin',' said her mother. 'You're a clever girl and no mistake. All done and a month to go. And I don't see that you had to be at college to do this. When I think of all those other lovely dresses you've made you didn't need no extra learning. And all of that time you wasted being taught sewing when you already know how to do it perfectly well.'

'It wasn't just sewing, Mammy.'

'No?' Her mother raised an eyebrow.

Vicky gave up. It wasn't worth arguing. Her mother thought that art was nothing more than pencil sketching and textiles was just dressmaking. And it was the knowledge that studying textiles wasn't the same as just being able to sew that had kept her at college just a few weeks longer. What Mrs Mead had said to her had hit home and had made her think hard about the rest of her life. With years of being a housewife ahead of her she'd decided that maybe it was worth trying to juggle living in two worlds for just a few more weeks before giving it all up. Whether or not her year of studying textiles would ever do her any good she couldn't tell, but she didn't think that, on balance, it could do her any harm. And she could put up with a few harsh words from the likes of Chloe just like she could ignore a few jibes on the trailer park for the next couple of months because in a few years' time who the hell would remember?

Vicky shook out the dark green skirt and then found a stout wooden hanger to hang it on. Carefully she pinned a label to it with the name 'Shania' on it. With each dress made-to-measure she didn't want them to get mixed up.

'I'll take it over to Liam's trailer in a little while.'

'Just as well you've got that place standing mostly empty. Lord knows where we'd put that lot if you didn't.' Even the one dress hanging off a cupboard door seemed to take up a lot of space.

'Wait till I get going on the underskirts. And with all that I've already got stored in Liam's trailer, there won't be room for those.'

'Have you got time to do the petticoats?'

'Mammy, they're dead simple. No hemming, no embroidery, no zips. I can whizz them up in no time, honest. It's just finding room to work on them and keep them that's the problem.'

'So what are you going to do?'

Vicky swung her legs out from under the table and began to pack up her sewing machine. 'There is a solution.'

'And?'

'And I don't think you'll like it but I can't see what else we can do.'

'Go on,' said her mother doubtfully.

'Kelly said we could put the petticoats in her loft.'

'Her loft.'

'Yes, it's dry and warm and there's heaps of space.'

'How would you know?' said her mother suspiciously.

'Because she's told me about it.'

'You've not been there, not after your daddy said you weren't to visit.'

'No, Mammy, what do you take me for?' asked Vicky with a frown. 'Dad said I wasn't to go to see her so I didn't.' She slipped the cover over her machine and lifted the seat of one of the bunks to stow it away tidily. She banged the seat down again noisily. 'I'm a good girl.'

'I know you are, sweetheart, it's just . . .'

'It's just?' Vicky stood with her hands on her hips looking down at her mother.

'You're not like Shania.'

Vicky bit back the comment that at least she had a skill, some ambition and a brain in her head, because she knew that being bitchy wasn't going to help matters.

'No, well, that's as may be,' she said instead. 'But it doesn't solve the problem about the underskirts and where we're going to store them.'

'Your dad won't like it.'

'So ask him to come up with a solution.'

'Don't be cheeky. As if a man should be bothered with where we're going to put some dresses.'

'Then what?'

'You sure there's not space in Liam's?'

Vicky shook her head. 'Not without getting everything horribly creased. And how will we get it all straightened out again?'

'And Kelly says it's all right to have them at her house?'

'I said, didn't I?'

'And her parents are nice – wouldn't mind?'

'How would I know? I've never had the chance to meet them, remember.' Vicky glared at her mum.

Mary-Rose looked away. 'I suppose storing the petticoats there might be okay.'

'Look, Mammy, if I go round with an armful of net petticoats I don't think they're going to kidnap me and sell me off to a pimp. If they agree and Daddy does too, he could drive me round with the petticoats as I make them, we pop them in their attic, Daddy drives me home again and that's that. Nearer the time I go and get them back, give them to all the bridesmaids and then they all bring them with their own dresses to the hotel and we get ready together. What's to go wrong?'

'It's just you know how he feels about gorgios.'

'But you like Kelly.'

'I know, she's a grand girl—'

'And Dad's met her.'

'Ye-es.'

'So help me to convince him.'

'I'll see. No promises, mind.'

'Otherwise we'll just have to tell him that he's got to come up with a better idea, because, Mammy, I can't think of anything. And I don't think you can.'

Knackered after her final four-hour practical exam, Vicky made her way to the canteen to meet Kelly as they'd agreed. This was her last day in college and she wanted to nail some memories and say some goodbyes before she turned her back on education for ever.

'So what are you doing tonight?' said Kelly. The pair of them were sitting at their usual table.

Vicky shook her head. 'Nothing.' She stirred her coffee.

'You are joking me. You've finished your exams and you just plan to go home and watch TV.'

'That's about the size of it.'

'Can't you even have a celebration with your family?'

'It's no big deal to them. We do christenings and marriages, not this sort of thing. Besides, we're all off to the Cotswolds at the weekend. They're all looking forward to that. The boys are totally overexcited about the trip. What with that and my wedding next month there isn't time for much more in the way of parties.'

'Going out for a drink isn't a party.'

'Maybe,' said Vicky, not wanting to pursue the subject. She changed tack. 'I got the last of the dresses finished at the weekend.'

'That was Shania's?'

Vicky nodded. 'And I'm going to start on the petticoats when we get back from Stow. I'll need to meet you somewhere to give you a final fitting with it under the dress.'

'Have you thought any more about using our loft?' asked Kelly.

'I'm waiting for the right moment to talk to Dad.'

'Talk to your dad? *Hello*? This is *me* offering *your* family a favour.'

'I know, I know, but you've met Dad. You know what I'm up against here.'

'So now my house isn't good enough for his precious daughter to set foot in, it's also not good enough for his precious daughter's frocks.' Kelly looked daggers at Vicky.

'It's not like that.'

'Oh really? It looks exactly like that from here. He's never even seen where I live and he's judging it as unsuitable. Well, thanks a bunch.' She folded her arms and turned away from Vicky, looking hurt.

Vicky pushed her coffee cup to one side and leaned across the canteen table. She touched Kelly's arm but her hand was shrugged off.

'No, you can go to hell,' snapped Kelly. 'I don't know why I bother with you, Vicky. I've tried, I really have, to be a friend and to understand what's going on in your life, but whatever I do just seems to get thrown back in my face.'

'It's not you.'

'No, it's not *just* me. It's Jordan as well. Look how he's stuck up for you over the last year and what thanks has he had? All you've done now for weeks is blank him completely and pretend he doesn't exist.'

'I haven't.' But Vicky knew that there was more than a grain of truth in what Kelly was saying. She didn't dare let herself get anywhere near him in case her feelings ran amok again. And she was still racked by guilt over allowing him to kiss her like that.

'He lost Chloe because of you,' Kelly said again.

'I don't call that a hardship. She was a bitch and I don't see what he saw in her.'

'From what I heard from the college football team, she's great in bed. They've all said so,' said Kelly with a dead straight face. A second later both of them were laughing.

'Miaow.'

'But seriously,' said Kelly, wiping her eyes, 'maybe if I come round for a dress fitting I could meet your dad again. Maybe if I ask him myself about storing your stuff at mine he'll find it hard to say no. Because if you can't use our loft, I don't know what you will do with all those dresses and petticoats. My mum's cool about it, we never go up there ourselves but it's got floorboards and there's plenty of light so it would be perfect.'

'We'll have to wait till after the weekend.'

'Oh yeah, you're off to the Cotswolds. Why?'

'Horse fair.'

Kelly nearly choked. 'A horse fair?'

'Kelly, we're Irish travellers, we live and breathe horses.'

'Can you ride?'

'Of course. Can't you?'

Kelly shook her head. 'I live in a town, where the fuck would I learn to ride a horse?'

'When you come round for your fitting we'll have to get you up on one. There's only one problem, though.'

'What's that?'

'We're not big on saddles and stirrups.'

'Then you can forget it. Sorry, but I'm not risking breaking anything before your wedding.'

'Suit yourself.'

A bell rang and Kelly looked at her watch. 'Shit, I've got my practical in twenty minutes. I've got to fly, babes.'

'Look, as I don't have to be in college again, I don't suppose I'll see you before the weekend. Good luck with your exam, I know you'll ace it, and I'll text you about that fitting next week.'

The girls gave each other a quick embrace before Kelly raced off for her exam. Vicky sat back down to finish her coffee. Her dad wasn't due to pick her up for another half-hour.

When she'd drained her cup she wandered back to the textiles room. She had no reason to come back to the college now her exams were over. She wasn't going to be doing the A level proper, so there was no point in coming back for the last weeks of term to start the next bit of the syllabus, although part of her really wanted to. But in deference to her mother's insisting that she concentrated on what was really important – her wedding – she'd given in. Peace at home with her mother and father was more important than squeezing out the last drops from her course. Mrs Mead was busy making a display of the best of her students' work. Naturally Vicky's output featured prominently.

209

'I've come to say goodbye.'

Mrs Mead turned from her work. 'Oh Vicky, this is a sad moment. You know how I feel and I won't say it again. But I will say how much I'm going to miss you.'

'Thanks for everything. I've really enjoyed the last year, despite some of the girls being a bit tricky about me being in class.'

'I'm glad they didn't frighten you away and you finished the year. I'll see you back here for your results, though, won't I?'

'I don't know, miss. I'll see.'

It'd be up to Liam whether or not she could go and get them. Vicky didn't want to make a promise she mightn't be able to keep.

'Then take care, Vicky, and good luck for the future. I hope everything works out well for you, and your wedding day is a wonderful one.' Mrs Mead went round to the back of her desk. 'I hope you don't mind but I've got you a little wedding gift.'

Vicky was astonished. 'You shouldn't have, really.'

Her tutor handed her a present, wrapped in pretty silver paper, about the size of a shoebox.

'Can I open it now?'

'If you like,' said her teacher with a smile.

Eagerly Vicky ripped off the paper. Underneath was an exquisite little workbox with needles and pins in special compartments, spools of thread, a tape measure, scissors, a crochet hook and all sorts of notions and ribbons and bits and pieces. 'Oh, it's beautiful. I love it.'

'Something by which to remember your time here. Maybe something to inspire you to keep up your skills.'

Vicky turned her shining eyes from the box to her tutor. 'It's the loveliest thing ever. I'll use it every day, I just know it.'

'Good.' Mrs Mead gave Vicky a quick hug. 'Now be off with you and if you ever want to drop in, you'll always be welcome.'

Vicky left before she began to cry.

She wandered back through the almost empty college. Most of the students had finished their exams or were off revising if they still had some left to take. She had almost reached the front door when she heard her name being called. She turned.

'Jordan.'

'Hi, Vicky. Trying to escape without saying goodbye?'

She shook her head. She hadn't been – well, not consciously.

Jordan walked across the atrium until he was right beside her. 'So this is it. You're off.'

Vicky nodded.

'When will I see you again?'

She shrugged. 'I don't think it's likely. Do you?'

'It would be if you wanted it to be.'

Jordan leaned towards her and Vicky took a step back. He raised an eyebrow. 'So that's how it is, and more than that, you don't want to say a proper goodbye.' His voice was chilly.

'Come off it, Jordan. You know how it is.' She stuck her hand out.

'You think I want to shake hands?' he snapped. 'You think that's all I want? You know something, Vicky, you can get stuffed. After all I did for you and you're

211

offering me a handshake.' He turned on his heel and stormed off, while Vicky was left holding back tears, upset that their parting had been so bitter.

Vicky didn't have time to spare in the rest of the week to think about college or her last words with Jordan as she, like everyone else on the trailer park, was swept up getting everything ready to travel to Stow-on-the-Wold for the horse fair. Her family weren't taking the big trailer they lived in but a much smaller one they kept for such events. That one had to be cleaned out and stocked with tins of food and essentials, personal possessions and clothes had to be moved over and everything made ready for the journey and the weekend stay once they got there.

Billy and Jon-Boy were beside themselves with excitement and could talk about nothing other than the races they were going to enter their ponies in and the fun they were going to have there. Johnnie was rarely around as he was occupied with getting horse boxes organised, transport arranged for the sulkies, sorting out harnesses and trying to keep his overexcited sons under control. Shania, when she wasn't working out what outfits she was taking with her, was making lists of stuff she still needed for her bottom drawer. The horse fair was going to be packed with traders selling everything a girl could need in that department, and it was an ideal opportunity for her to finish kitting out her future home.

'For God's sake, Shania,' said Vicky. 'Will you shift yourself.'

Once again Shania had a catalogue spread out over the main table.

Vicky, busy with polish and a duster, resented the fact that while she was grafting, Shania seemed to be taking it easy.

'What do you think?' said Shania. 'I love these. Won't they look grand around my home when I'm married.'

Vicky flipped the catalogue round the right way so she could see what was so appealing. It was a selection of brightly coloured decorative plates, each with a different picture of a horse in the centre. The rims of the plates were in bold block colours and then edged in gold.

'Lovely,' agreed Vicky, 'but this isn't getting this place clean. You know Mammy said she wanted it done by the time she gets back from the supermarket.'

'She'll be ages yet.'

'That's no excuse for you not helping me now.'

'And why should I? All the time you were at college doing that stupid course, who helped me?'

'It was so not a stupid course. Look at all those frocks I've made for you over the years.'

'It still doesn't let you off the hook for not cleaning this place for the best part of a year.'

Vicky wasn't going to concede that her little sister had a point. 'I helped out when I could.'

'Not much you didn't.'

There was a knock.

'Where's my best girl?' a voice called in through the open door

Shania leapt up in excitement. 'Your *best* girl? Your

only girl, I hope. What sort of a thing is that to be saying to your fiancée now, Mikey? And come in. Vicky and I were just about to put the kettle on.'

Mikey climbed into the trailer while Shania fussed around him like they were already married, taking his coat, tidying his shoes away and giving him the most comfortable corner of the bunk to sit on. Vicky hid a smile. There was no doubt that Shania was born to be a wife and mother.

When Mikey was comfortable and had his mug of tea, Shania began showing him all the things she planned to try and buy at the Stow fair. To give Mikey his due he did try to look interested but it was fairly obvious his heart wasn't in it.

'If it makes you happy, buy whatever you like,' he said as Shania turned yet another page of the catalogue.

'But will you come around the stalls with me at the fair, Mikey?'

He squirmed. 'Must I, Shania? I'll need to help Dad with the horses and I really don't know if I'll have that much free time. Can't Vicky go with you? She's got much more idea about this sort of thing than I have.'

Vicky was tempted to say that she'd rather eat glass but given the argument they'd just had maybe this was a moment to build bridges not tear them down. 'Of course I'll help you, Shania, haven't I finished my own bottom drawer?'

Of course, the promise, easily given, meant that Vicky was saddled with the reality of tramping up and down the field full of stalls, with Shania constantly dragging her from one side of the grassy aisle to the other as various traders' goods caught her eye. The air was filled with the calls of the stallholders, shrieks from over-excited children, the sound of a distant steam organ playing and the smell of frying onions, popcorn and hot spun sugar. The sun was shining, though the breeze was chill, but Shania, looking amazing in a skimpy yellow top that showed her bare midriff, white pedal pushers and sky-high wedges, didn't seem to feel the cold. Vicky wasn't risking pneumonia though and had on a hot-pink sweater and black jeans, but despite the fact that she was largely covered up she was drawing just as many admiring glances as her scantily clad sister. Every couple of hours they were forced to return to their trailer to dump their purchases and ease their aching feet. Shania, determined that they shouldn't miss out on any bargains, had insisted they'd hit the fair as soon as it had opened. *It's going to be a long day*, thought Vicky. It was past lunchtime and Shania showed no signs of flagging or running out of items on her 'must have' list, despite the fact that she'd been spending the money her dad and Mikey had given her like she was single-handedly trying to drag the whole country out of the recession.

'Isn't this fun,' said Shania with a laugh as she piled yet more bags of goodies into the back of her father's van.

'Wonderful,' replied Vicky, trying to sound enthusiastic.

'Are you tired?' Shania obviously hadn't been taken in.

'A bit. I'd quite like to go and see how Liam and his dad are doing. They've got a pitch here.'

'I'm up for that. Any idea where?'

'I'm going to text him and find out. Maybe he can give us a pointer. I've done enough walking round this fair. I'm dead on my feet.'

'You wuss. And you wearing flat pumps and all.'

Vicky shook her head. She didn't know how her sister did it; she never seemed to feel the cold, her feet didn't ache, whereas she suffered from both – it wasn't fair. Vicky sat on the floor of her dad's van, slipped off her shoes and massaged the circulation back into her toes before she got out her mobile and texted Liam. Then, sheltered from the breeze by the van's open rear doors, she basked in the sun till she got a reply.

'Okay,' she said, jumping up feeling faintly energised by her brief rest. 'Liam says it's not far. He says there's a stall right by him selling kites and flags and loads of New Age crap, and they've got them flying high over their stand. He says if we home in on those we'll be there.'

The vans and trailers were all parked up on the side of a hill above the main ground of the fair. The two girls scanned the array of stalls, tents and attractions spread out in the field below them, shielding their eyes against the bright May sun.

'Could that be it?' said Shania pointing to some brightly coloured strips of fabric fluttering in the breeze.

'Can't see anything more likely,' said Vicky. She slipped her shoes back on and the two girls locked up Johnnie's van before heading down the slope once more and back into the throng of people.

It took them a while of shoving, squeezing and

pushing to get to where Jimmy and Liam had set up their pitch. They were both working on lathes, turning chair legs. In a neat pile beside them were the seats they had already crafted and at the front of their stall were several finished traditional bentwood chairs. Around them were a group of interested bystanders watching the two craftsmen working. A sign at the front told the passers-by that they took orders.

'Yeah, but once they've got the money, will they deliver?' Vicky overheard one fairgoer say to another.

'Doubt it, they're gyppos, aren't they? Take the money and run, they will.'

Shania didn't have red hair for nothing. She rounded on the pair. 'How *dare* you?' she screeched at the surprised couple. 'How dare you say that? You know nothing about Mr Connelly and his son. Nothing at all. You're bang out of order making a remark like that. It's libel, that's what it is.'

'Slander, actually,' said the woman with a sneer, who had now recovered some of her composure.

'Whatever it is you can't say what you just did.' Shania was hopping with indignation.

Vicky took her arm. 'Leave it, love,' she said softly, but the couple were already walking away.

'Argh,' stormed Shania. 'It's so unfair. How can people get away with being so horrible?'

The short commotion had attracted Liam's attention, and he wandered over to the two girls. He was shirtless and his smooth skin was tanned to perfection. He leaned forwards and gave Vicky a quick kiss on the cheek.

'Thanks, Shania,' he said. 'Thanks for sticking up for us, but I don't know it does that much good.'

'Well, I wasn't going to let that stupid bastard get away with it.'

Liam shrugged. 'You can't change people's attitudes by shouting at them.'

'No, but it made me feel better,' said Shania stubbornly.

'So how's trade?' asked Vicky.

'So-so. We've covered the cost of the pitch and we've got a few orders. I think Dad's pleased enough. There's been enough people here who do trust us to deliver their order to have made it worthwhile. It seems that not every gorgio thinks we're scum. Anyway, I can't stand around gossiping with you all day; I've got chairs to make. Although you could do something for me and Dad.'

'What?' Vicky was only too pleased to help.

Liam slid his hand into his jeans pocket and hauled out a roll of notes. He peeled off a couple of tenners. 'There's a stall along the way selling teas and coffees and stuff. You couldn't get me and Dad a couple of teas and a bite, could you? We're starving here.'

'Sure.'

Liam peeled off another note. 'And get something for yourselves.'

'Thanks.' Vicky took the offered money. 'I'd forgotten about lunch,' she said as they walked away. 'I'm starving too.'

They found the food stall easily enough and bought the teas, some slabs of pork pie, a couple of filled rolls, two steak pies and some doughnuts. 'The men can choose what they want and we can picnic on the rest. I'm sure Liam won't mind us camping in a corner of their pitch while we get ourselves on the outside of this lot,' Vicky said to Shania.

Jimmy and Liam decided to carry on working while they ate and were more than happy to allow Shania and Vicky to sit in a sheltered corner of the open-sided tent that formed the back wall of the stand. Out of the wind it was warm and the girls munched happily.

'Do you love him?' asked Shania, out of the blue.

Vicky nearly choked on a mouthful. 'Of course I do. Why wouldn't I?'

'But how do you know?'

'Because when I look at him I feel all warm inside. Don't you feel like that about Mikey?'

'Yeah, I suppose.'

Vicky chewed for a bit. 'It's enough, isn't it?'

Shania nodded. 'I don't want anyone else. That's enough, surely.'

But Vicky wasn't so certain. She knew what she'd felt when she'd been kissed by Jordan. Supposing when Liam kissed her properly for the first time she felt nothing. Would she always be haunted by thoughts of Jordan and wonder if she'd settled for second best? She put treacherous thoughts of Jordan to the back of her mind and concentrated on watching Liam work; his muscles moving and bulging under his tanned skin, his stomach flat and toned, a line of hair running down from his belly button to his waistband on his jeans. He was lovely and she was happy with the idea of marrying him but . . . but . . . *did* she love him? And what if she didn't?

She made up her mind: she had to get Liam to kiss her properly, and soon.

# 11

'The bus'll be at the gate in about five minutes,' Kelly said to Vicky over the phone.

'I'll run down to meet you.'

'You don't have to. I know the way to your caravan.'

'Trailer,' corrected Vicky. 'But it'd be better if I did. Honestly.'

'Okay, have it your way.'

Vicky severed the connection and ran down to meet her friend.

'I'm longing to see my dress now it's completely finished,' said Kelly after the two had hugged each other. They began walking back through the park, avoiding a group of young lads hurtling about on bikes followed by a pack of small yapping dogs. 'And I asked Mum about storing some of them at ours and she said that better than the loft you could use the spare room. I told you she'd be cool about it.'

'So now we just have to convince Dad.'

Kelly shrugged. 'I don't know why you think this is going to be such a mission. It's just a place to hang a few dresses.'

'Yeah, you're right.' At least, Vicky hoped Kelly was right. 'Anyway, come on.'

The pair hurried up to Vicky's trailer and let themselves in.

'Everyone's out so we've got the place to ourselves. The boys are off with Dad to collect a couple of horses they bought at the fair, and Shania, Mum and Kylie have gone visiting. They've gone to talk to a couple of her bridesmaids, although they'll be back in a little while.'

'It's all go on that front for your ma, isn't it?'

'It'll be a long while before Kylie gets wed, as she's only two and a half, so she'll get a breather for a few years.'

'She'll need it. Right, let's get me into this frock again.'

Vicky pulled the hanger with the dress on it off the back of a cupboard door and put it in her bedroom. Already laid out on the big double bed was the underskirt she'd made and the bodice.

'If you get down to your bra and knicks,' she told Kelly, 'I'll help you into the underskirt and then put the dress on over the top. Then you can get into the bodice and I'll zip you up.'

'That's a lot of petticoat,' said Kelly, eyeing the mound of tulle and net suspiciously.

'I know. It'll make the dress look gorgeous.'

'The dress is gorgeous already.'

'But wait till you see it properly.'

Kelly didn't look convinced but started to get undressed anyway. Vicky helped her into the vast creation that she'd made and then slipped the wonderful green silk skirt over the top. She did up the fastenings and arranged the fabric so it hung properly over the petticoats underneath.

'Now put this on,' said Vicky, handing over the bodice. 'I'll turn my back.'

There was some rustling then Kelly asked her to zip her up, which Vicky did. She stepped back.

'That is amazing! It's just how I wanted it to look,' she said, clapping her hands.

'Are you sure?' asked Kelly.

'I've put a long mirror out in the main room,' said Vicky, 'so you can see yourself better. It's too cramped in here for you to get a proper view.'

'If I can get through the door,' muttered Kelly.

Vicky helped her squash down the yards and yards of fabric so she could manoeuvre her way into the lounge.

'Turn around,' said Vicky. 'What do you think?'

'Dear God,' said Kelly. Her mouth formed a perfect 'O' of horrified astonishment.

'It's fantastic,' said Vicky, wriggling with happiness at the way the dress had turned out and completely failing to pick up on Kelly's reaction.

Kelly continued to stare, slack-jawed, at her reflection.

At this point Shania bounced back into the trailer.

'Ooh,' she cried. 'Oh my God, that dress is amazing. It's wonderful. You are so clever, Vicky. Wait till Mammy sees it!'

Kelly remained silent as Vicky walked around the dress, twitching the fabric so it hung perfectly.

'Gorgeous,' she muttered. 'Perfect.' After a little while she noticed Kelly's silence.

'Aren't you thrilled?'

Kelly took a deep breath. 'I think,' she said slowly, 'that less is more.'

Vicky was confused. 'I'm not with you.'

'The dress looked perfect in that picture you showed me. But now . . .' Kelly plucked at the skirts. 'Why don't we get rid of some of the petticoats?'

'What?' Vicky was gobsmacked.

'Try it like it was before,' she ploughed on.

'No,' said Vicky, her voice high-pitched with indignation. 'No. It's grand as it is. Really. Isn't it, Shan?'

Shania nodded vigorously.

'Don't you think it's a bit over the top?' said Kelly.

Vicky looked at her friend, her forehead creased with worry. 'Over the top?' Was it really? She gazed at her creation, trying to see it through Kelly's eyes.

'A bit . . . a bit freaky?' Kelly added.

No – freaky it definitely wasn't. She flipped. 'Freaky? *Freaky!* Don't be stupid,' snapped Vicky. 'There's nothing "freaky" about this dress. If you hate it so much I suggest you take it off and forget about being my bridesmaid.'

'I was just saying,' said Kelly, defensively. 'This isn't normal, you know. Bridesmaids' dresses are never this big. This is . . .' Kelly searched for the right word but the best she could think of was, '. . . stupid.'

'No, no. Just get the fucking dress off and get out,' screamed Vicky. 'Go on. How *dare* you be so rude about it? How dare you! This is how *I* want *my* wedding. This

224

isn't about you, this is about me. You can do what you want when you get married but this is *my* day. You can dress your bridesmaids in the sort of stupid shit your sort like, but I want mine like this. Understand?'

'I didn't mean . . .'

'Didn't you?'

'The dress is big, though,' said Kelly.

'That's how we like them,' said Shania. 'It's how we do things. Not that you'd understand. You don't belong at Vicky's wedding. I don't know what made her come up with the daft idea that it would be good to have an outsider there. Well, at least we know what you're really like, what you really think of our ways before we get there. Probably best if you don't come at all because you'd only hate it. Sneer at us too, probably.'

Kelly, her face white, bit her lip and turned around, with some difficulty. 'You'd better unzip me,' she said quietly.

Vicky leaned forwards and tugged on the zip. 'Come on, Shania,' she said. 'Let's leave Kelly to get changed into something she is happy to be seen wearing. Something that doesn't make her into a freak.'

The pair left the trailer and shut the door behind them.

'Typical bloody gorgio,' said Shania, as they stamped across the park to get right away from their trailer and Kelly. 'She thinks she's so much better than we are. She was so rude about that dress and it's beautiful. It really is, Vick.'

'Leave it,' said Vicky. She didn't want to dwell on Kelly's reaction. What was wrong with having big fluffy

225

petticoats? They looked wonderful. She couldn't believe how rude her friend had been about the dress. Friends didn't say things like that to each other, not about their wedding plans. But then she'd been pretty rude back to Kelly – and Shania hadn't helped.

*What a fucking mess*, she thought as the sisters sat on a bench in the sun, both simmering with indignation and anger. Vicky wasn't entirely sure that all her anger was with Kelly – just most of it. But Shania needn't have weighed in and she herself had made things worse. Gah – it was just an all-round sodding shambles.

Despite her anger at what Kelly had said and her cruel criticism of the dress, she couldn't bear the way that she and Kelly had left things. This was so wrong – all those years of friendship blown away by a stupid row over petticoats. Vicky got her phone out and rang Kelly's number.

Straight to voicemail. She was being blanked.

Vicky wasn't having this. She had to make it up with Kelly right now. She couldn't have Kelly going off like this. She had to make it up with her before the wedding. They *had* to make up before the big day. Maybe Kelly wouldn't be completely happy about wearing a traveller bridesmaid's dress, but Vicky was sure she could talk her round – if Kelly let her talk to her – and explain it from a traveller's point of view. The trouble was, if Kelly continued to blank her phone calls there was nothing she could do. Vicky realised with a sick feeling that she didn't even know where Kelly lived. She only had a mobile number for her and no other information at all.

There was no way she was going to lose Kelly. Don't

226

let the sun go down on your anger, her mother always said. Vicky recalled that she once asked her mother 'Why not?' after a particularly bruising spat with Shania.

'Because with every day that passes it becomes twice as hard to make up again,' she'd said. 'You get more and more convinced that you are right and your sister is wrong and she feels the opposite, just as strongly, and neither of you backs down and, to be sure, by the time a week has passed you never will and you'll end up hating each other till you go to your graves. I've seen it in other families. It's how feuds start.'

Vicky had been so scared of her mother's dire warning that she always tried to take heed of the advice. There had been that one time she and Shania had really fallen out, back in the previous summer, but they'd made up the next morning. And since then they'd had the odd row, but they'd never fallen out really badly. Not like she and Kelly just had. She had to make up with Kelly – and quickly. She and Kelly had too much history, too many shared memories for them to part on such bad terms. Vicky jumped up and raced back to the trailer but when she got there the dress was back on the bed and the place was empty. Kelly had fled.

Vicky sat on the bed and began to cry.

It had all come to a head. She was so tired. She had worked so hard on the dresses and her college course; the weekend at the horse fair had been exhausting and now this. It was the final straw. It was her wedding day in only a few weeks, she should be on cloud nine, ecstatic, but instead, recently, she spent half of every night awake, racked by doubts about her and Liam, she'd just fallen out with her best friend and to cap it all she'd been told her dresses were freakish and stupid.

Miserably she tried to get hold of Kelly again and once again her call was blanked. She sighed. Sitting here feeling sorry for herself wasn't going to solve anything. Maybe she ought to go and see Liam. He'd cheer her up, or maybe he'd know how she could make it all better.

She wandered over to his shed where he and his dad were busy working on the orders they'd taken at Stow.

'Hiya,' she said as she went into their workshop.

Jimmy took one look at her sad face, muttered something about a tea break and left the pair of them alone.

'What's up, hon?' asked Liam, laying down his plane.

Vicky sighed. 'I've just had a row with Kelly.'

'Oh babe, I'm sorry. What's she done now?'

'She hates her bridesmaid's dress.'

'Why? I mean, what brought this on? She's seen it before.'

'Not completely finished. Not with the petticoats and everything.'

Liam didn't understand and he rubbed his face as if that would make everything clear. 'But that doesn't make it so very different, does it?'

'According to her, she now looks like a freak.'

'Stuff her then.'

'But she's my friend.'

Liam looked sceptical and sighed. 'I know you *think* she is but I've always had my doubts.'

Vicky nodded sadly.

'Her life and ours,' Liam went on, 'they're just too

different. And now she's made you miserable. Maybe this is for the best. Maybe you'll be happier if you never see her again.'

'No,' whispered Vicky. 'Just because she didn't like the dress it doesn't mean that she'd try to do me down. She's my mate; it's just the dress she doesn't like, she's not waging a war against me.'

'It's enough for me that she's upset you. And I don't want her to be able to do that to you again. I don't want you seeing her, you hear me? I don't want to risk her making you unhappy ever again. I hate it when you're sad, Vicky, I really do. This is for the best, Vick, trust me.'

'But . . . but you've always trusted *me* in the past, you've always been on *my* side. I thought you liked her. Liam, I don't want to lose Kelly's friendship. Just accepting that she's gone really isn't a solution. I thought you'd tell me how to put it all to rights.' Vicky stared at him, bewildered. What she'd wanted from him was a hug and a bit of sympathy, not to be ordered to stay away from Kelly. She had every intention of making it up with her best friend. She didn't know how, and it was probably going to take a while, but she was going to do it. Or rather she *had been* going to do it. But if Liam was going to be like this, Vicky's friendship with Kelly was becoming even more precarious. Vicky didn't know what to say and having just had a bruising argument with Kelly she certainly wasn't up for one with Liam.

'Right,' she said, trying to put a brave face on things. 'Best I make plans for just six bridesmaids then.' She

229

knew she might sound as if she didn't really care but inside she felt as if she were being torn apart.

And who could she talk to about this? Shania was livid with Kelly; Liam didn't understand; her father hated all gorgios and her mother would side with her husband. The one person she could have relied on to talk through such a problem was Kelly – how ironic was that?

When she got back to the trailer, Kelly's discarded dress was there as a reminder of their row. It was also a reminder that she now had a storage problem for all the petticoats. She didn't have any room for this petticoat, let alone another six – no, she only needed space for another five now. There was no way she'd be able to fit all of them in the family trailer. There was nothing else for it: she'd have to go against what Liam had said and she'd have to make it up to Kelly. She was sure she'd be able to persuade Liam that Kelly wasn't so awful when she'd succeeded. And she didn't want to make it up with Kelly *just* because of those damned petticoats. Yes, of course it was an excuse but she really wasn't that shallow. There was also the stark realisation that Kelly represented a part of her life she didn't want to leave behind completely. If Liam really put his foot down and refused to let her see Kelly again she'd lose touch with her altogether – for ever.

Feeling completely blue, Vicky hung up the green silk skirt, folded up the bodice and began stuffing the net underskirt into a bin bag. It wasn't ideal but at least it crushed it down small enough to shove in a cupboard. Not, she thought sadly, that it would matter if this one got crushed beyond recognition, not if Kelly really wasn't going to come to her wedding.

She tried ringing her again: nothing. There had to be a way of getting an apology to her. An idea zoomed into her brain. Jordan! Excitedly she dumped the petticoat, which instantly exploded out of the bin bag, and scrolled through her phone. Somewhere in the phone's call history had to be that text that Jordan had sent her the day she'd got her results. It was nearly a year ago. Would her phone still have it? She scrolled through the 'Inbox' file. Almost every text had come from a named friend but then she came to one that had come from an unknown person, a text that her phone could only identify by the caller's own number. It had to be it. Vicky scrabbled around in her brain but she couldn't think of any other messages that she might have made to or received from people who weren't already in her phone's address book. This had to be Jordan.

With a slightly shaky finger she hit 'call'.

'Vicky?'

'Jordan?'

'Of course it is. Who did you think you were calling?'

'I'm sorry, of course it is.' She paused. Now what did she say?

'What's the matter, Vick? To be honest I wasn't really expecting to hear from you again.' Even over the air-waves his voice sounded a bit cool. 'Does your fiancé,' he sounded as if he were spitting the word, 'know you're calling?'

'Jordan . . . Jordan, please don't be like that. I'm sorry, I really am.'

'Really? Sorry for the way we parted? It wasn't how I'd planned it you know. That poxy handshake, was that all our friendship meant?'

'Yes, I am *really* sorry. What happened between us never should have done. I was as much at fault as you – more so, as I should never have let you kiss me. And I didn't know how to handle it. I'm sorry if I hurt you but I thought it'd be easier if I just kept right away from you from then on. But I couldn't go without saying goodbye – and you wanted more than that. And I . . . I . . .'

'Leave it,' said Jordan. 'Just forget it. So why the call? You want something from me, is that it? Got a use for me?'

'Don't, Jordan, I don't know who else I can ask. You're my one and only hope.' Jordan didn't say anything so Vicky ploughed on. 'Look, I've really screwed up. I've had a row with Kelly and I need to apologise.'

'So go ahead and do it. All you have to do is say how sorry you are, maybe grovel a bit. Now if that's all the advice you need—'

'No! You don't understand. She won't answer my calls. If I knew where she lived I'd go and see her . . .'

'Really? I thought you lot had rules about that sort of thing. You see, since I found out about you I've been reading up about travellers. Can't think why – some random idea that I might find out what made you tick, I suppose. So now I know how strict the rules are for you traveller girls.'

'You're right about the rules. And they're really tough, but I'd be prepared to break them for Kelly.'

'You wouldn't break them for me. I'll be straight with

you, Vicky, I really fancied you and I thought you had something, something special. Despite the rules I thought you had the brains to try to break out, be different, *do* something. And I could have helped you if you'd let me. But hey, you blew me out, so why should I care any more?'

'I'm sorry Jordan, really, but you're a boy and I couldn't cut myself off from my family. Because that's what would have happened if my folks had found out about you and me. No ifs or buts. I didn't have the courage to risk it. I'm engaged, remember. It wouldn't matter how much I like you, there are some rules I really can't break.' She let the silence hang for a few seconds. 'But Kelly isn't a boy. And she was my friend.'

'Okay, okay. So why are you calling me?'

'I'd like you to go and see Kel for me, or phone her. Tell her I'm so, so sorry. Tell her I couldn't bear it if we don't make up. Tell her . . . I don't know. Just tell her I couldn't bear it if she didn't come to my wedding, that it would ruin my day.'

'Anything else?'

'I think that's enough.'

'I'll see what I can do. I can't think why, though, given the way you treated me.'

'I don't deserve your friendship, Jordan. I'm so sorry.'

'As I said, I'll see what I can do. I'll be in touch.'

Vicky put her phone down in her lap. So it wasn't just Kelly she'd completely pissed off, it was Jordan too. She was the worst friend in the world.

'And just who is Jordan?' said Liam.

Vicky jumped so much she actually left the bed and

233

her phone spun off her lap and onto the floor, skittering away from her. Liam picked it up. With his face set like stone he handed it back. 'You haven't answered the question. Who is Jordan?'

'A friend from college.'

'A friend, I see.' He sighed. 'A boyfriend?'

'What do you take me for?'

'"I don't deserve your friendship, Jordan. I'm so sorry,"' mimicked Liam. 'I don't know, Vicky. I really don't know what I should take you for.'

'Don't, Liam.' Tears started to run down Vicky's cheeks. 'He was just a guy at college. He stopped some people from bullying me. He looked out for me because he's a nice guy but that was all there was.'

'So why are you phoning him? I don't get it.'

'Because I want him to tell Kelly I'm sorry. She won't take calls from me and I don't want to stop being friends with her. I thought he could be a go-between.'

'But I told you what I thought. Didn't I just tell you to forget her? Didn't I say that once we're wed she won't be welcome?'

'But she's *my friend*, Liam.'

'Correction. *Was* your friend.'

'You can't tell me who I can and can't be friends with.'

'Not yet I can't but you wait till June.'

'But there's no reason for you to be like this about Kelly. This stupid argument we had was just about some net petticoats. If I wasn't so tired it would have all blown over and I wouldn't have told you and you wouldn't be like this.'

'Really?'

'Really. Please, Liam, Kelly's my best friend and if you loved me you wouldn't stop me from seeing her.'

'And if you loved me you wouldn't be so disobedient.' He turned on his heel, leaving Vicky pale and sobbing behind him.

If she'd thought life was a complete mess before her row with Kelly, it was nothing compared to how it was right now. Liam didn't trust her, she'd just discovered how much Jordan hated her, Kelly wasn't speaking to her . . . it seemed that everyone she cared about – or *had* cared about – was against her. She couldn't do anything right, she'd made a complete mess of everything. Even her precious bridesmaids' dresses were 'freaky'.

*Oh God*, a thought struck her. What if Liam told her dad about her talking to Jordan on the phone? *Shit, he'll go mental*. He'd never hit her, although he'd slapped Billy once, but there was always a first time. He had a ferocious reputation on the site for prizefighting in his youth and she knew for a fact that he'd settled a number of disputes with his fists since. The thought of the possible row to come from her father was the last straw.

She pulled up one of the bunks in the sitting room and rummaged in the space under it. She was sure there was a backpack in there that the boys had used during the brief spell they'd attended school. She found it under a pile of winter coats that were being stored until they were needed again. Not perfect and a bit dusty but it'd do.

She dashed back into her bedroom and pulled open the drawers in her chest to find a few pairs of clean pants, a couple of tops and a sweater. She stuffed everything in the bag. On top of these she flung her hairbrush, her make-up bag and her washing things. She gazed at her precious sewing box, her wedding present from Mrs Mead, but told herself no. And frankly, if she was abandoning her family and her entire way of life then what was a sewing box when everything else was taken into consideration?

She grabbed a jacket off the hook and then went to the kitchen. Her mother had a jam jar where she collected spare two-pound coins. Vicky took five. That should pay for the bus fare into town and buy her supper. Then, closing the door of the trailer behind her, she took off, trying not to think about how she would cope if neither Kelly nor Jordan wanted anything to do with her. And given how she'd behaved towards them she wouldn't blame them one bit.

# 12

Keeping her head down, Vicky made her way towards the gates at the front of the compound. It was getting on for teatime and lots of the mothers were indoors cooking the evening meal while the kids watched TV. There were a few lads about, some dealing with their horses and some having a kick-about, but they didn't pay any attention to Vicky as she slipped past. At the top of the park was the site manager's trailer but either he and his wife were busy indoors or they were away for the day as there wasn't a sign of life. Keeping a sharp eye open, Vicky scooted past and out onto the main road beyond.

She ran to the bus stop and then had a second thought. She couldn't wait for the 68 at this one; someone from the site, returning home after a day out, might see her. She shouldered her backpack and headed along the grass verge the half-mile to the next one, keeping her collar up and her head down. As she walked a bus swooshed past. Vicky could have cried. *Shit*. If she'd risked staying put she'd have been on it. How long would it be till the next one? How long would she have

237

to wait at the next stop, her chances of getting spotted were going up second by second?

When she got to the next shelter she studied the timetable and glanced at her watch. Twenty minutes. She have to pray she'd get lucky but at least, tucked into a corner of the wooden shelter, the chances of anyone who might know her seeing her had lessened.

She sat on the uncomfortable wooden bench and clutched her backpack on her lap, trying to slow her breathing and calm her nerves. She was scared: scared of getting caught, scared of being alone, scared that she mightn't hear back from Jordan and scared Kelly mightn't want anything to do with her.

What if Kelly didn't? What then? Did she crawl home, take the row from her father, face the disapproval of the whole community? Would Liam break if off with her? Would she be disgraced? Well, she knew the answers to those questions. Shit, she'd burned her boats this time and no mistake. At the thought Vicky felt quite sick with nerves yet again. What had she done? What had possessed her?

She glanced at her watch and then hazarded a peek round the side of the shelter. She couldn't risk missing the next bus as well. She might need to stay out of sight as much as she could but she'd have to make sure she kept a sharp eye out too.

By the time the bus arrived Vicky was shaky with fear and worry. She'd tried texting Jordan to find out if he'd had any luck with Kelly but he still hadn't replied and when she'd phoned Kelly again she was still being directed straight to voicemail. However, she couldn't go back to the trailer park so she had no option but to get on the bus and hope to God that when she arrived in the town centre she had either come up with a plan or that Kelly or Jordan was going to be able to bail her out. She paid her fare and went up the stairs. She didn't want to risk someone on the pavement or in a passing vehicle recognising her. Up on the top deck she'd be pretty much invisible. The bus ground on along the road, carrying her away from her home, security and everything familiar. As the miles went under the wheels Vicky's worries went round and round in her head.

She jumped off at the town hall and found a café. Although it was May, it wasn't especially warm and Vicky's jacket was only thin, besides she didn't want to hang about on the street. Taking out her precious stash of coins she spent a few more on a big mug of tea and a muffin then took herself to the top floor to hide in a corner once again. She put her snack down on an empty table, got her phone out and tried Jordan's number again.

She felt wobbly with relief when he answered.

'Jordan! Did you get hold of her?'

'Yeah.'

'And?'

'And what do you think? She's completely pissed off with you.'

Vicky let out a low moan.

'But – and you know, I have no idea why I did this, Vick, as I feel the same way as Kelly – but I persuaded her you really need a friend right now.'

Vicky felt a sob of relief well up. 'Oh, Jordan.'

She heard a snort down the phone. 'Ain't I the fool? Anyway, if you ring her you can tell her yourself.'

'Jordan, I don't know how to thank you, really I don't.'

'You can thank me by not treating Kelly like that again. She's a good friend, Vicky, she's always stood by you, so don't you lay into her like that again.'

'I won't, Jordan, I promise.'

'Good, see you don't.'

They said goodbye with Jordan still sounding pretty stiff and unfriendly. As Vicky stared at her mobile she wondered if she'd ever be able to do anything to make things better. But, realistically, what could she do? Not that the traveller rules that she'd been brought up to obey mattered much now. She'd cut herself loose from all that and there was no going back.

She drank her tea and took a bite of her muffin to steady herself before she hit the button to call Kelly. She answered on the second ring.

'Vicky. Jordan said you needed to talk to me.'

'Did he also say that I know I've been an arse?'

'He said something of the sort, yes.'

'Because I have been. A total, thoughtless cow. I should never have said those things to you.'

There was a pause. 'And maybe I was out of order about my dress.'

'No, it is big. You're right. Maybe I should have told you how we like to do things.'

'Maybe I shouldn't be so judgemental.'

'Oh, Kelly. I am so sorry.'

'I am too, Vicky. I am too.'

'Kelly, I don't want to talk on the phone. Could we meet?'

'Vick, I really don't want to trek over to the trailer park again right now. I've not long got home.'

'No, you don't have to. Could you meet me in town?'

'When?'

'Now?'

'Now!'

'I'm at the Market Café.'

'But . . . but . . .'

'Can you get here? I'll explain everything when I see you.'

'I suppose. I'll be about half an hour. Is that okay?'

Vicky checked her watch. 'I don't know if they'll still be open after six but if they're not I'll be waiting in the bus shelter outside.'

'I'll be as quick as I can.'

Vicky dragged out her muffin and coffee as long as she could, but as she feared, the café closed before Kelly arrived.

'I'm not hanging out in a bus shelter,' said Kelly firmly when she found Vicky. She grabbed Vicky by the arm and steered her into a nearby pub. 'What you drinking?'

'A Coke please.'

Kelly ordered the Coke and a large white wine for herself.

'But you're not eighteen,' said Vicky, horrified.

'Barman's a mate,' she replied. 'You can have a proper drink if you'd prefer.'

Vicky, even more horrified, shook her head. She

241

might have kicked over the traces but some rules were just too ingrained. And drinking alcohol as a single girl was one step too far.

'So what's this about? Why are you in town on your own?'

Vicky took a deep breath. 'I needed to see you to really convince you how sorry I am. And, well . . . I've run away from home.'

Kelly, who'd just taken a gulp of wine, splurted it across the table in shock. Wiping it up with the sleeve of her top, she stared at Vicky. 'Fucking hell, Vicky!'

'I know, but I had to.' She explained about Liam refusing to let her see Kelly again and then catching her on the phone to Jordan.

Kelly shook her head in disbelief. 'But running away, Vick. That's one hell of a step to take.'

'And I can't go back. I've been out unchaperoned. I could have got up to anything. I'm fallen, ruined . . . as far as everyone on the site will be concerned when they find out, I'm now nothing better than a harlot.'

'Don't be daft.'

'It's true.'

Kelly's eyes widened. 'But you've only been gone a bit and it's broad daylight. Besides, you're a Catholic. Can't you just go to confession and get absolution or something?'

'It won't wash with Liam's family. He won't want me now. Damaged goods, that's what I am.'

Kelly shook her head. 'Blimey.' She took another slug of her drink. 'So I suppose you need somewhere to stay.'

Vicky nodded her head.

'I expect Mum'll be cool. We've got a spare room you could have. And I see you've got some kit with you.'

Vicky nodded again. 'Will your mum mind that I'm a . . .'

'A pikey?' said Kelly with a wicked grin. 'She won't know, will she. She knows I've got a mate called Vicky but she's never asked where you live or nothing. No, it'll be fine. Our little secret,' she added.

Vicky sagged back in her chair. Things weren't perfect, far from it, but at least she wasn't facing the prospect of sleeping rough on top of everything else.

Her phone bleeped at her. She checked the messages – a text from Shania.

'Where r u.' She stared at the message.

'Problem?' asked Kelly.

Vicky turned the phone round so her friend could read it. Kelly took it out of her hand and switched it off.

'It's how I dealt with a situation I couldn't cope with.'

As if Vicky didn't know. 'But it doesn't solve anything, does it?'

'It gives you time to think. Come on, drink up. I want some supper even if you don't – I expect Mum'll be able to make whatever we're having stretch.'

'I'll get chips on the way. I can't put your mum to any trouble.'

'Don't be daft.' Kelly drained her glass. 'A nice supper, an early night and I bet things'll look a bit better in the morning.' Vicky finished her drink too and followed Kelly out of the pub.

Better in the morning? She very much doubted it but

she'd made her decision so however things turned out she was stuck with it.

'Mum, this is Vicky. Vicky, Mum.'

'Hello, Mrs Munro. Lovely to meet you.' Vicky stuck out her hand, which Mrs Munro took and shook.

'Nice to meet you, and it's Betty.'

'Betty,' repeated Vicky.

'Vicky needs a bed for a couple of nights,' said Kelly. 'Her parents have had to shoot off to look after a sick granny.' She shot Vicky a warning look not to contradict the story. 'It's okay if she stays with us till they get back, isn't it?'

'I suppose.'

'I'll make up the spare bed,' volunteered Kelly.

'I don't want to put you out, Betty,' said Vicky.

Betty gave her a look that implied that she was, but didn't say anything.

'And there'll be enough supper,' said Kelly hopefully. 'If there isn't, Vicky and I'll go to the chippy.'

Betty sighed. 'I could have done with a bit of notice. I don't mind having your friends to stay, really I don't, but if I know a day in advance it's a help.'

'I knew I should've bought chips on the way here,' said Vicky. 'I am really sorry, I've put you out.'

Now Betty had made her point she backtracked. 'No, it's fine. Don't mind me. Kelly, you take Vicky upstairs and show her the spare room. I'll put some more spuds on.'

Kelly led Vicky to where she'd be staying and shut the door behind them.

'I should have warned you. Mum always likes to play the martyr for a minute or two, just to make sure none of us take her for granted. Once she's made her point she's fine.'

Kelly went out of the room and returned with an armful of bedding. A few minutes later the bed had been made up and Vicky's few possessions were stowed in the chest beside it.

'Time to give you the guided tour,' said Kelly. She showed Vicky the bathroom and loo, 'And don't worry, you're only sharing it with me. Mum and Dad have an en suite,' and then took her downstairs to show her the kitchen, sitting room and dining room. Vicky couldn't believe how much space the three people in the Munro family had to rattle around in. When she thought about the place she shared with four siblings and her parents, this semi seemed palatial.

'It's not that big,' said Kelly. 'Mum says it would be so much nicer if we had a conservatory.'

Vicky raised her eyebrows. What the hell did they want with yet another room? They already had plenty to spare. And couldn't they turn the heating down? It was tropical in the house. She returned to her bedroom and slipped off her jacket before she passed out with heat exhaustion and then joined Kelly in her room where they lay on Kelly's bed and watched MTV until her dad got in from work and Betty called them down for supper.

Vicky was introduced to Brian, who seemed more interested in pouring himself a beer than meeting one of his daughter's friends, which suited Vicky because she was having to deal with too many new things all at once. If he ignored her it was one less.

Betty called them into the dining room for supper and they sat down at the table.

'You been away on holiday?' said Betty, eyeing Vicky's tanned bare arms, after she had dished up a chicken casserole and mash.

'Holiday?' Apart from trips to Stow horse fair and going shopping with her mother and sister, Vicky had hardly ever shifted off the trailer park in her life. And she'd certainly never been anywhere for any length of time.

'You're very brown given that we haven't seen much of the sun yet this year.'

'It's fake,' said Kelly, quickly.

'And are you sure you're warm enough?' asked Betty, who was wrapped up in a thick sweater, as were both Kelly and Brian, despite the radiator that was throbbing with heat in the dining room.

'I'm fine, honest,' she replied, wondering why on earth with central heating they needed jumpers as well. What was wrong with these people? Soft or what?

The chicken casserole was delicious but by the time Vicky had finished eating the combination of hot food and an exhausting and traumatic day caught up with her completely. She was shattered but it was in her DNA to help with the housework.

'Let me help you with the dishes, Betty,' she offered.

'Mum can cope,' Kelly assured her before Betty could accept or decline the offer for herself. 'She'll just bung them in the dishwasher. Come on, let's you and I go upstairs to watch TV.'

Stunned, Vicky allowed herself to be dragged into Kelly's room.

'Don't you help your mammy clear the table?' she said.

'Help her? Why? Mum's just a housewife so what else has she got to do all day?' Kelly mightn't have meant to sound callous but Vicky was horrified.

'But what about the housework and all, don't you lend a hand?'

'I've got school work.'

'Not now you haven't, or not much, your exams are finished. Don't you ever do the cleaning or anything, even in the holidays?'

'No, that's Mum's job. Why should I?' Kelly sounded bewildered by the notion.

Vicky couldn't believe her ears, but being desperate not to fall out with Kelly again she shut up. A monster yawn threatened to dislocate her lower jaw. 'I'm sorry, Kelly, I'm going to hit the hay soon.'

'But I thought we could go out on the town together, have a bit of fun.'

The idea of anything other than sleep made Vicky feel even more exhausted. 'Kelly, I'd love to,' she lied. 'But I'm shattered. Today has been a mare, the weekend was knackering and I've not slept through the night for ages.' She saw the look of disappointment on her friend's face. 'Maybe tomorrow.'

Kelly shrugged. 'Whatever.'

'And tomorrow I've got to think where I go from

here. I'm too tired to plan tonight but we'll have to think of something soon. You'll help me, won't you?'

Kelly nodded and then gave Vicky a hug. 'Yeah, of course I will. You sleep well now and I'll see you in the morning.'

Vicky cracked another yawn, hugged Kelly goodnight and went into her own room.

The double bed in the spare room seemed awfully big and she was going to be sleeping in it on her own. Without Shania. Vicky couldn't remember a time when she hadn't shared a room. And she missed the faint roar of the dual carriageway and the other normal noises of life on the trailer site. Suddenly she felt desperately lonely. The world seemed big and scary and she was all alone – cut off from her family, her traveller friends and all her other relations. Sitting on the edge of her bed, she wondered what the hell she'd done.

'I'm going to have to find a job, aren't I, Kel?' said Vicky through another yawn as she sat on the end of her bed after breakfast the next morning. Despite how tired she'd been was the evening before, she hadn't had a good night and had spent a lot of it wide awake, feeling terrified and cast adrift in equal measure. And the trouble was that in the dead of night, with nothing else to think about, her situation had become more and more monstrous and the consequences more and more dire until she'd been been in a complete panic. And maybe it had been a mistake to check her phone before she went to sleep. There were about twenty messages from Shania, getting more and more frantic, and a load of missed calls from Liam. She didn't dare look at any of the messages nor ring Liam back. Maybe if she ignored it all, as Kelly had already advised her, it would all just go away. Miserably she switched her phone off and then felt even more lonely.

If she'd had Shania next to her she would have been comforted but she was never going to have Shania next to her again. So she'd lain under the covers, rigid with fear and unable to sleep, until the sky had lightened. As the sun rose her fears seemed to shrink into the corners of the room and she'd finally slept but too late to get any real rest. Then Kelly had come bouncing in, full of life and plans, and all Vicky had wanted to do was put her head back under the duvet. And she would have done but Kelly insisted that they had to sort out Vicky's immediate future and they'd get down to it just as soon as Vicky had showered and eaten.

So now Vicky was being forced to face up to her situation and find solutions to the fact that she was jobless, penniless and virtually homeless.

'Yup, I'd say a job is your first priority. If you don't plan to go home, I'd say you have to find one. And get somewhere to live.'

Vicky nodded. 'How long do you think I could stay here with you?'

Kelly wrinkled her nose and pouted as she thought about it. 'Maybe a week. If you got a job and offered Mum some rent money we might be able to persuade her to let you stay a bit longer.'

'You reckon?' Vicky was doubtful. It was a lot to ask.

'Dunno. Worth a shot.'

'So, jobs . . .'

'What can you do?'

'Sew.'

'Obviously. Anything else?'

'Cook, clean. I'm not afraid of hard work.'

'Maybe we could get you a job as some sort of home-help, or office cleaner.'

Vicky shrugged. *That'd be okay*, she thought.

Kelly flipped open her laptop and began tapping the keys. 'Let's see,' she said, peering at the screen, 'what's available round here. Of course, what would be ideal would be a job as a live-in housekeeper but you're probably too young for anything like that and you don't have any references.' She prodded a few more keys and then scrolled down the screen using the touch pad. 'Nothing much,' she pronounced after a few moments of silence. She tried again and again. Then she sighed. 'We might have to get the bus to go to the job centre, see what they've got. There must be someone round here who needs a bit of unskilled labour.'

Vicky didn't want to dampen her friend's enthusiasm for finding her a job but the prospect filled her with dread. What did she know about doing a proper job? And what were the chances of her getting anything? As soon as they guessed who she really was she just knew all the normal prejudices would kick in. She was sure Kelly was wasting her time. There was no way anyone in the area would employ her once they knew she was a refugee from the trailer park.

'If we find something, we'll give them this address,' said Kelly as if she were reading Vicky's mind. 'Even if we've had to find somewhere else for you to stay I can pass messages and anything on to you.'

'I suppose.' Vicky wasn't convinced.

Between them Vicky and Kelly spent the entire morning trawling through recruiting agency websites trying to find something suitable. By lunchtime both of them were starting to lose heart.

'There must be something,' sighed Kelly, getting irritable with frustration. 'Something that's local and only needs a bus journey to get to at the most.'

'But there doesn't seem to be. Not a sausage.'

'Then it's plan B tomorrow.'

'Plan B?'

'We go into the job centre first thing and then we go round town and into every shop or business and ask if they've got a vacancy. Someone, somewhere must need a shop assistant or a cleaner or a waitress . . .'

'You think?'

'I'm sure.'

But Vicky didn't think her face reflected her positivity. Either way they'd both had more than enough of job-hunting for the day.

In the afternoon the girls moped around the house, which they had to themselves as Betty had gone to do a supermarket run, muttering about extra mouths. Vicky said she was too tired to keep ploughing through recruiting websites and had a nap for an hour while Kelly gave up too and got busy with Facebook. When Vicky woke up, feeling slightly less downbeat, Kelly was getting stir-crazy.

'Come on, Vick, we've been stuck in all day. I love you

251

to bits, babe, but I could do with seeing a few other friendly faces. What do you say?'

'Maybe.' In Vicky's experience there weren't many friendly faces off the trailer park – not if you were a traveller there weren't – but she didn't want to sound like a wet weekend.

'So why don't I text a few people and we go out on the lash tonight?'

Vicky's eyes widened involuntarily. 'Out?'

'Yeah, you know. To a club or somewhere, get hammered, have fun.'

'Hammered?'

'Oh, come on, Vicky. Learn to live a bit. You're not on the caravan site now, no one is going to see you. If you're going to be accepted by people you've got to start to behave like a normal one.'

Vicky wanted to say that as far as she was concerned she was perfectly normal and getting hammered didn't sound right for girls of their age but she was still wary of upsetting Kelly again. She owed Kelly too much, she *needed* Kelly too much to risk getting on the wrong side of her again.

'What did you bring with you – clothes-wise?' Kelly asked.

'Not much,' admitted Vicky. 'I didn't hang around to find out what my dad would say about me talking to Jordan.'

'Assuming Liam told him.'

'I dunno. He might have done. I think he would have done if I'd stayed. Now I haven't a clue what's going on there. Shania's sent me a few messages.'

'And?'

'And I don't want to read them. Not just yet.' She was scared she'd break down or lose her nerve or both. 'Maybe tomorrow.'

'I'd leave them well alone if I were you. You've escaped, you don't want any emotional blackmail to make you go back.'

But it wasn't about escaping. Kelly had it so wrong. Kelly made it sound like she'd been some sort of prisoner, that she'd been trapped, and Vicky didn't have the first idea how to start telling Kelly that it wasn't like that. Maybe another time. Vicky thought she was just putting everything off. The list of stuff she was going to deal with later was getting huge. *The coward's way out*, she thought.

After supper the two girls went back to Kelly's room to 'slap up', as Kelly put it, and change into something suitable for a night out. To Vicky's horror she had also nicked a bottle of her dad's wine, which she opened and poured into a couple of tooth mugs.

'Given the cost of booze these days, we're going out pre-loaded. Drink up, Vick!'

Vicky took the glass like she expected to receive an electric shock off it.

'Cheers,' said Kelly, not noticing and clinking hers against it. She took a swig and shuddered. 'Mightn't be so rough if it was cold but never mind.' She eyed her friend. 'Come on, get it down you. It's not that bad.' She took a second gulp. 'And it gets better as you get used to it.'

Vicky took a sip and tried to look as if she liked it. It

253

was much nastier than communion wine, which she didn't really like either but it would be rude to say so. 'Cheers, Kelly.' She put her glass down as Kelly turned up the music and then began to go through her wardrobe, hauling things out that might do for either of them between taking further slugs of wine.

Kelly found a pair of lime-green shorts and black leggings for herself with a skimpy orange top and then she picked out a chiffon blouse that was verging on transparent and a micro skirt, both in red, for Vicky. Vicky eyed both outfits warily – they were even more microscopic and revealing than the sort of things that Shania wore.

'The red'll look fab on you,' said Kelly, refilling her glass. 'And you need to wear these with it.' She handed Vicky a pair of sky-high heels.

By the time both of them were ready at nine o'clock, Kelly had had several glasses but seemed pretty sober considering, while Vicky felt distinctly wobbly after just one and a bit – and she knew it wasn't the stilettos.

The bus driver gave both girls a leer as they got onto the bus that took them to the town centre, which made Vicky feel uneasy. It was one thing dressing provocatively on the trailer park and being stared at by the boys there. There were rules there and everyone knew what they were. But here, on the outside, it was a whole different matter and Vicky felt very uncomfortable at the way the driver looked at her tits. She gave him a cold look and followed Kelly to the back of the bus.

'Look, Kelly,' she said when they'd sat down. 'I don't think this is such a good idea. Apart from anything, I'm skint. I can't afford a night on the town and I've no idea when I'll be able to pay you back.'

But Kelly was mellow from drink. She waved a hand. 'When you've got a job, babe. Wait till then.'

'But . . .'

'No buts. You're seventeen, almost eighteen, for fuck's sake. It's time you had a good time.'

But Vicky had had loads of good times, it was just they hadn't involved getting off her face and she wasn't sure she wanted to now. But if she didn't join in she'd annoy Kelly and she couldn't risk that. Not again.

The girls walked into the club and Kelly surveyed the scene with an expert eye. The noise was deafening and the place heaved with scantily clad girls gyrating madly while bored boys propped themselves against the walls and swigged pints.

Apart from the fact that Vicky didn't know a soul, from the amount of flesh the girls had on show, plus the amount of make-up they had on, this could have been a traveller party. Only it definitely wasn't, as one girl stumbled past her, her hand to her mouth and obviously about to throw up in the Ladies.

Kelly pressed her mouth against Vicky's ear. 'What do you want to drink?'

Vicky felt they'd both had enough but that was going to be the wrong answer. As was 'Coke, please.'

'White wine would be nice.'

'Good choice. Now we just need to get someone to buy them.' Kelly cast her eye round the room again then grabbed Vicky's arm. 'Come on,' she yelled as she tugged her through the throng.

Vicky followed, not having much choice. She was close behind Kelly and couldn't really see where they were headed until Kelly stopped suddenly. Vicky looked past her.

'Jordan!'

## 13

Oh no. Just when she thought life couldn't get any more complicated or difficult. She shot a look at Kelly. Had this been planned? Had Kelly meant to meet up with Jordan all along? She couldn't judge whether the broad smile on Kelly's face was just one of straight pleasure at seeing a friend or whether there was a hint of triumph that a plan had come together. Not that it really mattered, because as far as Vicky was concerned Jordan was the last bloke she wanted to run into. It was just too embarrassing given everything: that kiss, that awful goodbye, to say nothing of his coldness on the phone the previous evening, which clearly told her that he was still livid with her. But someone had to make the first move and behave in a civilised way, otherwise they'd just spend the evening circling each other like a pair of cats shaping up for a fight.

'Hi, Jordan,' she yelled over the throbbing drum and bass. He gave her a chilly stare and nodded in her direction. *Still in the doghouse*, she thought. 'I'm sorry,' she shouted. 'Really. I behaved badly.'

He just nodded back.

'Get us a drink, gorgeous,' hollered Kelly. 'We're on white wine.'

Jordan raised his eyebrows but disappeared off towards the bar. Kelly tugged on Vicky's arm again and pulled her further into the club. They rounded a corner and the music suddenly diminished to an almost manageable level. In this part of the club there were low tables, soft lighting and loads of comfortable seats. There were a few groups of people chatting but it was mostly empty. It was too early for most of the clubbers to want to take a break; they were there to dance and drink and maybe pull. Sitting out wasn't going to achieve any of that.

Kelly flopped down on a squashy sofa and Vicky sat on a big beanbag next to her.

'Will Jordan find us here?' she said.

Kelly nodded. 'It's where we generally hang out. Easier to talk. I know it's pathetic,' she added, 'but having to shout all the time does my head in.'

'So did you know Jordan'd be here?' She hoped she didn't sound too accusing.

'I thought he might. Let's face it, there aren't many decent places in this town for people our age to go.'

Vicky shook her head. 'How would I know, re-member?'

'Oops, sorry.' Not that she sounded it.

'I wouldn't have come if I'd known he'd be here.'

'You're joking me.'

'No.'

'But you fancy him.'

'No, I don't.'

'So what was that kiss about?'

'It was a mistake.'

Kelly's eyebrows shot up. 'Like it looked like it.'

'I'm engaged, remember. I love Liam.'

Kelly, emboldened by booze, said, 'Shouldn't that be, I *was* engaged and I *loved* Liam.'

Vicky was spared having to respond by the reappearance of Jordan with two glasses of wine and a lager for himself loaded onto a tray. He passed one glass to Kelly and then silently handed Vicky the other one. She took it and said thank you and then stared into the straw-coloured liquid, thinking that the awful thing was, part of what Kelly said was true. She probably *wasn't* still engaged. If Liam knew that she'd run away – and why wouldn't he by now? – there was no way he'd want her. But there was no way she was going to consign her love for Liam to the past. She did still love him and she missed him as much as she missed her family. The thought that she'd completely wrecked everything between the pair of them hurt horribly – a sickening, dull ache that was interspersed with occasional panicky interludes when the awfulness of her situation hit her. And it was a panicky moment that hit her right then, making her feel shaky and sweaty all over again.

*No point in crying or worrying, though*, she told herself angrily. She'd made her bed and even if it was a long way from being a bed of roses it was still chock-full of nasty, sharp thorns. And every time she remembered what she'd lost and left behind it was like being stabbed by one. She wondered, morosely, if the pain would ever go away.

She took a big swig of her wine. Maybe that would help. And then another when it had no immediate effect. She didn't know whether the wine she was drinking was better quality than the stuff Kelly had nicked off her dad or whether it was because it was chilled or maybe it was just that she was getting a taste for alcohol but she actually found herself enjoying this drink. She slugged back another gulp.

Jordan, sitting opposite her, raised his eyebrow. 'I didn't think you were allowed to drink.'

'That was then,' said Vicky. 'This is now.' She giggled, thinking what she'd said was quite profound and clever.

A youth approached their corner and said something to Kelly.

She instantly dumped her glass on the table beside her and with a casual 'Laters' skipped off to the dance floor. Which left Jordan and Vicky alone.

'So what's going on? Out with the likes of Kelly and me, drinking. Seems to me you're breaking a lot of rules.'

'I've run away.'

Jordan's drink slopped over the edge of his glass. 'Run away? Why?'

'Complicated,' she said.

'Obviously. I don't suppose you ran away on a whim. Not,' he added, 'when you consider how dangerous you lot seem to feel the outside world is. So, if taking your chances with the likes of Kelly and me is better than staying at home, things must be tough.'

Vicky nodded and had another slurp of wine. 'It wasn't good.'

'And this Liam bloke that you're engaged to?'

'I dunno,' she said miserably to her glass.

'So you've not spoken to him.'

She shook her head and thought about all the missed calls from him and unanswered messages from Shania.

'Don't you think you should? I mean, speaking from experience, blokes don't like finding out that the girl they thought they really liked suddenly isn't that interested. But it's better to be told outright than to be led on.' He gave her a meaningful look.

'I've said I'm sorry.'

'Yeah.' He didn't look like he reckoned it was much of an apology.

'Don't be like that, Jordan. If I could turn back time I would and then I'd make sure that kiss didn't happen.'

'It was that bad, was it?'

'No!' She glared at him, angry that he was deliberately misunderstanding her. 'No, it wasn't and you know it.'

'And I know how you reacted afterwards.'

'But it wasn't because the kiss was awful.' She held his gaze. 'I don't want you to think you did anything wrong; it was all my fault and I'm really sorry. But it was one of those moments that oughtn't to have happened. Maybe if circumstances were different . . .'

'So are the circumstances different now?'

Vicky had another swig of wine while she gathered her thoughts. Shit, she'd drunk the whole glass.

'I'll get you another,' said Jordan, standing up.

She had plenty of time to think while he was gone. Yes, circumstances were different. Everything was

261

different, but the trouble was, even if Liam never ever wanted anything to do with her again, she still loved him. Inside, despite running away and knowing that she'd ruined everything, she still hoped that maybe, just maybe, he'd do the knight in shining armour thing; that he'd gallop up, sweep her off her feet and carry her off to some private place where they could live together without anyone interfering. Because even if Liam, as a result of some miracle, forgave her, she doubted if the elders or the old women on the trailer park would ever let her forget she'd disgraced herself and her family.

She snorted. *Yeah, in my dreams*. Liam wasn't going to come and get her and that was that. The only route open to her now was to try to make a go of living with gorgios and fitting in with their world.

She looked about her at the other people in the club. Were they so different? They were human beings, just like her. She'd coped at school and at college so maybe she could cope again.

Jordan returned with another large glass of wine. As she leaned forward to take it she felt quite wobbly. She blinked and straightened up.

'You all right?' asked Jordan.

The feeling passed as quickly as it had come so Vicky took a drink of her wine just to steady herself. 'Fine.' She smiled at Jordan and waved her glass at him. 'And thanks for the drink. You're kind.'

Jordan leaned his forearms on his thighs and looked directly into her eyes. 'So what's the plan now?'

'Get a job, find somewhere to live. It sounds simple but . . .' She shook her head.

'But it isn't.'

Vicky nodded. 'Kelly and I looked today, it's hope-less.' She swirled her wine round her glass and then took a gulp. 'Either I'm too dim or too young or the job's too far away.' All the things that were wrong with the job market plus her own shortcomings were exaggerated by the effect of the wine she'd drunk. Despite her very recent resolve not to cry, the wine had got to her, as had a huge dose of self-pity. She began to sob.

Jordan took the glass from her hand and moved in to put his arm round her. She shook it off.

'Come on,' said Jordan. 'Don't be like that. I'm here.'

'But you're not Liam,' she snuffled, searching her handbag for a tissue. Finally, she found one and blew noisily into it.

Kelly arrived back from the dance floor, pink and flushed. 'What have you done to upset her?' she stormed at Jordan as soon as she realised her friend was crying.

'I didn't do anything.' He lowered his voice. 'I think she's a bit pissed.'

'Is that another glass?' said Kelly, taking in the nearly full one on the table.'

Jordan nodded.

'And she had a bit before she left mine,' admitted Kelly. 'Oh God, I should have told you.'

'I'll take her outside,' said Jordan. 'Fresh air might sober her up.'

'Good idea.'

'You want to come?'

'You don't need me, do you?' Kelly was afraid that Vicky might hurl when the fresh air hit her and she really didn't want to be around if that happened.

Vicky was still weeping fairly noisily into her soggy tissue.

'Come on, Vick,' said Kelly. 'Fresh air will make you feel better.'

'N-n-n-nothing's going to make me f-f-feel better,' she sobbed. 'It's all c-c-c-crap.'

'No it's not,' said Kelly firmly. 'Have a walk around outside and you'll see.'

It took some persuading but eventually they managed to get Vicky to her feet whereupon she swayed alarmingly. The booze – well over half a bottle of wine – was now really kicking in. Jordan put his arm around her to keep her upright as he walked her through the crowded club to the main door.

The air outside was remarkably brisk compared to the stuffy fug inside and the effect of it seemed to make Vicky drunker still. She swayed and staggered and Jordan held her tighter to keep her upright.

'Le' me si' down,' she slurred.

Jordan looked about for somewhere suitable. About twenty yards away was a shop doorway with three steps leading up to it. Ideal. He managed to steer her to it, wavering and weaving, where she collapsed in a saggy heap, leaning against the doorjamb, her head lolling. Jordan sat beside her to stop her falling over. She was still hiccupping and snuffling but her sobs seemed to be subsiding.

'How do you feel now?' he asked.

'Crap,' she moaned. 'I've ruined my life and Liam's. But I can't go back.'

'It can't be as bad as that.'

'You don't understand,' she said through another sob. 'None of you understand.'

'Try me.'

Vicky blew her nose and hiccupped again. 'I could've been up to anything while I've been gone.'

'But have you?'

Vicky sat up as straight as she could and gave Jordan a filthy stare. 'What do you take me for?'

'So tell them you haven't.'

'But they won't believe me.'

'Why not?'

Vicky shrugged and slumped back against the door. 'There'll be rumours. Whispers.'

'So your word means nothing, is that it?'

She nodded miserably and shivered, the cool night air finally getting through the insulation the booze had provided.

Jordan put his arm round her and drew her close. Instead of leaning on the door she leaned on his shoulder. She sniffed and blew her nose again.

'No,' she said. 'My word means nothing at all. As much as that.' She clicked her fingers, several times, till she succeeded properly. 'Nothing.'

'Poor baby,' said Jordan, rubbing her shoulder with his hand. Vicky snuggled closer.

'It's all such a mess,' she wailed as another wave of self-pity engulfed her.

He moved his hand off her shoulder and stroked her

cheek. Vicky put her hand up and held his, till Jordan released her hand and moved his to press against her lips. She kissed it.

Very slowly and gently Jordan shifted until he could bring his face beside hers and then he turned her.

'May as well be hung for a sheep as a lamb,' he said quietly.

'Wha'?' said Vicky, her brow furrowed. She knew she'd drunk too much but the wooziness she felt was almost as comforting as being in Jordan's arms. And although she knew she oughtn't to be doing this, the white wine had almost shut down her inhibitions.

And then Jordan kissed her for a second time.

Suddenly Vicky's worries seemed to lift. Jordan loved her; Jordan would take care of her. He wouldn't be kissing her like this if it wasn't so. Maybe she didn't love him back but Jordan wouldn't mind that, would he? He'd taken care of her at college, he'd look after her now too. She gave a little moan of relief.

Jordan's hand moved from her face to her shoulder and then down to her breast.

*Dear sweet Jesus*, thought Vicky as her body seemed to leap as his thumb rubbed gently over her nipple. A jolt of lust bolted from her breast to her groin and muscles there, which she didn't know she had, tightened deliciously. She pressed against Jordan, willing him silently to keep going. That feeling was unbelievable and she was desperate for more. Her encouragement was unmistakable, although Jordan barely needed it.

Then he gently pinched her nipple between his thumb and forefinger. An exquisite surge of pleasure made her whole lower half crunch. She writhed and clung to him as if she wanted them to melt into each other.

Jordan's hand slipped lower down her body, caressing her through the flimsy fabric of her blouse. His kiss was deeper, more urgent, his tongue exploring her mouth while his fingers explored lower on her body. He reached her thigh. He rubbed his thumb over her leg, easing down to the hem of her skirt and then gently he slipped his hand under the fabric so it was resting on her bare flesh.

Vicky, her misery forgotten, was swept away by this completely new set of sensations and experiences and responded to Jordan's caresses with another quiet moan.

He moved his hand back up her leg until it lay on the joint between her body and her thigh. Deftly he slipped his thumb under her knicker elastic and touched the moist cleft between her legs.

The intimacy of his touch was a step too far. Kissing was one thing but she didn't love Jordan enough to let him do *this* to her. The only man she wanted to teach her about sex was Liam. She didn't know if she ever had a chance to get back with Liam, but carrying on like this certainly wasn't going to help. She slapped Jordan's hand and pulled away from him.

'Gerroff,' she slurred.

'What?' said Jordan. 'What's the matter?'

'Stop,' said Vicky, panting with a cauldron of mixed emotions and grabbing his wrist to stop him moving his hand back where it had been. 'Stop right there.'

'But you wanted me. A second ago you couldn't get

enough.' In his frustration Jordan's rage began to boil over.

'Wrong. I've now had enough. I didn't say you could do that.' She glared at him, using anger to cover her embarrassment at what she'd let him do, how far she'd let him go. Kissing was one thing but getting into a heavy petting session was another.

'But . . . but you liked it. You were all over me.' Jordan couldn't believe it. 'For fuck's sake, Vicky, what are you on?'

'You went too far,' she said.

'Too far? Come off it, Vicky, it's just a bit of fun. And anyway, you were enjoying it right up until a moment ago, you know you were. You can't just stop like that,' said Jordan. 'You can't lead blokes on and then slam on the brakes.' He grabbed her shoulders and pulled her roughly towards him again. 'It doesn't work like that, I've gone too far to back off now.'

Vicky wrenched herself out of his grasp. 'Tough, because that's how it's going to be. I don't want you doing that to me. It ought to be Liam.' She staggered to her feet.

Jordan looked up at her, his face in an ugly grimace. 'I don't know what I ever saw in you. You think you're so special but you're not. You're just a pikey and Liam's welcome to you, you frigid cow.'

Vicky lunged away from him, his horrible words following her.

'You're a prick-tease, Vicky O'Rourke,' he yelled at her departing back. 'A cheap little prick-tease. What do you think Liam will say when I tell him about you, eh?

He'll never want to touch you again, not even with a nine-foot pole. That should make you happy.'

She shot back into the club, thankful when the deafening music obliterated Jordan's cruel words. Running away was such a huge mistake. If she hadn't, she wouldn't be in this dreadful mess now. And would Jordan really carry out his threat? God, what if he worked out how to meet Liam and told him what she'd done? Supposing he ran into him somewhere. Or got to him via the Internet? He was angry enough, she supposed. Even through the haze of drink she understood just how angry she'd made him.

If he did then it really would be curtains for her and Liam.

Oh Liam. She realised with a deep ache just how much she loved him and she was wrecking everything. And if Jordan went around telling everyone what had happened just then . . .

Terrified of what Jordan might do she staggered from area to area in the club, desperate to find Kelly. Kelly would know what to do; Kelly might even be able to calm Jordan down. Driven by a booze-fuelled panic, Vicky pushed and stumbled her way past dancers and drinkers, searching for her friend. They frowned and muttered nasty comments about drunks and pissheads as she barged past but she didn't care. Where was Kelly, where had she got to? She forced her way through to the chill zone but Kelly wasn't there either. The panic rose and got worse the longer it took her to find her friend. Then a dreadful thought struck her – supposing Kelly had left without her? The combination of fear, embarrassment and alcohol made the tears start to flow again, in earnest. She staggered on further to the back of the club, sobbing hysterically, where, finally, in a dark recess, she found Kelly wrapped around the man she'd danced with earlier.

Vicky, bawling and drunk, shook Kelly's shoulder to get her attention. Kelly swivelled her eyes sideways to see who was interrupting her.

'Fuck off, Vicky,' said Kelly amiably. 'Can't you see I'm busy?' Then she clocked Vicky's face. She gave her bloke a shove and stepped backwards. 'Vicky, babes! What's happened?' She threw an arm around Vicky, mouthed 'sorry' to the guy she'd been kissing and dragged Vicky over to a quiet corner. 'Babes, what's happened? Tell me.'

Vicky began to cry all the harder, this time with relief. 'It was . . . it was . . . it was Jordan,' she finally got out.

'The bastard. What's he done to you?'

But now Vicky was sobbing so hard that there was no way she could talk.

'I'm taking you home right now,' said Kelly. Vicky was obviously completely pissed but Kelly knew it wasn't just that that was making her cry so badly. Something had happened, something that had really frightened and shocked Vicky and, realistically, Kelly could only think of one thing.

She grasped Vicky by the hand and dragged her towards the exit of the club, as Vicky, terrified of running into Jordan again, hung back.

'For God's sake, Vicky,' snapped Kelly as she tried to

get her out of the front door.

'But Jordan,' squeaked Vicky, her face white and haunted.

'What about him?' Although Kelly thought she could guess, and it made her furious. How could Jordan have taken advantage of Vicky when she was so pissed? And to think she'd trusted him to look after her friend. What a bastard!

'Is he out there? I can't see him, I can't. Not after . . .' She whimpered. 'I just couldn't bear it.'

Kelly propped Vicky up against a wall near the cloakroom while she checked outside. 'Nowhere in sight,' she reported. With that reassurance Vicky finally allowed herself to be led outside.

The combination of being extremely upset coupled with drunkenness meant that leading Vicky along the pavement towards the bus stop was a complete mission for Kelly. She didn't try to talk to Vicky about what had happened. Vicky was still crying her eyes out and Kelly was having to concentrate on stopping Vicky from cannoning into street furniture or falling off the pavement and into the road. Finally they got to the stop and she dropped Vicky onto the bench before sitting down beside her with relief. She glanced at her watch. A bus was due in about ten minutes. Thank God for that.

'Want to tell me what happened, Vick?' she asked gently.

Vicky shook her head and mopped at her face with a soggy tissue.

'I blame myself,' said Kelly. 'It's all my fault. I should

have been the one to take you outside, but I thought we could trust Jordan. I never believed he would have . . . have attacked you.'

Vicky shook her head and sobbed again. 'He didn't attack me.'

'He didn't? Then what the fuck . . .?' Maybe Jordan wasn't as bad as she thought.

'I upset him. Again.' She sniffled. 'Kelly, it was awful. We got a bit carried away and then I realised it was all wrong. I want Liam, Kelly. I don't want Jordan and I told him.'

Kelly rolled her eyes. 'I can see that would go down like a bucket of sick.'

'Oh Kelly, he's threatened to tell Liam that I'm a prick-tease,' she sobbed.

'He won't,' she said reassuringly and with a confidence she didn't really feel.

Poor Vicky – and her such an innocent. Okay, so Jordan hadn't raped her but just because he hadn't managed to get into Vicky's pants didn't mean he had to be such a bastard. Poor Vicky, she didn't need more shit in her life, she had enough crap to deal with as it was. Maybe she'd have a word with Jordan in the morning, try to make him see sense.

The bus finally appeared. Kelly pulled Vicky to her feet and somehow managed to haul her friend into it.

'Two singles to Lambourne Road,' she said to the driver, plonking a couple of pound coins under the Perspex barrier.

'Nah,' he said. 'I'm not carrying you. I don't have

drunks on my bus. No way. Off you get.'

'But,' said Kelly, 'she's upset, I need to get her home.'

'Not on my bus you don't.'

'But . . .'

'Off or I'll call the police. This bus ain't going nowhere till you two get off.'

The other passengers were starting to give Kelly and Vicky evils and muttering to each other. It was obvious that the two girls didn't have them on their side either. Wearily, Kelly took back her money and dragged Vicky off the bus. As soon as they were on the pavement the bus doors hissed closed and off it went.

'Bastard,' Kelly yelled after it. 'Come on, Vick, Shanks' pony for us.'

She hooked her arm round her friend's waist and set off to walk the two miles back to her parents' house. It was a real struggle to keep Vicky moving and to keep her upright. And it didn't help matters that in her drunken, upset state she seemed to have lost all concept of road safety. Whenever they came to a junction or road to cross, Kelly would stop to check it was safe while Vicky just seemed to want to plough straight over.

'Hell's teeth,' said Kelly as a white van swerved, hooting, as Vicky launched herself between a couple of parked cars. The van squealed to a halt thirty yards along the road and then the reversing lights came on. Kelly pulled Vicky back onto the safety of the pavement as the van raced backwards towards them, the engine note rising as the driver accelerated. He stopped opposite them and wound down the passenger window so he could yell at them.

'You stupid, drunken cows,' the driver shouted. 'I nearly killed you, so I did.'

'I'm not drunk,' countered Kelly.

'You mightn't be but your friend is pissed. Pissed as a fart.' He leaned over. 'Look at her. She's a disgrace.' He narrowed his eyes as he stared at Vicky, then shook his head. 'Fuck me,' he said.

'Not in a million years,' retorted Kelly but the bloke didn't listen to her. Instead he shook his head again, muttered something she didn't catch and drove off.

'Come on, Vicky,' said Kelly. 'Not far now. Let's see if we can get you home without you killing either of us. And let's hope nothing else awful happens tonight.'

It was almost midnight when they finally got to Lambourne Road and Kelly was exhausted. She still had another couple of hundred yards to go to get to her parents' house but she needed a breather before she made the last push with Vicky. For such a slim person the girl was a deadweight. Kelly's shoulders ached and burned like she'd undergone some ghastly medieval torture and it didn't help matters that she had a blister that smarted and throbbed on the sole of her left foot. At the corner of Lambourne Road and the one that led to her parents' house was a low wall. She sat Vicky on it and then plonked down beside her while she took off her shoe and massaged her foot. At least Vicky had finally stopped crying. She was still pretty pissed but she was now a quiet drunk. Kelly slipped her shoe back on and rolled her shoulders to ease them. As she did she heard the tap-tapping of high heels approaching.

She glanced up and saw a faintly familiar face approaching. It was a girl she'd seen around college a few times. Some mate of Chloe's? Or Vicky's? Nope, she couldn't remember but it didn't matter. Time to get Vicky on the move again but she'd wait for this girl to pass before she got Vicky vertical.

'Hiya,' she said as the person drew close.

'Hiya,' she replied, giving a fleeting smile. Then, 'Oh hi! I know you from college, don't I?'

Kelly nodded. 'Kelly,' she volunteered.

'Leah,' the girl in high heels responded. 'Didn't know you lived round here.'

Kelly pointed down the road. 'Down there a few hundred yards.'

The girl stared at Vicky, who was slumped, apparently looking at the pavement, but at that moment she stirred and went to rest her head on Kelly's shoulder.

'Is that Vicky?' she said.

Kelly nodded.

'You're not friends with *her*, are you?'

'Yes.' And Leah's point was? Not that it really mattered. 'I don't suppose you could do me a favour. She's a bit upset and had a bit too much to drink. I'm trying to get her home. You couldn't . . .' Kelly looked at her new acquaintance, pleadingly.

'I suppose,' she said, giving Kelly an odd look. 'She staying with you or something?'

Kelly nodded again as she started to manoeuvre Vicky off the wall.

Five minutes later Kelly had Vicky back at home safe and sound. Now it was just a question of getting her upstairs and into her bed. She wasn't going to attempt to undress her friend, she'd just have to sleep in her clothes. Kelly looked at her mate, sprawled over the bed, face down with a bowl she'd placed 'just in case' beside her. *Poor kid*, she thought. *What a shit day she's had.* And tomorrow wasn't going to be much better, not with the hangover she was going to have.

## 14

Vicky slowly came round. And then wished she hadn't. Apart from the most awful taste in her mouth, her head throbbed, her eyes felt like someone was trying to grind sand into them using a stiletto heel and her stomach was churning. She swallowed and wondered hazily if she was going to be sick. If she lay absolutely still would the feeling go away? Or would it be better to head to the loo just in case? What the hell was wrong with her? She'd never felt like this in her life. Was it something she'd eaten, she wondered woozily. Or drunk?

Drunk.

Oh God. How much . . . ? She tried to think. A glass and a half before she'd set out with Kelly and then one huge glass at the club and then . . . Had there been another? It was a bit hazy.

She forced her brain to clamber slowly back over the events of the night before. She started at the point where she and Kelly had gone into town. Then they'd met Jordan, then she'd got weepy and then Jordan had taken her outside.

And then . . . and then . . . and then she'd led him on until . . .

A feeling of cold shame began to well up from her stomach along with a feeling of total nausea. Vicky bolted for the bathroom. Sometime later she was sitting on the edge of the bath, sipping a glass of water, trying to rinse the taste of vomit out of her mouth. Now she'd actually been sick, she felt less dreadful. Or she did until she remembered Jordan's reaction. She groaned and shifted uncomfortably. Well, she couldn't blame him. She leaned her aching head against the cool tiles as she felt shame wash over her. He hadn't deserved to be slapped down like that, not when she'd led him on, behaving like a hooker, making him think he was in with a chance.

She heard a quiet knock at the bathroom door.

'Vicky?'

She stumbled to her feet and unlocked it.

'You all right?' asked Kelly gently.

Vicky shook her head. 'Not really.' She hoped she didn't reek of vomit.

'We need to talk,' said Kelly.

Did they? But Vicky was feeling too fragile to argue and allowed herself to be led into Kelly's room where an empty bottle of wine and two used glasses reminded her silently of her wickedness.

She sat on Kelly's bed with her back to the glasses – she knew she was bad without it being rubbed in by the previous night's leftovers.

'Vick,' said Kelly. 'Vick, what happened last night? Was it just you and Jordan having a row? About him calling you a prick-tease?'

'What do you mean?'

'Vick, you came to me in the club, crying and in a complete state. I can't believe that was all it was about.'

'What do you mean, "all it was about"? That's enough, isn't it? He's threatening to tell the whole town, Kel.'

'He won't. He'll get over it.'

'You weren't there, you didn't hear him.'

'So he hoped to go all the way and you said no. He's not the first bloke that's happened to. In fact, it's probably happened to him before. He'll live.'

'But he hates me so much now.'

'Look, he went ape, of course he would, but so what? Just because you're all wrapped up in cotton wool on the trailer park. It's different out here in the real world. Most of us girls don't see anything wrong with letting a lad have a bit of a feel. Some of us,' Kelly gave Vicky a thin smile, 'quite like it. It's not just me saying this, think about Chloe.' This time Vicky returned the smile with a hint of one of her own. 'Jordan was expecting you to be a bit more like her. I don't suppose he's ever met someone quite like you, quite such an innocent. But hey, it's no big deal in the long run.'

Vicky shook her head. Things certainly were different and she wasn't sure she liked them. Suddenly she wished she was back on the trailer park where she was safe, where no boy would ever think of behaving like that, where she understood the boundaries and where she was treated like a princess. Another surge of nausea rolled around her stomach. And if she were there, she wouldn't now be feeling so shite because she wouldn't have got hammered.

'Can we drop it now?' said Vicky. She gazed at Kelly, willing her to leave the subject well alone. Apart from feeling filthy from sleeping in the previous night's clothes, she'd been sick too. She felt completely disgusting. 'I think I'd like a shower, if that's all right.'

Kelly leaned forwards and gave her friend a hug. 'Of course. And then we'll get you some paracetamol and a nice cup of tea to make you feel better, how about that?'

As Vicky went into the bathroom and closed the door behind her she heard a phone ringing. For a second she hoped it might be someone from her family trying to get hold of her. But of course it wasn't. She felt a physical reaction to homesickness that was almost as bad as her hangover. She dropped her washing kit on the counter and stared at her reflection. This was hopeless, she told herself. She didn't have a clue about life off the trailer park, she didn't fit in and she wasn't sure she wanted to. Last night had been a complete revelation and not one she had enjoyed. In fact, it had been a total nightmare. She switched on the shower to get the water warm while she undressed.

The hammering on the bathroom door made her leap out of her skin. The hammering was almost drowned out by shouting.

'Leave her, Mum. Leave her alone,' she heard.

'Get out of there, you filthy pikey!' She recognised Betty's voice.

*What?* Then the penny dropped. Betty knew who she

was. Vicky turned off the shower and unlocked the door.

'How dare you,' railed Betty, her face red with anger. 'Get your stuff and get out.'

'But . . .'

'No buts. Sling your hook. I'm not having a thieving gyppo in my house. And you, Kelly, you should be ashamed of yourself. Lying to me like this.'

'I didn't lie,' protested Kelly.

'You didn't tell the truth, that's just as bad.'

Despite her hangover, or more likely because of it, Vicky just wanted to get away from this.

'Don't worry, I know where I'm not welcome,' she said, looking Betty in the eye. She grabbed her washing kit and pushed past to the spare room. Slamming the door behind her she stripped out of her grubby outfit and into fresh clothes, stuffing all the rest of her possessions into the backpack as she went. She checked the cash she had, a shade over four pounds. She felt hopeless. How could she survive on that?

No job, no money, no shelter, no prospects. She was in such a bad place and as soon as she went out from this house it was going to get a whole load worse. But she had to leave; she had no other choice.

On the other side of the door she could hear the row raging on. It seemed that by leaving the trailer park she hadn't just wrecked her own life, she'd got Kelly into trouble too. If she went, maybe Betty would stop laying into her daughter.

She caught sight of her phone in her backpack. It was her one and only link with her family and everything that was safe and familiar. She stared at it for a few seconds before she tentatively picked it up and switched it on. It rang instantly.

She had such a fright she dropped it but luckily it landed on the bed. She grabbed it again. Shania.

Should she answer? She hesitated for a moment and then she had an overwhelming desire to talk to her little sister.

'Shania?'

'Vicky. Oh thank God, you're alive.'

The relief in Shania's voice got to Vicky. She swallowed a sob. 'Of course I'm alive, sis.'

'I was going out of my mind. And as for Dad and Mammy. We didn't know what to do, who to turn to . . . Vick, we've been out of our heads. It was only when I saw you'd taken your washing stuff . . . but even so, off the park and on your own, you could have been in terrible trouble.'

'Shan, I am so sorry.'

'Where are you?'

'Safe,' she lied.

'Vick, you've got to come back. Mam and Dad just want you home. It doesn't matter where you've been, what you've done, just come back. Truly.'

'I can't. I can't face what people will say.'

'That's it, Vick, no one knows.'

'What? What are you saying, that's impossible. Surely Liam . . .'

'We told him you've got food poisoning and can't see anyone. Vick, we can't keep that up much longer. He's going to get suspicious soon and then . . . well, you just need to come home.'

Oh, God. She could go home. She hadn't completely ruined everything, or not yet. Except sneaking off the trailer park was one thing, getting back in with no one spotting her was a whole other issue.

'How, Shan? How am I going to sneak back?'

'Dad'll come and get you in the van. I'm sure we can do it, honest, Vick.'

But Vicky was attacked by her guilty conscience and fear at facing her parents. The row would be awful. And Liam was bound to have told her folks about her phone call to Jordan. Even if her family kept it quiet about her running away, Liam wasn't going to want her. She'd been chatting to a gorgio behind his back. He'd have every right to think she was a slapper. He'd break off their engagement and for the rest of her life she'd be on the shelf. Damaged goods. The woman no one wanted to marry. Maybe it would be better not to go back.

'I don't know, Shan. I've made too much of a mess of everything.'

'No you haven't.'

But Vicky thought that if she told Shania everything, getting drunk, snogging Jordan, her sister would soon change her tune. She wouldn't want to be associated with such a trollop either.

'It'll be a five-minute wonder,' insisted Shania. 'And that's if the story even gets out. Which it won't.'

Vicky still hesitated as another jolt of guilt rocked her. What if Liam ever found out about Jordan. Never – it must *never* happen. She would never tell anyone. *In fact*, thought Vicky, *I won't even tell the priest at confession.* What she'd done was going to go to the grave with her.

Her penance. A lifetime of guilt was going to be her punishment.

'What made you go, Vick? I've been going over and over and I can't see why some stupid comment from Kelly made you take off like that.'

'It wasn't what Kelly said. Besides she's apologised. It was Liam.'

'Liam!'

'He said that because Kelly had upset me I wasn't to see her ever again.'

'That's a bit harsh.'

'He doesn't like my college friends.'

'He'll get over it,' said Shania breezily. 'It isn't as if they'll be hanging around here once you're wed. But that still doesn't explain you taking off. Look,' she said, 'talking on the phone isn't solving anything. Come home, once you're back we can get it all sorted out properly.'

Shania was probably right and Vicky desperately wanted to go back but she felt as if she were trapped between a raging bush fire and a precipice. If she stayed where she was, she was doomed, but if she jumped . . . If she jumped, she might be doomed or she might just survive. Two chances of things getting worse, one chance of making it better.

'I'll come back.'

Shania's sigh of relief whistled down the mobile with the strength of a gale. 'Where are you?'

'I'm not quite sure but the house is near a bus stop on Lambourne Road. I'll wait for Dad there.'

'Thirty minutes?'

284

'No problem.'

Vicky swiftly stripped her bed and piled the neatly folded bed clothes with her towel and the outfit she'd borrowed off Kelly on top of it, made sure the room was tidy before she left it and headed for the stairs. Now she not only had a hideous hangover but the churning in her stomach was made worse by butterflies. The row between Betty and her daughter had either moved out of earshot or died away while she was talking to her sister but Vicky had a horrid feeling that her reappearance was likely to kick it off again.

Betty was waiting for her at the bottom of the stairs, her arms tightly crossed. Vicky made her mind up to say her piece first.

'I'm sorry, Mrs Munro, for putting you out and I'm sorry you didn't realise who I am so I'll go right now. I've left my room tidy. You can check it if you like to make sure I've not taken anything.' Betty sniffed and coloured slightly. Vicky felt a tiny surge of satisfaction that she'd scored a hit. 'Kelly's always been a good friend to me. You should be proud of her, Mrs Munro, she's a lovely girl. Very kind and caring. Anyway, I'm off now, so you needn't worry.'

'Good,' was all Betty Munro said before turning on her heel and stamping into the kitchen.

Vicky let herself out of the house and made her way along the street to the junction with Lambourne Road. She'd almost reached the bus stop when she heard someone running behind her.

'Vick!'

She turned. Kelly was pounding towards her.

'You can't go without saying goodbye.' Kelly panted up to her and enveloped Vicky in a big hug. 'I shut myself in my room to get away from Mum and then I went into yours and you'd gone.'

'I couldn't stay.'

'No.' Kelly paused, looking so apologetic she didn't need words. 'She was just shocked, I think. And it's mad because she liked you when she met you, before she knew that you . . .' Kelly's voice petered out. 'Maybe she'll come round.'

'No, Kelly, I don't think she will.'

'But you can't just leave. You've nowhere to go.'

Vicky shook her head. 'I'm going home. You've been a star but I'm going home.'

'It's all that fucking Leah's fault,' said Kelly out of the blue.

'Leah?'

'Leah from college. She recognised you last night when I was taking you home. She must have rung Mum this morning. Or told someone else who did.'

Vicky rolled her eyes. 'She's hated me ever since she found out I'm a traveller. Spiteful cow.' She sighed. Why did some people feel they just had to make life difficult for others? Or was it just the likes of her that always got the rough deals?

'So how are you getting home? Want me to come with you?'

'Dad's fetching me and it's a kind offer but I'll be all right.'

'You sure?'

Vicky smiled. 'To be honest, no. But having a gorgio

286

hanging about probably won't help. Or that's how my dad'll see it. I'd love you to be there but . . .'

Kelly gave her another hug. 'You've got to keep in touch, babes.'

Vicky nodded, feeling emotional. 'And if you can get your mum to agree and I can get mine to, I still want you at my wedding. You don't have to be a bridesmaid though and wear that freaky dress.'

Kelly gave her a watery smile. 'Vicky O'Rourke, if I'm allowed to be at your wedding it's entirely on condition that I *can* be a bridesmaid and wear that absolutely *beautiful* dress. Although I think you'll have to find somewhere else to store them. Sorry, but Mum . . .' She didn't have to say any more, Vicky understood. She gave her friend another hug and a kiss. 'You'd better get going if you don't want your dad to see you hanging out with rubbish like me.'

'Oh Kel. I so owe you.' She pecked Kelly on the cheek and turned the corner. She knew she would always love Kelly. And if Liam forbade them to meet she'd just have to find another way of keeping in touch.

Her father didn't say much as she climbed into the van apart from directing her to sit in the back. 'Don't want anyone to see what I'm dragging back, like the cat.'

So Vicky made herself as comfortable as she could on the floor of the Transit, trying to brace herself as Johnnie swung it round corners with no apparent thought about the comfort of his cargo.

She could tell when they reached the park as the van bounced and jolted over the tussocky grass to reach their pitch. Johnnie stopped the van, then engaged reverse. When he flung open the door at the back Vicky could see he'd parked so close to the door to the trailer all she had to do was take one step on to the grass and then she was in through the door and back home. Mammy was waiting for her.

Tired, emotional and feeling like death, Vicky just burst into floods of tears and ran into her mother's arms. Mary-Rose hugged her close and once again the smell of Devon violets seemed to sum up everything that was right about being at home. Never mind the awfulness of the last couple of days, home was perfect. Mary-Rose stroked her daughter's hair and murmured things about being pleased to have her back and then she held her away and had a good look at her.

'Well, you look like you've been poorly so not a word of a lie there.' She sighed. 'So dare I ask what you got up to? Do I need to be ashamed of my own daughter?'

The trailer rocked and Vicky, her conscience making her jumpy, spun round to see who had come in. It was her dad. But Mary-Rose shook her head and he stepped out again. 'Best you and I talk, woman to woman,' she said. 'Now, answer the question.'

'Not very,' said Vicky.

'How much is *not very*?' said Mary-Rose, sitting on a bunk.

Vicky sat down opposite. 'I was out unchaperoned, it's true, but I was with Kelly.'

Mary-Rose's eyes narrowed. 'And just what does she know about our ways?'

'Not much, but she's a good friend.'

Mary-Rose's snort suggested she didn't entirely

agree. 'So you were out and about with Kelly. Doing what?'

'Drinking,' whispered Vicky.

'Which explains the way you look now.'

Vicky nodded. 'Mammy, I'm so never going to drink again.'

'Good, because if you do I will wash your mouth out with carbolic. Anything else?'

'No,' lied Vicky. 'Just drinking. That's enough, isn't it?'

Mary-Rose nodded. 'More than enough, if you ask me. But it could have been worse.'

*It so nearly was*, thought Vicky. *It so very nearly was.* 'Shan says Liam doesn't know I lit out.'

'Your daddy thought it for the best that we tried to keep it quiet, if we could. Liam thinks you're poorly and if he sees you looking like you do right now he'll never guess we lied.'

'There might,' said Johnnie from the trailer door, 'be a problem with that.'

'How come?' said Mary-Rose.

'Fergal was coming home late last night and saw Vicky off her face with drink, so he did.'

'Fergal. Dear Lord above, that's all we need. Can we deny it?'

'He nearly ran this pair of drunks over so he went back to have a go at them. He's in no doubt. Saw her as clear as day. He's just asked me what I was thinking of, letting my daughter roam the streets like a tart.'

'He never,' said Mary-Rose, shocked.

'He did so. I told him she was ill in bed but he

wouldn't have it.' He looked at his daughter, disappointment clear on his face. 'Why Vicky, why? Why did you run away?'

'I had a row with Liam.'

'That's no cause to go off like that.'

'I thought he'd tell you why we rowed,' Vicky mumbled. She was going to have to admit to the phone call now. Her daddy was going to go mad.

'And just why was that?' asked her dad with a scarily calm voice.

'I was talking to a college friend. A boy.'

'A boy! Vicky.' Her father looked at her sadly. 'Where did we go wrong with this one?' he asked his wife. 'I knew she should never have gone to college. All that learning, all that freedom, that was her undoing to be sure.' His disappointment was almost worse than full-on anger. Vicky thought she could cope with a bawling out but this awful sadness that his daughter had utterly failed the family, let everyone down, was worse.

'We can't put the genie back in the bottle now,' said Mary-Rose.

'So you rowed with Liam, then you took off. Why?'

'Because I was afraid of what you'd say,' she almost whispered.

'As well you might.' Johnnie shook his head. 'Jeez, we knew school would corrupt her, and so it did, but we never thought it would go this wrong. So who was this boy and why the need to talk?'

'I just wanted him to tell Kelly I was sorry about the row. She was blanking my calls and I just had to apologise.'

'You wanted to apologise to Kelly. After what Shania said she said to you! Sweet Mary and Jesus, she said horrible things to you. Why on earth . . .?'

'And I said horrible things back. But she's my best mate. And you always told me, Mammy, never to let the sun go down on my anger.'

'She's not a traveller,' said Johnnie. 'And she's never your friend. She let you get drunk and you were seen in that state.' He spat out the last sentence.

'We'll just have to convince Fergal that he was wrong. After all, no one except us knows she left the site,' said Mary-Rose.

Johnnie shrugged. 'I don't think it'll work. He's certain he saw her.'

They were interrupted by a tapping on the trailer door. Mary-Rose got up and opened it.

'Liam.'

'I heard . . .' he started. He peered round the door and saw his fiancée. 'Vicky! Vicky, are you feeling better?'

'Not really.' At least that was one question she could answer truthfully.

'You really don't look right,' he said, his brow furrowed. 'So, it's true then, you really have been poorly. Are you sure you ought to be out of bed?'

His concern just piled the guilt on Vicky all the more.

'So Fergal's definitely lying,' he added.

'Lying about what?' asked Mary-Rose, innocently.

Vicky couldn't believe her mother was prepared to lie on her daughter's behalf. More guilt was loaded on.

'Fergal said he'd seen—' Liam paused, pink with

291

embarrassment at what he was about to say. 'He said he saw Vicky very drunk. But no way. I mean, if you've been ill in bed you couldn't be up and about at the same time. Besides, I know you,' he glanced from Johnnie to Mary-Rose, 'wouldn't let Vicky out alone at night. You just wouldn't. So I told him straight he had it wrong.'

*Dear sweet Liam*, thought Vicky. *He's so trusting, so nice.*

Mary-Rose nodded. 'You're a good lad, Liam.'

'I told Fergal, I told him straight, if I hear any more talk like that I'm going to fight. I won't have him saying things that dishonour my girl.'

'Liam! Please don't,' said Vicky, racked with yet more guilt. Dishonour her? That was a joke – as if Fergal could say anything that could make her feel more dishonourable than she already was.

'Why not? It's my girl he's lying about. I'm not having anyone saying those things.'

'But Fergal . . .' Fergal was over six foot and built like a heavyweight boxer. He was covered in tattoos, which only served to emphasise his huge muscles. To have Liam and Fergal fighting was going to be like pitting a Labrador against a Rottweiler in a dogfight. 'Liam, you can't fight Fergal. He'll kill you.'

'I won't have him telling lies about you, Vick.'

Vicky shut her eyes. Should she tell him that they weren't lies, should she tell him not to fight for her honour? She wasn't worth it. She was a dirty little baggage and Liam should let her stew in the mess she'd made.

'Vicky,' Liam said, 'I love you more than life itself. If

I can't defend you, then I don't deserve you. And if I win, then no one can say anything against you again.'

Vicky gazed at him. He loved her *that* much? And she'd jeopardised it all. She didn't deserve him, no way and yet she couldn't face owning up and losing him for sure. She suddenly realised, with absolute truth, that she loved him utterly and completely. It wasn't just that he was prepared to fight for her, it wasn't that he loved her so unconditionally, it was that she just couldn't imagine a future that didn't include him. To belong to Liam for the rest of her life was the only ambition she had now.

But what if he lost? What then? Vicky couldn't bear to think about that.

'God and the Blessed Virgin Mary will look after me,' said Liam, fervently and with conviction, crossing himself. 'They know Fergal's wrong and They'll side with what's right and true.'

*But They won't*, Vicky longed to say, thinking her heart was about to break. *They won't because I'm a liar and a slut and a drunk and I don't deserve you. I don't deserve anyone.*

After Liam had left their trailer a ghastly silence descended with both her parents staring at her.

'So he's going to fight for your honour,' said Johnnie. 'That's rich.'

Vicky fought back tears. 'I can't let him. I've got to tell him the truth.'

Mary-Rose grabbed her arm. 'Oh no you don't, missie. If you do, it won't just be you who'll be shamed; you'll shame the whole family. You can't do this to your sisters, or to your dad and me. So, you'd better get down on your knees and pray that Liam wins if it turns out he has to fight. Because if he doesn't, all those dresses you made will be only good for dusters. They certainly won't be getting worn, that's for sure. Your dad and I are utterly disappointed with you. Lord knows what came over you, but it's up to you now to try and make things better – and apart from anything else, that means doing as you're told. Understand?'

Vicky nodded miserably. Her mother was right: if the whole truth came out Shania would be in the same mess as her big sister – and she'd never made a false step. She got up and went into her bedroom and shut the door. She flopped onto the bed feeling wretched. Her head hurt so much it seemed to block out all thoughts, which was just as well, because the future was too bleak and too uncertain to think about.

## 15

Shania bounced into the bedroom.

'Jeez, but you're a stupid cow and no mistake,' she hissed, her eyes narrow with anger. 'Is it true?' she spat.

'What?' groaned Vicky. She still felt evil and she really didn't need yet another row.

'About you being drunk.'

'What do you think?' said Vicky.

Shania sat down on the double bed. 'You never told me that when I called.'

'It was hardly something to brag about,' groaned Vicky.

'What possessed you?'

Vicky began to shake her head but stopped. The pain behind her eyes was so bad she felt that death would be a good option. 'I don't know. I didn't set out to get drunk, it just happened.'

Shania sighed. 'It's all over the trailer park, you know. Everyone is talking about it. Mammy and Dad are saying it's rubbish, that you were ill in bed, and Liam is getting mad at anyone who repeats the story.'

'Oh God, this is awful. He said that he'll fight Fergal over this, to defend my honour.'

'Defend your honour? *Your honour?* Does he know?'

'Know that I was drunk? Of course not, no.'

'That's just great then. My sister – a liar *and* a drunk. You don't deserve that boy, you know that, don't you? He's going to risk getting mashed by that brute Fergal and you're going to let it happen.'

Vicky felt tears begin to well up again. 'I don't have much choice, do I. Whatever I do I'm in the wrong. All I do know is that Liam loves me more than I could have ever thought possible. More than I deserve.'

'Then you're going to have to make it right to him, if he still wants you when all this is over. You've got to be the most perfect, the best wife a man has ever had. Because, so help me Vicky O'Rourke, if you're not, I shall be reminding you every day of what he did for you.'

'I've already worked that out,' said Vicky. 'No more ideas about dressmaking, no more ideas about college, that's it. I'm just going to settle down and look after him.'

'You could do *some* dressmaking,' said Shania, giving Vicky a hint of a smile.

Vicky shook her head. 'Nope, not me. Wife and mother – that's all I want to do.'

'That's a shame. And there was me hoping you'd make confirmation dresses if I have any daughters.'

'Oh Shan, of course I'll make those for you – as many as you want.' Vicky felt a tiny glimmer of hope. At least Shania still seemed to want to know her, be a friend. Her mother and her father had left her alone all morning. She'd heard them come and go from the trailer but they hadn't spoken one word to her. Too ashamed of her, she supposed. The very sight of their own daughter probably just made them feel sick with disappointment. She'd let them down, she'd let Liam down . . . She was a waste of space.

There was a pause in the conversation as Shania sat on the bed, fiddling with the tassels on the edge of the coverlet, and Vicky shut her eyes and wondered when her head would stop hurting.

'So what was it like?' said Shania in a low voice.

Vicky snapped her eyes open – her guilty conscience lurching to the fore, wondering just what Shania was referring to. 'What was *what* like?'

'Getting drunk, of course.'

Vicky kept her sigh of relief to herself. 'Not that great. Crap, actually. For a start I can barely remember anything, and I didn't like the booze much.'

'Then why did you drink it?'

'Because it was there. It seemed rude not to as Jor . . .' Shit, no she couldn't let on Jordan had been buying her drinks. Allowing a non-traveller man to get her drunk – she couldn't face seeing the disgust on Shania's face if she knew. Oh God, another secret to keep. 'As *just* about everyone else was drinking.' She glanced at Shania – it seemed that she had got away with the lie. 'I felt okay to start with but then I got all dizzy and funny. I felt as though my brain and my body weren't quite together. And then I found I wanted to cry about everything. And when I woke up this morning – oh, Shania, I was so sick. I hurled and hurled.'

'Sounds like a great laugh,' said her sister, wrinkling her nose in disgust. 'I can't say you've sold it to me.'

Vicky shook her head carefully. 'Take my advice, you're better off without it.'

The pair of them heard the door to the trailer bang open. Shania clicked open their bedroom door to see who had come in and saw their brothers scrabbling about under a bunk in the sitting room.

'Oi,' said Shania, round the half-open door. 'Don't you two make a mess. What do you want anyway?'

'Looking for my camera,' said Jon-Boy, not taking his head out of the storage space.

'What on earth for?'

'Because pretty-boy Liam is about to get his face kicked in by Fergal and I want to film it.' Jon-Boy found what he was looking for and both lads thundered back out of their home, leaving the door swinging.

Vicky felt sick. No! Liam oughtn't to fight Fergal on her behalf, she wasn't worth it. This was so wrong.

'Bloody hell,' said Shania. She stared at her sister wide-eyed. 'He's going to do it.'

'I've got to watch,' said Vicky.

'You can't. You know the rules. No women allowed.'

'I know, but it's all my fault that he's having to fight. If I watch it'll be like my punishment. I can't let him do this alone.'

Shania snorted. 'Oh yeah? Your punishment? It won't be you taking the hits though, will it. And don't you think you've already caused enough trouble? If you get caught watching a fight it'll just make things even worse.'

'Shania, I'm in so much trouble with Dad right now nothing can make things worse. Besides I won't get caught. I know where the men go to fight and there's a bit of broken fence in that corner. I'll hide behind that, no one will see me.'

'But what if they do?' Shania was tearing at the tassel now, pulling bits of thread out of it.

Vicky shrugged. 'I'm going to take the risk. I can't let Liam do this without support from me. He won't know I'm there but maybe – I don't know – maybe if I'm close I can send him good vibes or something.'

'You're mad,' said Shania. 'Liam's going to need a bloody sight more than *good vibes* when he's getting thrashed by Fergus. If you're planning on sending him anything I'd go for body armour. And if that doesn't work you may have to send him a coffin.'

'Shania! That's an awful thing to say. How could you?'

'Sorry, sis, but you've got to face up to it. Fergal's twice Liam's size. Liam doesn't stand a chance. And rather than worrying about Liam, I'd worry about myself if I were you, because if Liam loses . . .' Shania let the words hang.

That decided Vicky. Disregarding her headache she leapt off her bed and shot out of the trailer.

Shania watched her go. She didn't want to see two grown men trying to destroy each other and she had no idea why Vicky wanted too. Besides, if Vicky wanted to get into yet more trouble then that was her lookout.

Vicky slipped behind the shower block and around the bunker where the bins were stored. From there she eased her way through a gap in the hedge and skirted around behind the outside boundary of the trailer park to the far corner. As she approached her goal she could hear a bunch of male voices either yelling encouragement, shouting or groaning. The fight must have started. Vicky felt even sicker than she already did.

In the far corner of the trailer park was a small electricity sub-station surrounded on all four sides by a six-foot fence. Vicky knew this area from when she'd tried a few illicit puffs on her first cigarette, egged on by some of the older girls. She also knew of the privacy the area inside the fence afforded and how easily accessible it was – providing you didn't mind taking a bit of a risk. Ignoring the signs that warned of death and high voltage Vicky jumped up, caught the top of the fence and then scrambled up it. Then she rolled over the top to land on the gravel surrounding the rather sinister grey box that hummed faintly from the power that went in and out of it.

Vicky kept close to the fence – even she wasn't so foolhardy as to want to touch the equipment – until she reached the side nearest the fight. One of the wooden slats was broken on that section of fencing, a fact she remembered from when she'd been experimenting with smoking, and it allowed a very good view of the back section of the park. When she'd been there, smoking her first-ever ciggie, she'd loved the idea that she could spy on her fellow travellers. She'd gone there a few times afterwards to watch some more. She hadn't done it for any other reason than the sheer devilry of watching what people did when they didn't know they were being observed: old ladies hitching up their stockings; men scratching their arses; kids picking their noses; a couple grabbing a kiss; all of it seen and noted by Vicky.

Only now she wasn't looking at the things people did in private, now she was looking at a full-on spectacle. Right now she had a ringside seat for a bare-knuckle fight, where every crunch and crack and thump was happening just a few feet away, close enough for the blows to echo in her head, to see the drops of sweat spraying off the men's faces, to hear their grunts of effort.

There was no ring except the one formed by the men surrounding the two boxers and it seemed the rules were as loose as the arena. Gouging and elbowing looked as if they were allowed as well as more conventional punches. Blows above and below the belt were fine, in fact the phrase 'no holds barred' had been invented for this type of fight. A referee tried to keep order but his job seemed to be more to keep the fighters from landing blows on the spectators rather than anything else.

Vicky watched in horror as Fergal aimed blow after blow at Liam's body. Already, there were puffy red weals and darker, more sinister marks where Fergal's fists had hit home. However, after a little while, Vicky noticed that Fergal was aiming a load of punches that didn't reach their target. Liam might not have had Fergal's reach, but he was lighter on his feet. More often than not, as Fergal swung wildly, Liam skipped backwards, just out of contact. She also noticed that now and again, Liam slipped in under Fergal's guard and managed to land a hit in retaliation. Liam was getting battered, there were no two ways about it, and Vicky winced every time he took another blow, but the fight wasn't entirely one-sided. And Liam had youth and fitness on his side.

Suddenly, Liam hobbled and yelped. Fergal had landed a cracking kick on his shin.

'No kicking, no fucking kicking,' yelled the referee but Fergal landed another kick regardless before getting Liam in a headlock. Vicky could barely watch; she was sure Fergal was going to twist Liam's head clean off his shoulders, but then Fergal let go and gave an anguished cry.

'The fecker bit me,' he shouted. 'He can't do that.'

'Kicking's not allowed either,' shouted back Liam defiantly, his chest heaving, sweat glistening all over his body.

Fergal launched himself at Liam again but Liam danced sideways and Fergal went headlong. Liam weighed in with a kick to Fergal's backside and then another, for good measure. The men watching hauled him off and the referee yelled at him for breaking the rules. Liam just shook his head.

'And you'll do what?' he yelled back at the ref.

But as he was arguing Fergal was up and at him again. A terrific crack made Vicky groan as Fergal's fist connected with Liam's jaw. He staggered. Fergal swung again and Vicky didn't dare look. She shut her eyes but the roar from the crowd told her the fight wasn't over. She peeked again. Somehow Liam had stayed on his feet, although from the way blood was trickling from a cut over his eye as well as out of the corner of his mouth.

Fergal must have landed yet another punch. Vicky's heart went out to her fiancé. He was being so brave and getting so damaged. Surely he wasn't going to be able to take much more. And yet she was only worried on his account – if Liam lost, God only knew what would happen to her and her reputation – but she wasn't thinking of that. That didn't matter a jot. It was Liam that mattered. Just how much did he love her that he was putting himself through this for her?

Vicky forced herself to watch, despite the fact that it was making her feel hideously ill. As she'd said to Shania, this was her punishment for what she'd done. She knew the images would stay with her all her life – a permanent reminder of her wrongdoings. But also it would be a permanent reminder of Liam's faith in her. It would be there in the back of her mind to nag her if she ever felt that her lot as his wife was less than perfect.

The fight rumbled on, blows being exchanged now more equally, and it was obvious, from the way Fergal was trying to keep out of Liam's way, and from the way his shoulders were heaving, that he was tiring fast. Age, experience and weight had been an advantage to start with but now they were counting against him. Liam, however, was still dancing on his toes and able to dart in, under Fergal's guard, landing the odd jab and punch here and there. And then, suddenly, it was all over. Liam dived in and hit upwards with his right fist just as hard as he could. It connected with Fergal's chin. His head snapped backwards, his eyes rolled up in his head and he went down onto the Tarmac like a felled pine. A cheer went up and Liam staggered away from the fight, blood streaming from the corner of his mouth and down his chin.

Vicky found herself crying but she didn't know if it was from relief or from the awfulness of what she'd just witnessed. But one thing she did know: Liam must truly, truly love her to have put himself through that for her sake.

She waited until the area where the fight had taken place was cleared. Fergal was dragged away by his supporters, groggy and semi-conscious, a couple of the men settled bets that had been placed on the outcome and then all was quiet. Vicky went to the rear fence and clambered back over then slipped back through the gap in the hedge and returned to her trailer.

She longed to go to see how Liam was but she didn't think either Bridget or Jimmy would be pleased to see her – when all was said and done, she was as much a cause of his injuries as Fergal.

'Did he win?' asked Shania, who was reading a wedding magazine.

Vicky nodded. 'But it was gross,' she said. 'Awful.'

Shania snorted. 'No sympathy for you. You wanted to go and see it.'

'I know. Part of me isn't sorry though. I need to know what Liam went through. In the future, if ever I feel sorry for myself, I shall think about today and what Liam did for me. And I shall have to live with what I witnessed for ever. That's my punishment, Shania: remembering what Liam did for me, when I didn't deserve anything – nothing.

\*

304

'You can count yourself lucky,' said Johnnie, later that day, returning to the trailer.

Vicky knew exactly what he was referring to.

'Although I've a mind to put you across my knee,' he said. His face was thunderous and Vicky thought for a second he really might. No matter that she was almost eighteen, no matter she was only a few weeks off being a married women, it was a very real possibility.

'I'm sorry, Dad,' she said.

'As well you might be.' He sighed, a deep sigh of utter disappointment. 'But your reputation is safe, thanks to Liam. Of course, never mind what he's done for you, people are still talking.'

'No smoke without fire,' murmured Vicky.

'Correct. But talk will die away. I suggest you stay out of sight for a few days. And tell that friend of yours Kelly to keep away. We don't want her running into Fergal, not till we've got you safely wed. If he sees her and recognises her it'll all kick off again, only this time a grand gesture from your fiancé mightn't be enough to save you.'

For a second Vicky wondered how they would keep Fergal away from her wedding if Kelly was allowed to be a bridesmaid but then an urgent need to know how badly injured Liam was shoved it away. 'How is Liam?' She had to keep up the pretence she knew nothing about the fight itself except that it had taken place.

'How do you think? You know the size of Fergal.'

Vicky nodded.

'He's a mess. You'd better hope the bruises have

faded before your big day otherwise you're going to have a permanent reminder in all of your wedding pictures.'

She already had a permanent reminder – in her memory bank – and one that was much more vivid and awful than anything that might appear in a photo. 'Dad – about the wedding . . .'

Johnnie's eyes narrowed. 'What about the wedding?'

'I want to ask you something.'

Johnnie looked even more suspicious.

'I'd still like Kelly to be a bridesmaid.'

'What? Kelly? That . . . that . . .'

'That friend of mine, that girl who stuck by me at college when the other girls were bullying me—'

'You got bullied? You didn't tell me.'

'And have you tell me I couldn't go?'

Johnnie rubbed his hand over his face. 'I sometimes wonder about you, my girl. To be sure I do. You're not like the rest of us and I don't know where you get your ideas from.'

'I just wanted to see what was possible,' said Vicky. 'I just wanted to stretch my wings just a little bit.'

'And you nearly tumbled right out of the nest with all that college nonsense.'

'Nearly crashed and burned. But at least I've discovered what really matters – you, Mammy, Liam, family.' She pointed out of the door. 'The park, all our neighbours.'

Johnnie nodded. 'Maybe it's better that you did what you did. Maybe you won't always be wondering what might have been.'

'No, that's for sure. Dad, I didn't like what I saw off the site. It was awful; I didn't understand their rules or the way boys treat women. It was all so . . . disrespectful.'

'Come here, Vicky.' Johnnie held his arms wide and Vicky let herself be hugged. A big, warm, safe, bear hug. 'You've learned a big lesson. We'll say no more about it. And if you really want this girl Kelly at your wedding – well, it's your big day and I always said that my girls will have whatever they want. If that's what you really want then so be it. I'll make sure Mammy agrees, and Liam of course. He should have the final say in all of this. Mind you, I don't know what we'll do about Fergal. We don't want him there making waves.'

Vicky nodded. *No, we certainly don't.* But she had no doubt her father would sort something out.

Later that day, under cover of darkness Vicky slipped out and ran over to see Liam. As she feared, Bridget opened the door, after she'd knocked.

'It's you,' she said, her face hard and unwelcoming.

Vicky nodded, squirming with embarrassment. 'I've come to see Liam.'

'Have you just.' Bridget folded her arms across her chest.

Vicky nodded again.

'Lucky for you he told me I was to let you in,' said Bridget. She stood back as Vicky climbed in up the step.

'Who's that, Ma?' called Liam from the back of the trailer.

'Vicky,' yelled back Biddy.

*At least she didn't add 'that tart',* thought Vicky.

307

'Go through,' said Biddy, sitting down on a bunk by the big front window.

*I'm not to be trusted with her lad on my own*, she thought. *Not surprising under the circumstances.*

She went into the little side bedroom, the one they'd earmarked as the nursery when their first baby arrived. Liam, as he'd promised, wasn't going to use the big cherry-wood bed till he could share it with his bride-to-be. Liam was lying on the bunk, his face a mass of reds and purples. Now the bruises had come out and spread his face looked even worse than it had straight after the fight. His eye was half-closed and his lip was split and swollen. It was an appalling sight.

Vicky's hand flew to her mouth. 'Liam!' Tears pricked.

'It's a mess, isn't it,' he said cheerfully.

She nodded, not wanting to speak in case she cried.

'How do you feel?' she whispered.

'Okay. It helps if I don't move or smile. But you should see the other bloke,' said Liam with an attempt at humour.

'You were so brave.'

'I was lucky. A lucky punch.'

'It wasn't lucky. Not at all.'

'And how would you know?'

'I watched.'

'You did what?' Liam sat bolt upright in bed, winced and scowled and flopped back on the pillows. He glanced at the door. 'You did what?' he hissed in a much lower voice. 'Good God, Vicky, how much trouble do you want to get into? You know the rules.'

308

'I couldn't let you go through that on your own.'

'Jeez.' Liam shook his head. 'I am just glad I didn't know. I wouldn't have been able to fight if I'd known you were there.'

'No one knew.'

'So how . . . where . . . ?'

Vicky described her vantage point.

'Well, don't you ever do that again. In fact, when I'm better, I'm going to get a plank and block up that hole so you can't.'

'I'm never going to watch another fight, cross my heart. It was gross.'

'It wasn't a picnic where I was either,' said Liam, wryly.

'Oh, babes.' She reached forward to take Liam's hand but he snatched it out of the way. Clearly he didn't want her to touch him.

With a lurch in her stomach, the thought that she now disgusted him raced through her mind. Maybe, now the fight was over and the pain had set in, he'd had time to think about the awfulness of what she'd done. Before he'd been carried away by some gypsy code of honour but perhaps now his blood had cooled, so had his feelings for her. Okay so he hadn't told her to get lost yet. But she was sure he would. She'd blown it. Vicky felt the threatened tears spill over.

'Hey, sweets, don't cry,' said Liam.

'But you don't want me touching you.'

'Only because I'm so sore. You wait till I'm better, then you can touch me as much as you like – and where you like.'

309

Relief made Vicky giggle despite her tears. Dear God, her emotions were on a roller-coaster ride! And the elation she felt that he wasn't about to tell her to sling her hook was all the sweeter because of the despair she'd felt just a second earlier. 'I'll hold you to that promise,' she snuffled happily.

'I'd do it again for you,' he said quietly, looking into her eyes. 'I'd do anything for you, you know that, don't you?'

Vicky nodded. 'Yes. And I promise I'm going to be such a perfect wife. I'm going to look after you so well I shall make every other traveller man mad with envy.'

'They're mad with envy already. They'd all give their right arms to be in my position, to be engaged to the most beautiful woman in the world.'

Vicky blushed.

From the living room they heard Biddy clear her throat noisily, as if to tell Vicky that she was outstaying her welcome. The two lovers looked at each other and burst out giggling.

Liam reached forward to stroke Vicky's face and she could see just what a state his knuckles were in. She gasped.

'Liam, shouldn't you get this seen to?' She pointed a shaky finger at his mangled hands.

'They'll be all right in a few days. They just need time to heal.'

'You're sure? Your hands are your living.'

'I'm a chippy, Vick, not a concert pianist, they'll be fine.'

Vicky longed to take them in her own and kiss them

better but she was scared of causing Liam any more pain. She'd caused quite enough to last him a lifetime. There was no way she was knowingly ever going to cause him any, ever again. She knew now, totally, completely and absolutely just how much Liam loved her and she loved him. And wasn't that all that mattered? What did making a few frocks compare to a lifetime of happiness?

## 16

Vicky moved across the deep blue carpet of her hotel room, stared at herself in the mirror and caught her breath. The ivory silk and dark green complemented her dramatic colouring, the sash made her already neat waist look minute, the choker made her neck look long, slim and elegant and the almost transparent veil over her hair gave her a dream-like quality. Either side of her the yards of fabric billowed out in a vast cloud and every move she made caused the silk to rustle like forest leaves. It was the dress Vicky had dreamed about having: the most wonderful, the biggest, the most beautiful dress she'd ever possess, and it was perfect. She turned slightly and the huge skirt, flawlessly designed to hang just half an inch above the floor, swished round, the folds and pleats rippling and the sequins in the delicate embroidery on the bodice catching the light. *Beyond perfect*, she thought, as she watched her skirts sway and settle.

Mary-Rose, looking fabulous in daffodil yellow, gave a sob, and even Biddy dabbed away a tear.

'Perfect,' said Vicky, under her breath. 'Just like a real princess.'

It was the look of the young girl in the portrait that Mrs Mead had shown her, the look she'd wanted to recreate. The look of a princess; not just a Disney, fairy-tale one but a *real* one. The sort of princess that Liam – darling Liam – deserved.

She glanced at her watch. 'Nearly time to go,' she said. She felt amazingly calm. This was her destiny, after all. She and Liam had been meant to be together since birth. And now they would be. *Till death do us part*, she thought.

There was a quiet knock on the door and then it opened. Kelly put her head round.

'Oh my,' she said when she saw her best friend. 'Oh Vick . . .' She smiled at Vicky, although her eyes were glistening with happy tears. She squeezed her dress through the door to Vicky's suite, pressing down the massive petticoats to get into the room.

'Don't cry,' said Vicky. 'Firstly you'll wreck your make-up and then you'll set me off.'

Kelly rustled across the thick carpet and took a tissue from the box on Vicky's dressing table, then carefully dabbed at her eyeliner.

Vicky had barely seen her best friend since she'd been taken home by her father in near disgrace. There were things she was desperate to say to Kelly, but in private. She nodded at the two mothers in the room. 'Mammy, Bridget, could we have a moment alone? Please?'

The women exchanged a look but said nothing as they left, shutting the door behind them.

'They still don't approve of me,' said Kelly with a sigh.

'They'll come round, honest.'

'No. They think I'm some sort of devil child for leading you astray with the evils of drink.'

'They so don't. For a start, Biddy knows nothing about my time at your house or what I got up to and Mammy . . . Well, Mammy will get over it.'

'And Liam?'

'Liam knows how much your friendship means to me.'

'Really?'

Vicky nodded. 'Truly. And I'm so pleased you're my maid of honour. And so is Liam.'

Kelly raised her eyebrows. 'Are you sure?'

'Are you joking me? When he sees you in that dress he's going to be blown away.'

'Don't talk daft, Vick. He's not going to have eyes for anyone else but you. I mean look at you!'

Vicky couldn't help glancing again at the mirror. 'But you're beautiful too.'

'Not freaky?' said Kelly with a naughty glint in her eye.

'Not freaky in the least. And I know I've said it before but I need you to understand just how grateful I am that you stood by me when . . . when it all got tricky at home.'

Kelly squeezed Vicky's arm. 'That's what friends do, Vick. Real ones, anyway.'

The door to Vicky's suite opened again and Mary-Rose appeared, now wearing a huge cartwheel of a hat that matched her dress and jacket.

'It's nearly time, Vicky darlin'. The car'll be here any minute. Biddy and I are heading off to the church now and your dad's waiting for you downstairs.'

314

Vicky suddenly felt a little tingle of excitement and nerves. This was it.

Kelly came as close to Vicky as their skirts would allow and leaned over to give Vicky a peck on the cheek. 'See you in church, babe.'

Vicky nodded. 'And remember,' she said, 'no snogging the best man before the ceremony!'

For a minute or two Vicky was alone in her room while she composed herself and made sure she looked perfect for Liam. Then slowly and with great care Vicky left the room and made her way along the corridor and down the wide stairs. At the bottom the staff from the hotel were waiting for her and they burst into a spontaneous round of applause as she glided past them and into the arms of her father.

'Vicky, me darlin', you're a beauty, to be sure.' He blinked back a tear and cleared his throat. 'The car's waiting. Are you ready?'

Vicky nodded. 'I've never been more ready for anything in my life,' she said with total sincerity.

When she arrived at the church, just half a mile from the hotel, her seven bridesmaids were there waiting for her and they too applauded when she emerged from the white limo. Kelly made sure her skirts were arranged to perfection while the photographer bustled about snapping the group as they got ready to make their grand entrance.

Little Kylie, bursting with pride, led the procession looking completely darling in her dark green frock. Then came Vicky, radiant, calm and happy, hanging onto her father's arm, her skirts filling the space between the pews, while half the congregation seemed to be in tears and the other half cheered. And finally Kelly and the six other bridesmaids, all looking stunning in their dark green frocks, followed her down the aisle.

Liam turned around when she was halfway to the steps of the altar and his face lit up. She didn't need to be able to lip-read to see he whispered 'Wow!'

He nudged his best man, who also grinned at Vicky before his gaze slid from her to clock Kelly and then he winked in approval. Vicky almost laughed and wondered if he knew that the bird he seemed to be already planning to cop off with was a non-traveller.

She arrived next to Liam, who was grinning like he'd won the lottery. His hand groped for hers among the folds of silk and then he twined his fingers in hers as Johnnie took her bouquet of cream roses and placed her left hand on Liam's right one before squeezing past her train of bridesmaids and taking his place beside a tearful Mary-Rose.

'I don't deserve you,' whispered Liam. 'You're far too beautiful for the likes of me.'

'And I don't deserve you,' whispered back Vicky. 'But I love you more than anyone on this earth.'

'Dearly beloved,' began the priest as Liam squeezed Vicky's hand again.

The wedding mass passed in a blur of sheer delight until the moment came and the priest said, 'You may now kiss the bride.'

Vicky, her veil already lifted back from her face, turned to her husband and gazed into his wonderful blue eyes. She felt his arms encircle her waist as he pulled her towards him before his lips met hers. It began as the softest, gentlest of kisses until she felt his tongue just flicker over her own lips. And as she parted them, just a fraction, she felt an explosion of warmth and joy surge through her.

Her kiss with Jordan might have lit her up like a sparkler but this was a huge great Roman candle – heat, light, fizzing electricity and unbelievable chemistry powered between them. She drew back, breathless, and then, almost unable to believe what she'd just experienced, to the whoops, whirr of cameras clicking and applause of the congregation around them, she leaned in to kiss Liam again.

How could she have doubted her decision, she wondered and why on earth had she not married Liam months ago? Her insides exploded with happiness as he led her off to the back of the church to sign the register where they were joined by her parents and his, all hollering, crying and laughing and grabbing kisses with each other.

The entire congregation erupted into cheers when she and Liam returned and made their triumphant procession back down the aisle before clambering into the limo to take them back to the country hotel.

As the car drew up outside the pale gold stone mansion Vicky was, once again, stunned at how beautiful the place was with its immaculate gardens and beautiful lawns. A flunky in a white jacket with brass buttons leapt to open the door of the vehicle and help her out. By the time she was out of the car and her skirts had been sorted out again, her bridesmaids were piling out of another limo and family members were starting to arrive from the direction of the car park.

Another waiter appeared with a tray full of brimming champagne flutes and began to offer around drinks as the photographer tried to get some semblance of order with the gathering of happy, noisy friends and relatives. He managed to get everyone together for a selection of group shots and as soon as he'd finished, most of the party disappeared round the back of the hotel to the converted barn, where the reception was to be held, searching for the bar, leaving Vicky, Liam, their parents, their bridesmaids and the best man to be grouped for a more intimate selection of photos.

'Cop a load of Jack,' whispered Liam to Vicky as they posed for yet another picture. She glanced over her shoulder at Liam's best man, who was gazing at Kelly like a dog hankering after a biscuit.

'Dear God, he's completely smitten,' said Vicky, stifling a giggle. 'His tongue's hanging out and he's almost drooling. You'd better tell him she's not one of us before his heart gets completely broken.'

'Let him have his fun tonight.'

'Kelly'll let him have that all right,' said Vicky good-naturedly. 'She's not all set about with rules like our girls are.'

'And smile,' said the photographer. Flash – another picture in the bag.

'You mean . . . ?' asked Liam.

'Smile again and look into each other's eyes.' Flash.

'It's not for me to say,' said Vicky, loyally.

'Wait till I tell Jack.'

Vicky laughed. 'Could be that he gets lucky tonight, just like us.'

Liam roared with laughter.

'Beautiful,' said the snapper, his flashgun going into overdrive as he captured the couple looking over the moon with happiness and laughter. He checked the digital display at the back of his camera.

'I think that's almost it. I'd just like a few of the bride and her beautiful chief bridesmaid.'

Vicky and Kelly posed together for the photographer while the others, thankful at being released, charged off to join the other travellers and find drinks. The sound of jollity drifted across the bowling-green lawns as the DJ began to pump up the volume from his decks and the party took off.

Finally the photographer finished and Vicky and Kelly made their stately way across the grounds towards the barn.

'Could you go in and tell Dad that I'm ready to come to the party now?'

Kelly nodded. 'Of course, hon.'

Kelly pushed her way through the big double glass doors into the seething melee inside. The sound of two hundred travellers having a whale of a time waited for her on the other side. She almost flinched at the din. And the colour was almost as loud as the racket with all the flashing lights from the disco coupled with the brilliant rainbow of outfits all sparkling like fireworks from the crystals and sequins. Above the throng was a glitter ball that added to the dazzling blaze of colour and light.

Kelly shoved her way across the dance floor, where all the young girls were swivelling, twisting and gyrating, to the bar area where Liam, Johnnie, Jack and Jimmy had swapped their champagne glasses for pints.

'Vicky's ready for you, Mr O'Rourke,' yelled Kelly.

Johnnie, full of happiness and goodwill, put his arm around Kelly. 'Call me Johnnie,' he insisted.

'Johnnie,' repeated Kelly.

'And you've met Liam's cousin Jack, here, haven't you?'

Kelly nodded. 'But we haven't been formally introduced.' She noticed his dark brown eyes and even white teeth and thought, not for the first time that day, that he was pretty fit. Fitter than Jordan, even. And this time there was no danger of Vicky coming between her and this hunk. Vicky was well and truly spoken for now, completely off-limits, so out of the frame when it came to being available. Unlike herself. And, thought Kelly, she could be very available where Jack was concerned. She flashed a smile at him.

'Then I'll leave Liam to do the honours,' said Johnnie. He put his beer glass down on the bar. 'I'm off to help my daughter make her entrance.'

He made his way to the exit via the DJ, who he had a quick word with en route.

Two minutes later the music suddenly fell silent.

'Ladies and gentlemen,' said the DJ into the hush. 'May I present the bride, Mrs Liam Connelly.'

The vast room erupted as Johnnie led his stunning daughter in her beautiful dress into the centre of the suddenly empty dance floor. Then he took her in his arms as the strains of Eric Clapton's 'Wonderful Tonight' filled the air.

'And you are,' he told Vicky as they waltzed together. 'I couldn't be more proud of you if I tried,' he said.

'Thank you, Daddy,' said Vicky, not knowing if she was going to laugh or sob with happiness. 'And thank you for making today so perfect. I can't get over how lovely this place is. It's been amazing.'

'It's your big day, it's no more than you deserve.'

'But I nearly didn't deserve it, did I, Dad?'

'Hey, none of that now. That's all in the past and no harm done.' He squeezed her arm. 'And what Liam doesn't know . . .'

Vicky gave him a rueful smile. 'Thanks, Daddy. And thanks for letting Kelly be a part of this.'

'Liam and I both agreed that it was the right thing to do if it would make you happy. Like me he didn't want anything to spoil your day so if you wanted Kelly here, then you were going to have Kelly here.'

The music drew to a close and Liam appeared beside them.

'I think this next dance is mine,' he said.

To wolf-whistles and huge cheers Johnnie handed Vicky over to her new husband as Whitney Houston began to belt out 'I Will Always Love You'. Vicky put her arms around Liam's neck and kissed him full and hard on the mouth.

'And I'll always love you,' she said, panting slightly. 'I can't tell you how much I do.'

Liam, speechless, just held her close as they danced together. The minutes passed in a haze of happiness until the music finished, another record was put on and the dance floor filled again but the pair of lovers were oblivious. On and on they danced with eyes for no one else, not spotting Mikey and Shania snogging, nor Kelly being grabbed by Jack and hauled outside, nor Kylie getting fed up with her big dress and ripping off the underskirts.

Finally Mary-Rose came over and suggested that she and Liam ought to cut the cake.

'Already?' said Vicky.

'Already? The guests have been here two hours and they're starving for something to eat.'

'Two hours? Surely not.'

Mary-Rose thrust her watch under Vicky's nose. Vicky blinked. Blimey. Of course, the photographer had taken ages but even so . . .

Once again the DJ was asked to call for quiet and Vicky and Liam made their way over to the big trestle table at the far end of the barn where her seven-tier cake, lit with fairy lights, glittering with edible gold foil and wreathed with dark green ivy and cream icing-sugar roses to match the dresses, towered over the buffet. She and Liam clasped hands over the handle of the big knife before making the first cut. Another cheer raised the rafters.

Johnnie banged a table. 'I'm not much of a one for speech making,' he said. 'And there's still a lot of money behind the bar that needs dealing with and there's a buffet here that needs eating, but before you do I'd like you all to raise your glasses to my beautiful, clever and wonderful daughter Vicky, and her handsome and talented husband Liam. The bride and groom,' he toasted.

'The bride and groom,' echoed everyone present with yet another cheer. Vicky and Liam kissed as a posse of waiters ferried the cake away to be cut up properly in the kitchens and their friends and relations surged forwards to attack the buffet.

When most people had been fed, Jack then made a speech during which he managed to reduce the audience to fits of giggles describing Liam's early attempts at carpentry – the only carpenter apparently who had ever managed to make a three-legged stool which wobbled – before he praised the beauty of the bridesmaids' dresses and then the bridesmaids them-selves, sending Kelly, Vicky noticed, yet another wink. A wink that was returned with a blatantly lustful smile.

Vicky felt her face flare red with pride as a couple of women in the audience shouted out that they wanted Vicky to make dresses for them.

'Your first orders,' muttered Liam beside her and giving her a squeeze.

*Maybe*, thought Vicky, *maybe but what does dressmaking compare with what I have now?*

Finally all the formalities of the wedding had been dealt with. The waiters filed back into the reception to hand out slabs of wedding cake and the music was racked back up as the party, now fuelled by a certain amount of beer and champagne, really got going.

'Mrs Connelly?' said Liam.

'Yes, Mr Connelly?'

'I'm not really hungry for cake.'

'Is that so?'

He gazed at her. 'But there is something I do want.'

Vicky raised an eyebrow. 'Really?'

'Mmmm. Can you guess?'

'Possibly.'

'We could slip off.'

'To our room?'

'I've got a better idea.'

Vicky's eyebrow went up again. 'Which is?'

'The limos are outside. I think we ought to get one of them to take us back to my place. I've got a bed that needs testing.'

'So you have,' murmured Vicky. 'It would be a crying shame if we found out there was something wrong with it; that it was faulty or lumpy. Best we find out sooner rather than later.'

'The trouble is, it's going to be hard to get away unnoticed.'

'I think if we mention that we're going for a walk in the garden no one will think much of it.' Vicky giggled. 'It'll be just like being grabbed all over again.'

'I don't think what's going to happen next is going to be anything like getting grabbed,' said Liam with a slow sexy grin.

Vicky felt her insides crunch in delicious anticipation. Dear God, this was it – or it would be shortly!

The pair made their way over to the bar where they mentioned casually to anyone who cared to be told that they were slipping outside for some fresh air.

'See you later,' said Mary-Rose, with a knowing look.

Vicky gave her mother a hug and resisted the temptation to tell her that she probably wouldn't, although she had a suspicion that her mother already knew.

On their way out they passed Kelly and Jack, who were locked in a kiss.

Vicky tapped Kelly on her shoulder as she passed.

'Sorry to interrupt,' she said.

Kelly pulled away from Jack and opened her eyes. 'Hi, Vick,' she said through swollen, over-kissed lips. Her pupils were dilated and she was breathing heavily. *She looks drunk on whatever she and Jack have been up to*, thought Vicky.

'Kelly,' she said. 'You know that phrase "get a room"?'

Kelly nodded. 'Sorry, Vick, we just got a bit carried away.'

'No, I don't mean it like that. But Liam and I are off. Which means my suite is vacant. That is . . .' She looked at Kelly and Jack. 'Well, it's up to you. It's room number forty-five, though, if you're interested.'

Kelly was already dragging Jack towards the hotel reception as she called 'thank you' over her shoulder.

'Waste not, want not,' said Vicky primly.

'What are you like?' said Liam, shaking his head and laughing.

'You're going to find out in about thirty minutes,' said Vicky with a wicked grin. 'I think Kelly is just about to make Jack a very happy man.'

'And you're about to do the same for me,' said Liam with a gleam in his eye.

Vicky giggled again as her insides squished in delicious anticipation of what she was about to experience. 'I'm glad she and Jack get on so well. Just think if they really, *really* get it together we might even end up neighbours.'

'I'd like that.'

Vicky stopped walking along the gravel path towards the hotel car park and the waiting limos. 'Do you mean that? Really?'

'Yeah. As I've said before, if Kelly being around makes you happy then it'd make me happy too.'

Just when Vicky didn't think her day could possibly get any better it just did. She leaned across her voluminous skirts and gave Liam another great kiss on the cheek. 'You are the most darling man and no mistake,' she said.

'And you're very lucky to have me,' he acknowledged.

Vicky was still laughing as she and her dress were piled into a limo for the third time that day. As the car drove away from the hotel, down the long gravel drive, she snuggled up next to her new husband and felt utterly content.

She felt even more content when she woke up the next morning. Beside the bed was a mountain of ivory silk and net underskirts that Liam had peeled off her layer by exquisite layer as he'd helped her undress. Any worries about embarrassment had been dispelled by his gentle caresses and kisses as he'd slowly sought out his prize, hidden under the yards of fabric. Once she was naked he'd picked her up and laid her on the bed before slipping out of his clothes and climbing under the covers to lie beside her.

Vicky had shivered at that moment, partly wound up with excitement and partly scared.

'Mrs Liam Connelly,' Liam had whispered as he'd taken her in his arms and began to kiss her. First her face then her neck, before his mouth had moved lower. The tenderness with which he'd explored her body had left her aching and longing for the moment of fulfilment and when it came, when he finally entered her, it was as if it was the moment her body had been waiting for since the day of her betrothal.

And afterwards, as they lay panting and satisfied, their bodies still intertwined, Vicky thought she might cry with happiness but instead, overwhelmed by the day and excitement, she'd fallen asleep with Liam's arm curled protectively around her.

Now wide-awake, Vicky looked across at her new husband. Pale lemony light filtered through the yellow curtains of their trailer and gave him a golden glow. She caught her breath as she remembered the previous night and thought that no one could be as happy as she was right now.

'Where's my tea, wench,' murmured Liam, looking at her through half-open eyes.

'Where's my tea, wench, *please*,' corrected Vicky with a giggle.

'Where's my tea, wench, or I'll have to carry on where I left off last night.'

Vicky's insides turned somersaults. 'Is that a threat or a promise?' she whispered.

'A promise,' murmured Liam back, his hand already slipping down her body as Vicky shivered with pleasure.

And she'd nearly jeopardised all this for the sake of making frocks. What had she been thinking about? A life, a future with Liam, a future of sharing his bed and loving him and being loved back in return was all that she wanted now.

She could see her future ahead of her and it was perfect.